"Whose baby is this?"

"Did you find some identification?" Neil asked tersely.

The single sheet of stationery, patterned in black and white with a caricature of a holstein cow in sunglasses, had a postscript that said, "My Life's an Udder Disaster." The handwriting was neat, large and to the point. *Neil*, it read, *a boy needs his father and I don't need this responsibility. So, I'm leaving the baby with you. Affectionately, Stephanie.*

"Stephanie?" Krista said.

"Stephanie?" Neil echoed Krista's question. "Who the hell is Stephanie?"

"Apparently she knows you."

Neil swung toward Krista. "This is someone's idea of a bad joke. I am *not* this baby's father."

Krista wanted to believe him. But a tiny doubt circled her thoughts, repeating the possibility that he could be the father of this bouncing baby boy. And is his eyes she s........................ ty.

D0834461

ABOUT THE AUTHOR

Karen Toller Whittenburg lives in the beautiful green country of northeastern Oklahoma. Her favorite pastime hasn't changed since she was a child—curling up with a good book. She divides her leisure time between a part-time job and family activities. She also scripts movies for the Narrative Television Network, a network for the blind and visually impaired. Karen and her husband love to spend weekends browsing through antique shops. He collects old cameras and she collects ideas for future books.

Books by Karen Toller Whittenburg

HARLEQUIN AMERICAN ROMANCE

197–SUMMER CHARADE
249–A MATCHED SET
294–PEPPERMINT KISSES
356–HAPPY MEDIUM
375–DAY DREAMER
400–A PERFECT PAIR
424–FOR THE FUN OF IT

HARLEQUIN TEMPTATION

303–ONLY YESTERDAY

Don't miss any of our special offers. Write to us at the following address for information on our newest releases.

Harlequin Reader Service
P.O. Box 1397, Buffalo, NY 14240
Canadian address: P.O. Box 603,
Fort Erie, Ont. L2A 5X3

KAREN TOLLER WHITTENBURG

BACHELOR FATHER

Harlequin Books

TORONTO • NEW YORK • LONDON
AMSTERDAM • PARIS • SYDNEY • HAMBURG
STOCKHOLM • ATHENS • TOKYO • MILAN
MADRID • WARSAW • BUDAPEST • AUCKLAND

If you purchased this book without a cover you should be aware that this book is stolen property. It was reported as "unsold and destroyed" to the publisher, and neither the author nor the publisher has received any payment for this "stripped book."

To my son, Paul,
who has blessed my life in so many ways

Published February 1993

ISBN 0-373-16475-0

BACHELOR FATHER

Copyright © 1993 by Karen Toller Whittenburg. All rights reserved. Except for use in any review, the reproduction or utilization of this work in whole or in part in any form by any electronic, mechanical or other means, now known or hereafter invented, including xerography, photocopying and recording, or in any information storage or retrieval system, is forbidden without the permission of the publisher, Harlequin Enterprises Limited, 225 Duncan Mill Road, Don Mills, Ontario, Canada M3B 3K9.

All the characters in this book have no existence outside the imagination of the author and have no relation whatsoever to anyone bearing the same name or names. They are not even distantly inspired by any individual known or unknown to the author, and all incidents are pure invention.

® are Trademarks registered in the United States Patent and Trademark Office and in other countries.

Printed in U.S.A.

Chapter One

Krista Hartley resolutely pulled a petal from the wild-flower she held in her hand. *He will beg me to stay.*

Another petal hit the ground. *He will say, 'Good-bye, good luck, and don't bother to write.'*

Krista counted the remaining petals. Three left. *He will beg me to stay.*

In a pig's eye, she thought, as she tossed the mutilated flower over her left shoulder and stuffed the remains of her lunch into a crumpled paper sack.

Dr. Neil Blanchard didn't beg. Orders were more his line. Orders, instructions and to-the-point questions. And he never, ever allowed emotion to interfere in business. He'd built Blanchard Pharmaceuticals from a two-bit operation, which sold aspirin and antacids to a multimillion-dollar laboratory, which manufactured a wide variety of prescription medications and over-the-counter drugs. To be sure, he'd inherited the lab and a sizable yearly income, but no one could accuse Neil Blanchard of resting on his laurels.

He was a classic type-A personality, a heart attack in the making. And to the women who crossed his path, he was a heartache waiting to happen. Her own heart was a little worse for the wear, but still in working order.

Her libido had definitely taken a beating during her two-year tenure as his assistant. It was a great job, possibly the best job she would ever have, but Krista had been with him long enough to know that if she didn't leave soon, she never would. And if she didn't leave, she would wake up one morning and discover all she had were unfulfilled dreams.

Krista got up from the bench on which she'd been sitting and started across the park toward the administrative offices of Blanchard Pharmaceuticals. So, she thought, she'd come to a decision. She would hand Neil her resignation and he would not beg her to stay on. He wouldn't say, 'Goodbye, good luck and don't bother to write,' either.

What the hell do you think you're doing? were probably the actual words he'd use. Though he'd get used to the idea of replacing her. He'd hate the inconvenience of training someone new, but in a matter of months, he wouldn't even remember her name.

Krista shuddered at that thought and wondered if she were out of her mind. But, no, resigning was the only sensible thing to do. She reached that conclusion as she pulled open the door of the building and prepared a smile for Heidi, the receptionist. But Heidi wasn't at her desk.

"Krista?" Mary Nell Campbell, Neil's personal secretary and the stabilizing force in the administration of the lab, stood just outside the doorway of Neil's office. "Would you mind coming in here for a minute?" she asked. "There's a...small problem."

"Small problem?" Krista echoed a moment later as she stood staring at the infant dressed in blue and strapped in the carrier seat in the center of Neil's large

desk. The baby raised a tiny fist and drooled. "But...
that's a *baby*."

Mary Nell nodded. "Definitely a baby," she said. "I
found him just a few minutes ago when I came back
from lunch. He seems pretty happy to be here."

"Yes, well, I don't think Dr. Blanchard will share his
excitement."

"Goes without saying. I've called security and asked
Howard to check around for a mother with a mis-
placed child. We can only hope she gets here to pick up
Junior before Dr. Blanchard gets back."

The purr of a big-engined car followed the words like
a bad feeling. Krista exchanged glances with Mary Nell.
"Where do we take the baby?" she asked. "Your office or mine?"

"I don't think it will make any difference," Mary
Nell fussed. "Dr. Blanchard will pass both offices on
his way in. He's bound to notice."

"We'll tell him the baby belongs to one of the employees."

"That won't help. You know how he feels about
children."

Outside, the automobile engine had stopped. Neil always parked in front. Krista knew they had less than a
minute and a half before he'd come striding into his office. Mary Nell was right. He would not be pleased to
find a baby on his desk. Or anywhere in the building,
for that matter.

"We'll just leave the baby where it is and tell Dr.
Blanchard the truth," Mary Nell said. "I'm certainly
not going to try to explain this."

"Ignorance is not always bliss, Mary Nell." Krista
pushed back a wayward strand of her dark hair and

stared at the baby. He offered her a toothless smile in return and her heart gave a curious little jump.

"Did I call this meeting or are you two plotting some sort of mutiny?" Neil Blanchard entered the office with a briefcase and a whirlwind of energy. He was halfway to the big leather chair behind his desk before he saw the visitor. "What is this?" he asked in a voice that could have chilled a dozen bottles of champagne.

"It's a baby."

"I can see that, Hartley. What is it doing here?"

Krista glanced from the infant in the carrier seat to her boss. His dark good looks were marred by a terrific frown. "I don't know," she said.

"Let me rephrase the question. Who does it belong to?"

"I don't know."

Impatience flickered in the depths of his incredibly blue eyes. "Mary Nell?"

The older woman shrugged. "I found him when I got back from lunch, Dr. Blanchard. I don't know how he got in here."

"He couldn't have walked in so the obvious answer is that someone brought him. Simply find that person."

"I've already called security," Mary Nell answered. "Howard says only employees checked in or out between twelve o'clock and one, but he's conducting a search of the premises."

"Have you asked the receptionist if she saw anyone? She is at her desk during the noon hour, isn't she?"

Krista and Mary Nell exchanged glances. "I'll go talk to Heidi," Mary Nell said as she headed out the door.

Neil stepped behind the desk and snapped open the clasps of his briefcase. The baby jumped at the metallic sound and its little face puckered with a frown a second before it began to cry. Impatience changed to annoyance in Neil's expression before he looked down at the contents of the briefcase. "Hartley," he said. "Do something."

A tinge of irritation lifted her chin. "What should I do?"

"Get it out of my office."

"He," Krista said. "Not 'it.'"

Neil looked up. "What?"

"He's a little boy."

He glanced at the child. "How do you know?"

"He's dressed in a sailor suit and that thing he's sitting in is covered in blue-and-white checks. I think it's fair to assume he's a male."

Neil's frown returned with a vengeance. "Hartley, I don't care if it's male or female. I don't care if it's dressed in purple polka dots. I just want it out of my office."

"Baby-sitting is not a part of my job description."

Neil's mouth tightened a little more. "I hereby appoint you vice president in charge of day care. Now will you pick it up?"

"You pick it up," she said without a qualm. "I have an appointment with Dalton from the FDA."

"What about Mary Nell?"

"She has a dental appointment this afternoon."

He frowned at the squalling baby and turned to the phone. Without lifting the receiver, he jabbed out a number and then waved a hand over his desk. "See if you can give it something to quiet the uproar, will you?"

Krista approached the desk and looked for a distraction that might end the crying.

A muffled ringing burred through the speakerphone and then a rough, gravelly voice answered. "Security."

"Howard, this is Dr. Blanchard," Neil said. "There is a baby in my office."

"Yes, sir. I'm aware of that, sir." Howard's voice jumped to attention. "We're lookin' for the mother. No mother is just going to walk off and leave her baby. She probably went to the ladies' room or somethin' like that."

"Keep checking, Howard." Neil jabbed a button and the phone went silent. "Did you search the ladies' room?"

"I did," Mary Nell said as she reentered the office. "No luck, and Heidi didn't see anyone during the lunch hour. What have you two done to this baby?" She advanced on the crying infant. "He was perfectly happy when I left."

"Why didn't you take him with you?" Neil lifted a stack of papers from his briefcase and dropped them on his desk. "Then, maybe, *I* would be perfectly happy."

"I don't know what to do for him," Krista said, stepping back to let Mary Nell, who had once been given a 'best grandmother in the whole world' sweatshirt, take charge. "He just keeps on fussing."

"Yes, he does, and the baby's not very happy, either," Mary Nell said under her breath as she reached for the crisscrossed straps that held the baby in the carrier. "There, there, little fellow. You're going to be all right."

The baby's sobs quieted the moment Mary Nell touched him, and Krista wondered if all he'd needed was reassurance. She wished she'd thought to offer it.

"Heidi didn't see anything?" Neil questioned, his voice brusque, his actions in tight control as he shifted a stack of papers. "How could she not notice some strange woman who walks into my office with a baby and walks out without it?"

Krista glanced up at Neil. "How do you know it was a strange woman? It might have been a friend of yours."

"No friend of mine has a baby." More papers landed on top of the stack with a frustrated plop.

The baby gurgled as Mary Nell lifted him in her arms. He kicked the air, his little toes curled. Krista had never seen anything so tiny and so perfect. She was an only child, born as a midlife surprise to a couple who'd given up on ever being parents. Before this moment, the closest she'd come to an infant was passing one in the mall. "He's so cute," she said softly.

"All babies are cute." Neil stepped from behind the desk. "That is their job. Our job is to find out what this baby is doing in *my* office."

"I'm sure there's a reasonable explanation." Krista reached out and touched the baby's bare toes. A pleasurable warmth flooded through her and resulted in an instant smile. "Howard's right. No mother is just going to abandon her baby. She'll show up in a few minutes, all tears and apologies. You'll see."

"What kind of mother would leave her child unattended?" he demanded. "She ought to be arrested."

"Then this little guy really would be unattended." Mary Nell rocked the baby, holding his baby head in one hand, his baby butt in the other. "I agree with Krista. The mom is bound to come back sooner or later. And she didn't leave him unattended, exactly. I found him and he hasn't been alone since."

"I only hope the mother isn't idiotic enough to sue us for some imagined damages." Neil drummed his fingers once against the solid wood desk. "Mary Nell, find someone to watch the kid until his mother returns and before you have to leave. Krista, bring me the résumés of the top five candidates for that lab position. I'll go over them while you're gone. And give Dalton my regards."

Krista made a mental note of his instructions as she watched Mary Nell put the infant back in the carrier seat. At the last minute, the older woman lifted the baby again and shifted him in her arms so she could pick up a piece of paper from the blue-checked seat. "What's this?" she said.

"What's what?" Neil asked tersely. "Did you find some identification?"

"I'm not sure. This was under the baby." Mary Nell unfolded the piece of paper, read it and handed it to Neil. "You'd better take a look." Krista moved closer to get a better view of the paper. It was a single sheet of stationery, patterned in black and white with a caricature of a holstein cow in sunglasses and a postscript which read, "My Life's an Udder Disaster." The handwriting was neat, large and to the point. *Neil,* it read, *a boy needs his father and I don't need this responsibility. So, I'm leaving our baby with you. I hope you like him. Affectionately, Stephanie.*

"Stephanie?" Krista said.

"Stephanie?" Neil echoed Krista's question. "Who the hell is Stephanie?"

"Apparently she knows you."

Neil swung toward Krista. "This is someone's idea of a bad joke. I am *not* this baby's father."

Krista wanted to believe him. But a tiny doubt circled her thoughts, repeating the possibility that he could be the father of this bouncing baby boy. And in his eyes, she saw a glimmer of uncertainty.

"I've got to meet Dalton," she said, as if the FDA meeting had priority in her mind, as if her gaze didn't keep shifting to the baby, looking for any resemblance. "I'm sure you'll figure out . . . something."

"We should call the authorities." Neil's voice didn't waver and Krista gave him full marks for composure. "Mary Nell . . . ?" he began. "No, I'll call."

Mary Nell nodded as she placed the baby in the carrier and picked up the entire bundle. "I'll take the baby with me. Someone out in the lab can watch him until . . . he's picked up."

"Good." Neil stood behind his desk, his brow furrowed in thought. "Hartley, I'll expect a full report on your meeting. Mary Nell, are you coming back to the office after your appointment?"

"I hadn't planned on it, Dr. Blanchard, but if you think it's necessary . . . ?"

"No problem. I can handle this."

No problem, Krista thought as she followed Mary Nell from the office. That was a man for you. Hand him a baby and he says, *No problem. I can handle this.* Well, this particular problem could be slightly more difficult than Dr. Blanchard anticipated.

"This could get sticky." Mary Nell echoed those same thoughts as they reached Krista's office. "Why, the baby looks just like him."

Krista's heart sank. "Do you really think so?"

"Here." Mary Nell extended the carrier. "Look for yourself. This little fellow has a dark complexion . . . like Dr. Blanchard's. And look at the eyes. Dark blue and gorgeous . . . like the doctor's." Mary Nell shifted so she could balance the carrier with one arm and use her free hand to tap the baby's chin. He responded with a frown. "Doesn't that look just like Dr. Blanchard?"

It appeared to be circumstantial evidence to Krista. Except, perhaps, for the eyes. "Oh, Mary Nell, I don't know. He sounded very sure of himself when he said he didn't know anyone named Stephanie. It might be a bad joke or maybe a case of—"

"Mistaken identity?" The older woman shook her graying head. "I suppose there's always that possibility. It could be some silly woman who thinks this is the way to become Mrs. Blanchard. But if that's the case, why didn't the idiot stick around? Did she think Dr. Blanchard would just take the baby home to raise?"

Krista leaned closer to the baby, fascinated by his movements and the endless array of expressions which crossed his face. "What will the authorities do with him?"

"I guess they'll come get him and put him in a foster home while they search for the mother." Mary Nell clucked her tongue. "What kind of woman would do something like this? *A boy needs his father.* Hah. She didn't know Dr. Blanchard very well, if she thought that, now, did she?"

Any woman who thought Neil could be tricked into a relationship would have a rude awakening. Krista had figured that out within twenty-four hours of meeting him and nothing had changed her mind since. He handled everything, including relationships, his way or not at all. "He could be a very good father if he wanted to be."

"*If* he wanted to be." Mary Nell gathered the baby carrier close to her body and turned toward the door. "There's always that catch. Well, I've got to find somebody to watch this little orphan. I'd better send someone to the store for diapers and a bottle." She smiled over her shoulder at Krista. "Maybe Dr. Blanchard will go."

Mary Nell laughed at her own joke as she left, but Krista was having a hard time seeing the humor. She pushed a strand of unruly black hair behind her ear and told herself this was not her problem. But she knew she'd worry about Neil and the baby for the rest of the afternoon.

NEIL PACED THE LENGTH of his office as he'd done every ten minutes for the past hour and a half. He did not know anyone named Stephanie. He could not be the father of that baby and he had no reason to feel guilty about calling the authorities. For all he knew, the baby might have been kidnapped from some loving family. Or it could have been left in his office by mistake. Certainly there were other Blanchards living in southern California. It was, undoubtedly, a simple case of mistaken identity.

The baby couldn't be his. Hadn't Melinda's twins hated him? Hadn't Melinda herself told him what a disaster he would be as a daddy? A paternal catastrophe, he believed she'd phrased it. He'd thought about that often in the two years since she'd married another man, a widower with four children. He didn't believe she was right about his lack of 'daddy potential,' but that was not a good reason to prove her wrong.

The baby couldn't be his. One-night stands were not his style. His relationships were discreet and short-lived but, if he put his mind to it, he knew he could remember the names of every one of the women he'd been with during the past year...perhaps even further back. And he always took precautions. In this day and age, a man would be insane not to.

The baby couldn't be his...and he'd done the right thing by calling someone who could locate the baby's mother.

Satisfied with his rationale, Neil returned to his desk. But five minutes later, he was striding down the hallway, past Krista's office, to Mary Nell's desk. It was empty, and he remembered, belatedly, that she'd gone to the dentist. He moved on to the main reception area.

The receptionist straightened at his approach and fluffed out her hair. "Hello, Dr. Blanchard. Can I help you with something?"

"Mary Nell...um, Mrs. Campbell...my secretary—?"

"She's gone to the dentist." The young woman looked as if she'd just given the winning answer on a quiz show. "I don't believe she's coming back, but if there's something you need, I'd be very happy to do what I can."

"I was wondering about the baby. Do you know if someone from the city came to get it?"

"I don't think so, Dr. Blanchard. Mary Nell took the baby back to Inez. Do you want me to call the lab and find out if he's still there?" The smile that curved the receptionist's lips betrayed an interest he did not want to encourage.

"No, thank you." He turned and walked toward the laboratories. He could imagine the gossip that was already circulating. Regardless of what might be said, he only wanted to make sure the child was in good hands.

He moved purposefully down the corridor, noting with satisfaction the activities which went on in the various sections of the lab. Noting, also, with deep displeasure, the areas where activity was sluggish and, in one section, nonexistent.

He heard the baby before he saw it. Actually, he heard the collective oohing and ahhing of half a dozen of his employees. They were grouped around the infant carrier and were carrying on like idiots, making faces and clucking their tongues. The baby certainly seemed happy enough. Neil moved to the edge of the group and stood there, rocking slightly on the heels of his custom shoes, his hands clasped loosely behind his back. Within a minute, two of the employees had scurried back to their respective jobs. Another employee glanced up, offered a sheepish smile and moved quickly away from the baby and back to work. The last two lingered for another few seconds before returning to work and leaving Inez Jimenez to face the boss.

"Baby break?" Neil asked in terribly polite tones. "I see no one has come to claim him."

"Not yet," Inez said. "But he hasn't caused a single problem the whole time he's been here."

Neil made an attempt at a smile. Problem, maybe not. Distraction, definitely. "I appreciate your taking care of him, Inez. Mary Nell and Dr. Hartley both had appointments."

"I don't mind, Dr. Blanchard." Inez smiled with her eyes and patted the baby's bare foot. "I have two children myself and I love babies. It's hard to imagine a mother just leaving her child like she did, isn't it? Some days it seems the whole world is full of crazies."

Neil could feel the curious glances of the other employees. He wondered if a rumor was circulating that this baby belonged to him. Mary Nell wouldn't have said anything and Krista was the most loyal assistant he'd ever had, but somehow he sensed that these peo-

ple knew. Or maybe it was simply a resurfacing of the
guilt which, he reminded himself, he had no reason to
feel. It was not his fault that this baby had a crazy
mother.

And then, out of the blue, it clicked into place.

The world is full of crazies.

My life is an udder disaster.

Stephanie.

Chapter Two

Krista tossed her briefcase onto her desk chair and checked the message light on the phone. Voice mail was the curse of the nineties, she thought, as she slipped off her jacket and unfastened the top button of her blouse. She stretched, hoping to dislodge the knot of tension at the back of her neck. Dalton had been dull to the point of tedium, but Krista couldn't blame him for her headache. She couldn't even, in good conscience, blame Neil. It had more to do with an abandoned baby and her resignation which was, even now, in an envelope on the top of her desk.

She had typed it out a week ago, a pleasant, upbeat, 'time-to-move-on' resignation of her duties at Blanchard Laboratories. She'd cried real tears over it, sealed it with her own determination and told herself she was happy with the decision. But every time she got close to giving the letter to Neil, she found some reason to postpone the moment of reckoning.

Until now. The incident with the baby had stiffened her resolve. Neil had just wanted the infant out of his office. He hadn't experienced even one of the swift and poignant emotions she had felt when the baby smiled at her.

She wanted children. She wanted a husband, a family and all the trimmings. She'd experienced life in the order prescribed by her parents. College, graduate school, an established career. And where was she? Top assistant to a man who made every other man she met seem lackluster and uninteresting. A man who thought of her as a human notebook and pen. A man who asked her opinion on the state of the economy, but who wouldn't notice if she wore a tiger-skin sarong to work. So, here she was, approaching thirty with no prospects for happily-ever-after in sight.

She picked up the envelope, spun on the heels of her practical navy pumps and walked the length of the hall to Neil's office. She walked in without knocking and stopped inside the doorway.

His big leather chair was pushed back and he was crouched behind the desk, his head and shoulders bent and just visible over the top of the desk. "Lose something?" Krista asked.

He straightened with a slight jerk and a frown. "Hartley," he said. "I expected you back sooner."

Krista shrugged. "Dalton was on a roll. I heard more about office politics than FDA policies."

Neil glanced down. "Yes," he said.

With a tilt of her head, Krista processed the visual clues and decided there was something wrong with this picture. He had discarded his suit jacket, draping it over the back of his chair. The cuffs of his white shirt were turned back and pushed halfway up his forearms, revealing a tantalizing section of beachcomber tan caressed with a fine covering of hair. The maroon-and-navy silk tie he'd worn earlier was nowhere to be seen. His dark hair was disheveled as if he'd pushed his fingers through it recently and more than once. His eyes, usually a sharp and focused ocean blue, were shadowed by distraction. And that, Krista decided, was the dead giveaway. She craned her neck, trying to see what might be on the floor behind his desk. "Did you...lose something?" she asked again.

He met her gaze...and if he had been anyone else, she would have thought he looked a little sheepish. "My tie," he answered. "I've lost my favorite silk tie."

Krista leaned across the desk and looked down. The carrier seat, complete with sailor-suited baby, sat on the floor at Neil's feet. The baby clutched a slobbery wad of maroon-and-blue silk and was making an all-out effort to stuff both tie and fists into his mouth all at once. Krista experienced a series of reactions, starting with pleasurable surprise and ending with weary resignation. "Let me guess," she said. "You do remember Stephanie, after all."

A trace of discomfort settled along his jawline. "In a manner of speaking."

"In a manner of speaking...." Krista repeated the words slowly and distinctly, disliking their innocuous sound. "Isn't it a little difficult to conceive a baby that way?"

"Don't give me a hard time, Hartley. It's been a long afternoon."

She could see that, but didn't feel much sympathy for him. "What happened to the child welfare people?"

"No one showed up." He glanced at his watch. "It's after five now. I doubt anyone is coming."

"Hmm. Don't you think that's odd? You put in a call about an abandoned child and no one comes to check your story?"

"There could have been any number of calls regarding abandoned children today. My call must have gotten lost in the shuffle."

Krista lifted an unconvinced eyebrow and Neil knew she wasn't buying one word. But damn, he didn't owe her an explanation. It was none of her business that he'd made two phone calls to the authorities...one to ask them to pick up the child and one to let them know that the first call had been made too hastily and that a parent had been located. He didn't know what foolishness had made him dial the number a second time, but whatever it had been, he was not going to confess to it.

"So," he continued. "The question is, what should we do with this little guy for tonight?"

"What do you mean...*we?*"

"I didn't think you'd want to handle it all by yourself."

"Oh, no." She backed up a step. "This is not my problem. I am not taking this baby home with me."

"I don't expect you to do that, Hartley." Neil moved around the desk, stopping just short of blocking the doorway.

"I don't know anything about babies," she said defensively, and Neil couldn't help but notice the soft rise and fall of her breasts beneath the creamy silk blouse she wore. He'd always thought she had a nice figure. Much nicer in many ways than Melinda's model-thin frame. Of course, it was because of what had happened with Melinda that he'd done nothing to get better acquainted with Krista's curves. One blighted romance with an assistant was enough, and when Melinda had left, he'd vowed not to repeat the mistake.

"Hartley? Did you know I almost didn't hire you because you were too attractive?"

Her expression went from defensive to annoyed in a split second. "Don't think you can toss out a backhanded compliment like that and get me to take that baby off your hands. It won't work, Neil."

He extended his palms in a gesture of innocence. "That was not my intention. I was simply—" He broke off the explanation, realizing she wouldn't appreciate the line of thinking that had led to the comment, either. "Perhaps we should discuss our options."

"Discuss our options," she repeated with irritating softness. "Well, this is my option and I'm exercising it." She slapped an envelope into his outstretched palms and he nearly dropped it, the action was so unexpected.

"What is this?"

"My resignation."

"Don't be ridiculous, Hartley. You don't want to resign because I asked you to baby-sit."

Her lips pursed into a humorless smile. "You have never *asked* me to do anything. And I had planned to give you this today even before...your son...made his appearance."

His stomach gave a lurch. "Don't say that."

"Why? He is your son, isn't he?"

Neil wondered at the intensity in her voice. Was she angry? "I don't know," he answered honestly.

She shook her head, setting a wave of silky black hair in motion. "Did you or did you not sleep with *Stephanie?*"

He rubbed a knuckle across his chin. "Sleep? Yes. That part I remember."

Krista's dark eyes flashed equal proportions of personal outrage and feminine pique. "Oh, you just woke up one morning and she was in bed with you and now, several months later, you have a baby who was—what? Conceived in your dreams? How special. Won't that make a great story to tell your grandchildren?''

Grandchildren? Now, wait a minute. "What are you so mad about, Hartley? I'm the one who's stuck with a baby, not you." He knew immediately it had been the wrong thing to say.

Her chin came up. Her shoulders went back. He thought for a second or two she might go up in flames. Passion suited her, he decided, regardless of its source. She'd never looked so angry or so beautiful ... at least, not in his office.

"Neil Blanchard," she said in a voice as tight as a good corkscrew. "You deserve to be *stuck.* I hope this baby grows up to be a real hell-raiser. And I hope he'll refer to you as ... as ... *Pop!*"

"Pop?" Neil murmured as she brushed past him and out the door. The baby began to fuss, a quiet, gearing-up-to-cry kind of noise. Neil glanced in that direction before he stepped into the hallway just in time to see Krista enter her office.

Why had she flown off the handle like that? *Pop?* Did she consider that a terrible threat? Was she upset because he might have fathered a baby? Or was she upset because he couldn't remember doing so?

Even from the distance between their offices, he could hear her tossing things around, opening drawers, closing them again with a slam, muttering to herself. She was behaving like a ... well, like a jealous lover.

That thought caught him off guard and produced tantalizing images which he quickly shook off as alien invaders of a wonderful working relationship. He tapped the envelope against his palm. Wonderful as far as he was concerned. Obviously, Krista hadn't been quite so impressed with their partnership. He moved purposefully to her office doorway. "Why do you want to resign?"

She looked up. "The reasons aren't important."

"I'd like to hear them."

"Look, Neil, you have other more important questions to answer. We can discuss this some other time."

He thought now was as good a time as any. "Have you been offered another position? Better pay? More responsibility? Greater benefits? What?"

"No," she said, wishing she'd waited to hand in the resignation. She did not want to talk about this. Not with Neil. Not after finding out he was the father of that baby. "It's just . . . time for a change, that's all."

"You're resigning because you want a *change?* What in hell does that mean?"

From down the hall came the unmistakable squall of an unhappy baby. Krista looked at Neil and wished . . . oh, a thousand wishes. "I believe someone else may be in need of a change," she said. "And his reasons take precedence over mine."

Neil frowned, glancing over his shoulder in the direction of his office, glancing back at Krista. "You don't really want to quit, do you, Hartley?"

No, she didn't. She wanted it all, but she was smart enough to know she'd never get it without making some sacrifice. And this was it. "I've given three weeks' notice." She pointed to the letter in his hand. "That should give you plenty of time to find a replacement."

For a moment, she thought he might actually ask her to stay, but he turned on his heel and left her office without another word. The baby's cries grew stronger, intensifying after each new pause for air. Krista felt a little like crying herself. Neil was *stuck* with a baby. And she was stuck with her decision ... for better or for worse. Sighing, she turned back to her desk and tried to recall what, exactly, she'd been looking for.

The baby's cries tugged at an already tender corner of her heart and she kept thinking how he'd stopped crying earlier when Mary Nell had touched him and spoken in a soft, reassuring tone. Would Neil ever think to do that? Did he know how to change a diaper? Or fix a bottle?

But ... this was not her problem. She resumed her search, moving files from one corner of her desk to another, shuffling papers, doing anything to keep from offering her help to the pragmatic male down the hall. The baby stopped crying for half a minute or so, then resumed wailing with renewed fervor. Krista heard the low rumble of Neil's voice and hoped he wasn't saying anything harsh. It wasn't the baby's fault he'd been abandoned.

She looked through a stack of manilla folders without knowing why. Neil should pick up the baby and hold him, she thought. It would do them both a world of good. It might be good for her as well. If she were going to have to deal with the idea of Neil as a father, the sooner he began acting like one, the better.

"Hartley!" His voice boomed down the hallway to her office, commanding and imperative. "I need your assistance."

She steeled her resolve. It was after five. She was off duty. Let him handle his own problems. She moved her briefcase and sank into the arms of her desk chair. No matter what he said, no matter what he did, she was not going to offer any assistance.

"Hartley? Are you still here?"

Krista gripped the arms of the chair and stayed where she was. He knew she was still in the building. Just as he knew everyone else in this section had long since called it a day.

The baby's crying stopped abruptly, sending a disconcerting silence barreling into her office. Okay, she thought. Neil had managed to do something. He'd either changed a diaper or given a bottle or was now holding the baby.

Neil wasn't the nurturing type, but, while he might lack patience, he was not short of human kindness and a good dose of basic responsibility. Witness the fact that the baby was with him rather than in the hands of the child welfare department. Krista had no doubts that was his choice, regardless of his pretense otherwise.

Not that he'd keep it with him long. Sooner, rather than later, that baby boy would be reunited with his mother. Neil, if convinced that he was the father, would affix a generous amount of support on the mother and child and then return to his unattached life-style.

She sighed. Neil was a father. And she was deep-down, green-to-the-core jealous of Stephanie...whoever she turned out to be.

"Hartley, you've got to help me." Neil stood at her door, looking harried, hassled and even a bit helpless. "I got the diaper off, but—" He looked down and Krista followed his gaze to the wide, wet spot on his shirt. The corners of her mouth twitched, but held firm as she matched his earnest frown with a questioning look.

"Don't...say a word," he warned. "I've already lost my favorite tie and a good white shirt. I think my temper may be next."

Krista lifted an eyebrow. "Do you want me to drop the shirt at the cleaners on my way home?"

"This shirt is the least of my worries. I've got to get the kid waterproofed before he floods my office."

She was tempted to rush to his aid, but, well, she had never changed a diaper, either. "It can't be that difficult," she said.

"Let's see you do it."

"Oh, no you don't." Krista stood, giving her resolve the advantage of a few extra inches. "*I* didn't sleep with Stephanie and *I'm* not changing any diapers."

He leaned a shoulder against the doorframe and crossed his arms at his chest, well above the wet spot. "What is your problem with this, Hartley? Are you mad because some crazy woman accused me of fathering her baby? Or are you mad because I admitted that I slept with her?"

"I'm not mad," she said, even though she was. "And it is none of my business who you sleep with."

"Very true." His blue eyes fastened on the pulse at the base of her throat and lingered there, before laying a path of warm awareness along the open V of her blouse. Krista had seen other men try the same technique, with less skill and considerably less hope of success, and she had laughed at their persuasive attempts. She did not feel like laughing now...even though she knew Neil was playing an old game in order to get what he wanted. And what he wanted was for her to take care of that baby.

"Neil, I..." She toyed with the edge of a folder on her desk. "I need to go. I...have a date tonight."

He seemed to consider that. "Help me get a diaper on the kid before you go...please?"

A request, Krista thought. He had actually asked for her help. He'd even said please. True, he was desperate, but she was a sucker for a man who begged. "One diaper," she said. "That's it."

"I'm giving you a raise, Hartley."

"I just resigned, Neil."

He acknowledged that with a dubious smile. "So you did." He turned and headed for his office.

"You do understand that I know as little about babies as you do?" Krista called after him, but he didn't answer and she had little choice but to follow him and hope the two of them together could figure out something as uncomplicated as diapering a baby.

Five minutes later, she admitted they were hardly a match for a baby who preferred being half-naked. The infant kicked, cooed, and generally thwarted their attempts to diaper him. "You're not keeping him still," Krista accused after a third bungled attempt. "You need to hold *him,* not the carrier seat."

"I'm afraid I'll hurt him," Neil said in his own defense.

"Grab his feet and lift," she commanded as she bent over the carrier seat, ready to seize opportunity the moment it presented itself. The disposable diaper rustled in her hand as she moved it closer to the chubby bare bottom. "One, two, three . . ."

Neil grabbed the ever-kicking feet and lifted. The baby slipped from the curve of the carrier seat and his bottom dangled precariously on the lower edge, his feet held in Neil's brown hands, his bare butt exposed to the office air. He looked uncomfortable and not a little surprised.

"Now look what you've done, Hartley. He's going to break his neck that way. We've got to get him out of this contraption. Pick him up."

"I'm not going to pick him up. You pick him up."

Neil studied the problem. "Maybe if I tipped this thing, he would slide out."

"I don't know...."

At her hesitance, Neil took the situation under control and readily let go of the baby to grasp the top of the carrier seat.

"Here we go."

"Wait," Krista said. "Let me get something to put under him. Then you can tilt the seat and he'll slide out onto the floor." She looked around for something suitable and relatively soft and spied Neil's jacket.

"No," he groaned as she pulled it from his chair and smoothed it into a cushion of sorts. "I really like this suit."

She argued him down with a hard stare and got the diaper ready. "Okay," she said. "Go."

Neil tipped the seat and the baby slid with a bump onto the jacket. He looked a bit startled, but adjusted quickly to the new position and began to pump his fists and feet with excitement.

"He didn't land on the diaper," Neil pointed out. "Do you think you can get it on before—?"

"Too late," Krista observed. "I'm sorry, Neil. I was sure he'd slide right onto the middle of it. Now, you'll have to get your jacket cleaned, too."

"Just don't expect me to hold him on my lap, all right?" With a frown, Neil sank back on his heels. "Maybe I should call a diaper service. You and I, for all our combined education, seem hopelessly inept at this."

"A diaper service only supplies linens. They don't change the baby for you."

"Why not? They could make a fortune."

Krista smiled and relaxed a bit. "Now that's he's lying flat, I think we'll have better luck. Want to try again?"

"I suppose so, although it doesn't seem to bother him to go without." Neil leaned over the baby and captured the little feet. "Okay, kid. Ready or not, here we go." He lifted and Krista slipped the diaper into position. In a few calculated moves, she had everything in place and taped for good measure.

Neil observed her accomplishment with a critical eye. "It's crooked."

"What do you mean, it's crooked? It looks fine to me." She glanced over her handiwork. "All the crucial parts are covered. What more do you want?"

He shrugged and shifted to a sitting position with his back supported against the wall and his long arms looped over his raised knees. "I don't know. An explanation, maybe. A psychiatric examination. Something dry to wear. What do you want, Hartley?"

She leaned against his desk and let her gaze be drawn to the details of his hands . . . the long, narrow fingers, the feathering of dark hair on the back, the well-cared-for nails, the outline of bones and veins beneath the skin. Contrasted against the smooth, pink skin of the baby, Neil looked very tan, and next to the baby, he seemed massive. Attraction wrapped around her in an unexpected swirl of emotions. She wanted this man. She wanted his baby. She wanted a nice, neat little family and a nice, neat little life in which there was no intrusive Stephanie.

"I want babies of my own," she admitted without thinking. "I want a house in the country and a husband who comes home at night with a smile on his face and contentment in his eyes."

"You're kidding. You?" Neil's lips curved with a slightly derisive amusement. "I never thought you'd buy into the Cinderella myth, Hartley. You've always seemed so...reasonable."

Embarrassment that she had confided her dreams and annoyance that he had discounted them teamed in a bloom of color on her cheeks. "Yes," she said. "Well, not everyone finds your life-style appealing. Personally, I'd prefer to remember the occasion on which I conceive a baby."

It was a low blow, but he took it without flinching. "I'm not sure this is my baby, Hartley."

"But you're not sure he isn't, either."

His only answer was to look at the baby, who was still boxing the air with his fists and feet.

Krista didn't know what to say. She admired Neil, had even thought at moments that she was half in love with him, herself. But to hear him admit that he could have created a baby with a woman he barely remembered was a slap in the face of her womanhood.

"What are you going to do now?" she asked.

"Invite you to come home with me."

The invitation created a stupid stir of interest in the pit of her stomach. As if he wanted her company, and not just an extra pair of hands for changing diapers. Krista straightened, scraping her back on the edge of the desk as she rose. "Thanks, but I have a—"

"—date tonight. I remember." Neil's smile faded as he stood. "You're not getting married, are you, Hartley? That's not the reason you resigned?"

She laughed without much humor. "That's not the reason I resigned."

"And you're *not* getting married?"

"No."

Neil experienced a surprising rush of relief with her answer. "Who's your date tonight? Anyone I know?"

Not unless he was acquainted with Vidal Sassoon, Krista thought. "I don't think so." She glanced at the baby. "So, you're going to take him home with you?"

"Unless I can spot an overnight nanny service on the way. You're sure your house isn't available?"

"Positive." Krista glanced at the baby and couldn't stop herself from smiling. "He is awfully cute."

"All the more reason you should spend time with him." Neil knew he could win Krista's cooperation. It was only a matter of figuring out the best way to approach her. The baby already had her number—Neil just had to get it. "Babies grow up so quickly, you know."

She shot him a pained glance. "I am not going to baby-sit for you."

"Why not? Afraid you'll get attached to him?"

The look she gave him was wistful and sad and caught Neil off guard once again. He'd never suspected her of harboring Cinderella fantasies. He'd never thought of her as the wife-and-mother type. But he was beginning to form a different, and not entirely comfortable, opinion of his competent assistant. "If that's a problem," he continued, "I'll be sure you only get to spend time with him when he's crying."

"Give it up. If you didn't want to take care of him yourself, you should have let the authorities come and get him." Krista pursed her lips and challenged him with a confident gaze. "Why did you tell them not to come, Neil? Guilt?"

It had been an impulse, a compelling flash of paternal responsibility. If this baby belonged to him, then it wasn't spending a single night in a foster home. "What makes you think I told them anything?" he asked in a voice that discouraged any discussion. "And I don't believe I owe you an explanation, either way."

Her mouth tightened and he cursed himself for forgetting that he was dealing with a woman whose help he intended to secure, one way or another.

"You're right," she said. "You don't owe me an explanation. The less I know about your affair with this baby's mother, the better." She turned to leave, but in one direction her path was blocked by the baby and his carrier seat, and in the other direction, Neil commanded three-quarters of the space.

He placed his hand on the edge of the desk and took control of the remaining quarter of escape route. "It wasn't an affair, Hartley," he said. "It was one night."

A pure and artless anger uncoiled inside her. One night. In one night he had slept with a woman, conceived a child and promptly forgotten the woman's name. She had the lowest opinion of men who committed such irresponsible acts. Her respect for Neil Blanchard was under severe attack. But yet, deep in her heart of hearts, she believed he would eventually offer an explanation that would satisfy her indignation. "That does not make me feel better about this situation," she told him. "And it doesn't make me feel hopeful about the baby's future."

"His immediate future, say the next twenty-four hours, is of more concern to me at the moment. I don't know what to do with a baby, Hartley. I need help."

"Call your mother," she suggested, none too nicely.

"She's in Florida. I don't have a sister. Mary Nell had a root canal and is paying homage to pain pills this evening. You're our last hope, Hartley." It was shameless, he knew, but he sent a calculated glance in the baby's direction. "Think of him."

Her glance followed his, and Neil could almost taste victory.

"No," she said, snatching it from his grasp. "You will just have to manage as best you can." She moved the carrier seat out of the way, stepped over the baby, and walked around the desk to freedom. She was out the door before Neil could think of a suitable epithet.

How could she desert him at a time like this? Couldn't she see that the kid needed a woman's touch? The baby gurgled and Neil looked down. "Why didn't you do something cute?" he said. "She'd have stayed if you had asked."

The baby batted the air, supremely unconcerned, and Neil frowned. "You'd better come up with a plan before she leaves the building," he advised. "Or you're going to be stuck with me—Disaster Dad—for the rest of the night."

As if on cue, the baby's face crumpled and he let out a healthy wail. Neil raised an eyebrow. They might pull this off yet. With a new plan in mind, he hurried to the door of his office. "Hartley!" he yelled. "I think he's hurt!"

She was in the office in ten seconds flat. Neil bent over the baby, hoping like hell he wouldn't stop crying too soon. "I was trying to put him back in his seat," Neil said. "I think he bumped his head."

"Oh." Krista knelt beside the infant. She touched the baby's hand and tossed an accusatory glance over her shoulder. "You should have been more careful."

"I'm not very good at this," he said, even though he thought he was doing okay so far. "Will you, at least, help me get him back in the carrier?"

"There, there," Krista cooed, her voice soothing, her touch calming the child's distress. "You're all right." As the crying began to subside, she faced Neil, eye to eye. In fact, Neil realized, he could have touched her with hardly any effort, she was so close. He could smell the scent of fresh air and wildflowers that hovered about her. Her hand was still wrapped around the baby's, and her voice retained its soothing tone when she spoke. "This is what Mary Nell did before when he was crying. She touched him and spoke softly. I think he just needs a little reassurance."

"Whatever you're doing seems to be working." Neil leaned a bit closer, toward the sound of her voice, toward the soft fragrance of her hair, as a renegade awareness crept up on him.

"You try it," Krista advised.

He thought about trying several things, none of them pertaining to the baby. But if he touched her, wrapped his fingers in the luxury of her dark hair, he'd be breaking a rule that had served him well. And she'd only accuse him of trying to coerce her into baby-sitting...which, he had to admit, was his first priority. He'd be better off to let the baby do the work and make any mistakes that were to be made. "He'll only start crying again."

"Don't be such a big coward." Krista grabbed his hand and guided it toward the tiny fist. "Touch him."

The baby's skin was smoother and softer than he'd ever imagined. Krista's skin was smooth, too. And soft. Sandwiched between the two—the baby's fist pressed against his palm, Krista's palm pressed across the back of his hand—Neil experienced two very separate, equally compelling desires. To stay right where he was. To retrieve his hand and put it safely in his pocket. Much to his relief, the baby made the choice. His cries escalated to full volume. "See," Neil said. "He doesn't like me."

"You're being ridiculous." She bent nearer the baby and lowered her voice to a whisper. "Shh. There, now. You're all right."

The baby kept crying, and Krista lifted dark eyes, filled with decision. "I think he'll stop crying if you hold him."

"You had him calmed down until I touched him a minute ago," Neil commented. "You hold him. Just for a minute. Give it a try, Hartley. For his sake."

She hesitated and then inhaled sharply. "All right," she said. "I'll hold him . . . but just for a minute."

Neil nearly sagged with relief. He would have picked up the baby himself . . . eventually. But his hands were very big and the baby was very small. And he didn't want to drop it. Or worse, feel some stirring of paternal pride and affection. That would be a disaster.

"Move the carrier," Krista ordered. "I'll just slip my hand under his head, the way Mary Nell did." She accomplished that with amazing ease, Neil thought admiringly . . . which proved that women were better at this sort of thing. "And then, I'll put my other hand here. . . ." She had the baby up and nestled in the curve of her arms in the space of a mother's heartbeat, and Neil realized he'd been holding his breath.

He rocked back on his heels and smiled at the Norman Rockwell scene before him—a woman, with a wondrous look on her face, and a little boy in a sailor suit who was no longer crying.

Score one for maternal instinct, he thought.

Way to go, Kid.

Chapter Three

"I appreciate this, Hartley."

Krista caught his glance in the rearview mirror and wondered how he had talked her into his car—into the back seat, no less, next to the baby. *You're doing so well with him, Hartley. Can you carry him to the car? You won't mind going with me as far as the house, will you? I'll get you a cab from there. I know you'll be late for your date, but women are never ready on time. You'll still make it. He's being so quiet now. You're very good with babies, Hartley.* So, here she was ... still angry in a muted sort of way and oddly proud of how good she was with the baby.

"Don't give it another thought," she said because she knew he wouldn't, anyway.

"I hope your date will wait for you."

"He has the patience of soapy water." She could see the quick arch of his brow in the mirror and she smiled to herself. "He'll wait forever, if necessary."

"I'm glad you're not in a hurry. We're going to have to make a couple of stops on the way home."

Krista frowned, but Neil had turned his attention to the road and was no longer looking in the rearview mirror. "What kind of *stops?*" she asked.

"The kid needs some stuff. He can't have steak for dinner, and look at him—he doesn't even have a pair of shoes."

She patted one bare baby foot and received a toothless and heart-winning smile for her effort. "He will need another bottle or two," she said. "And maybe some special food, but I don't think he needs shoes."

"They'll weight down his feet and make it easier to change his diaper."

"You'll get better with practice." Krista looked up, knowing he would be looking back, knowing that no matter what he said, he had no intention of changing any diapers. "By this time tomorrow evening, you'll be a pro."

"By this time tomorrow, he'll be back where he belongs."

Her heart fluttered a protest, but she buried the objection under a show of indifference. "In that case, he definitely won't need shoes."

"I'm buying him a pair of shoes, Hartley." Neil glanced over his shoulder at the baby. "At least I can keep his feet warm."

There was a serious note in his voice and a hint of fatherly concern. Krista decided that Neil was adjusting to the idea that the baby might be his. And that acceptance was drawing out a sense of responsibility and obligation. This baby boy needed more than a simple pair of shoes, Krista knew. But he was already making an imprint on the heart of the man who could be his father.

And where did that leave her?

Krista sighed. She would help Neil for the next hour or so. That was more than he had any right to expect, more than she had any obligation to give. And that was as much reflection as she intended to do on the situation.

"This will only take a minute." Neil parked outside the entrance of a shopping mall. "You don't mind staying with the baby, do you?"

Krista looked out the window. "Did you know this is a No Parking zone?"

"Is it?" He glanced at the entrance and then at the crowded parking lot several feet away. "Well, I won't be inside for more than a few minutes. How long can it take to buy a few things for a baby?"

Half an hour later a security officer told her to either move the vehicle or risk having it towed. She'd never driven Neil's car but he'd left the keys and she was ready to shift into drive when he came out of the mall, carrying one small package.

"You aren't going to believe this, Hartley," he said as he jerked open the car door. "Scoot over."

She looked at him, wondered how he could ignore the scowling security officer. But he simply stood waiting as she scrambled over the console to the passenger seat. "I was going to move the car," she said. "So it wouldn't be towed."

Neil nodded, tossed the package onto her lap, and moved quickly into the driver's seat. "It's no wonder retail sales are down," he said, shifting into drive and pulling away from the mall entrance. "Did you know that there wasn't a disposable diaper in that place?" He shook his head. "Clothes, yes. They sell clothes. And shoes. I did get some shoes. But the health-food store doesn't carry baby food. And the shoe store doesn't carry baby shoes. I had to go to some shop called Fashion Babes to find those." He waved toward the sack in her lap and she opened it and took out a small shoe box. Inside was a miniature pair of leather slip-ons.

"You bought him a pair of loafers?" she asked incredulously.

"What's wrong with that?"

"Babies don't wear shoes like this. They wear little white baby shoes. The kind that fit up high and keep them from getting pigeon-toed or bowlegged or something."

"Those will keep his feet warm and that's all I care about at the moment."

Krista placed one of the shoes in her hand and examined it before turning in the seat so she could see the baby. "These aren't going to fit him," she said. "They're too big."

"I got socks, too. We'll stuff cotton in the toes of the shoes if we have to, but I'm not going back into Fashion Babes." Neil hadn't known babies were so complicated. He was torn between feeling hopelessly inadequate and totally helpless. Melinda had been right. He was a disaster at this. "When we get to the grocery store, maybe you should go in."

She glanced in the back seat. "Are you going to stay in the car with the baby?"

Neil frowned. "We'll take him with us," he said. "That way, we can try things on for size."

"I don't think baby food is packaged by size," Krista said with a smile.

She wasn't smiling when they finally located the baby-food aisle inside the gigantic Food Emporium Grocery Outlet. "Good grief," she said.

Behind her, Neil pulled the grocery cart to one side and surveyed the variety of products stretching from one end of the aisle to the other. "We should be in the baby business, Hartley."

With a glance at the baby, who seemed to be enjoying his ride in the cart, she nodded. "I think we are, Neil. We're on the consumer side."

"Then, let's consume." He pushed ahead of her. "You take that side. I'll take this one. Anything you think looks good, put it in the cart."

"Strained asparagus," she said. "How can that be good?"

The baby gurgled.

Neil reached for a jar of carrots. Babies needed vitamin A. He put it in the cart.

"Krista?" A woman spoke from behind them, and Neil turned in unison with Krista. The woman was tall, with wispy beige hair. "Krista. Hi. Remember me? Suzan Shepley? Suzan...with a z? We used to be neighbors when you first moved to San Diego."

"Suzan." Krista smiled with pleasure. "Of course I remember you. How could I forget?"

Neil waited for the remembrances to subside and noticed how pretty his assistant was when she laughed. He couldn't deny being curious about Krista's private life and he realized, with some surprise, that he'd never before met a personal friend of hers. When Suzan turned her smile on him, he offered his hand with some eagerness.

"Neil Blanchard," he said.

"Suzan Shepley." She gripped his hand firmly before her gaze dropped to the baby in the grocery cart. "Krista, you lucky dog, why didn't you invite me to the wedding? I suppose this handsome little fellow is Neil, Jr.?"

The atmosphere in the baby-food aisle bubbled with a curious tension. Neil glanced at Krista, who looked at the baby before she turned awkwardly to him. "Uh...?"

"We call him Kid," Neil said, deciding he was under no obligation to make explanations to Suzan Shepley. Let her assume whatever she chose. "We're out shopping for some gourmet delights for his dining pleasure."

"I'll bet you're just thrilled to pieces with him." Suzan leaned over the cart and clicked her tongue at the baby. "How old is he?"

Neil exchanged glances with Krista. "He's...uh... older than he looks," he said with a shrug. "Six months. He's six months old."

"Really? He only looks about three."

"What am I thinking?" Neil shook his head. "I didn't mean to say six months. He is three months. Three months...and one week. That's why he looks older. He's a week older than three months." Neil kept smiling as he glanced at Krista. "Isn't that right, dear?"

"Three months." She smiled at Suzan and offered Neil a glare of brown-eyed annoyance. How had he failed to notice how very dark her eyes were? And how very expressive.

"Three months." Neil smiled and nodded.

Suzan laughed as the baby grasped her index finger. "He's so cute. Looks just like his daddy. Krista, really you should have let me know."

"Suzan," Krista said, and Neil knew by her tone of voice that she wasn't going to let the assumptions ride. "Neil and I aren't married."

Suzan's glance soared from the baby to Neil and then winged to Krista. "Oh," she said and then gave an awkward laugh. "Oh, well, what's a piece of paper, anyway? Obviously, you're crazy about each other and why should you bother with a ceremony when you have this little guy to bond you together?"

"Ceremonies are often meaningless," Neil threw in. "Nothing more than rituals for the benefit of a society that's overburdened with traditions."

"Too true," Suzan agreed readily. "I'm getting married in the fall, but we're keeping the traditions to a minimum and saving ourselves a lot of hassle." She turned to Krista with a second rushed laugh. "Listen, I'm just incredibly happy for you. I can't wait to have a baby myself. Let's keep in touch. Are you in the phone book?"

"Yes."

"No."

Krista and Neil spoke at the same time and Suzan laughed again, oblivious to the exchange of antagonistic glances between the happy couple. "It's in the book," Krista said. "Under Hartley."

Suzan reached across the cart and squeezed Krista's shoulder. "I always did admire your independence." She turned to Neil with a full display of her wide smile. "You're a lucky man and this little guy..." she transferred the smile to the baby "... is one lucky *kid*. I've got to run. I'm cooking dinner for my fiancé tonight and I'm running late, as usual." She waved a flighty goodbye as she rounded the edge of the aisle and disappeared from view.

"It's always nice to see an old friend, isn't it?" Neil pushed the cart a few inches down the aisle and scanned the shelf of pureed fruit.

"Why did you do that?" The words hit his back, somewhere just below his shoulder blade, with warmth and wrath. "How could you do that to me?"

He turned slowly, taking in with some small pleasure, the passion directed at him. From the jut of her chin to the fire in her eyes, Hartley was mad. He didn't really blame her. He hadn't meant to imply... well, perhaps he had... but Suzan had jumped to those conclusions on her own. "I wasn't going to explain the situation," he said.

"How am I going to explain the 'disappearance of Neil, Jr.,' the next time I run into her? Really, Neil. You should have said something, anything to keep her from thinking... well, what she was thinking."

"Why didn't you set her straight? You jumped right in there to let her know we weren't married."

"She talked so fast after that, I couldn't get another opening. Besides, he's your baby. It was your place to correct the misunderstanding."

"I did not confirm her assumptions."

"Is that right... *dear?*" With her hands on her hips, her head tipped back to look up at him, Krista looked shorter than usual. And he felt considerably taller.

"I call a lot of people 'dear.' That doesn't mean I'm married to them or that I had a baby with them." He turned back to the shelves and placed a jar of pureed pears in the basket. "If it's important to you, I'll go find her right now and tell her she jumped to the wrong conclusions. I'll explain that as far as I know, you are not the mother of this infant."

"Never mind, Neil. You'd only confuse the situation even more. I don't understand why you didn't just tell her that we're baby-sitting."

"It's none of her business. And frankly, I don't care what she thinks."

Krista leaned over the baby and adjusted the bottom of his sailor suit. "If I wasn't worried about the *Kid*, I'd give you a piece of my mind right here and now. But we are in a public place and I know he has to be getting very hungry, so I'll save my comments for later."

"Shall I make you an appointment?" Neil asked, enjoying her anger a little less now that she wasn't standing so close to him.

She straightened and fixed him with a sharp, 'I'm no fool' gaze. "I know what you're trying to do, Neil. I am onto you." She turned aside and he watched from the corner of his eye as she reached behind two jars of strained peas and picked a third identical jar from the shelf. "Just don't say another word to me until we get out of this place."

Neil would have been happy to abide by her request, except that she broke the silence first.

"What do you know about baby formula?" she asked.

"It's marketed in cans, mixed, ready-to-mix, powder, liquid and concentrate."

"I can see that. Which kind do I get?"

"One of each. Three of one, two of another. How do I know? Just put some in the cart and let's get through with this."

"We don't even know how old he is." Krista's voice hovered between a sigh and a reproach as she started placing cans of formula with the other groceries.

"He's three months," Neil said, taking Krista's arm and moving her, along with the cart, down the aisle. "Your friend said so."

"Three months. That means he would have been born in March. When, exactly, did you wake up in bed with Stephanie?"

Neil knew she was going to demand some kind of answer. Lord only knew why. "It was June, almost exactly a year ago."

"You remember the month, but you can't remember having sex with her?"

He leaned forward and buried his lips, and hopefully his words, in the silky swath of hair that covered her ear. "I am not going to talk about my sex life in the middle of the Grocery Emporium."

"Oh, I don't know." Krista swept a pointed glance past the baby supplies. "This seems an appropriate place."

He wanted to bust the argument wide open, then and there. Make her tell him why she was complicating his life with more tension. Find out just why she was so angry about the baby and Stephanie. But he was a strategist and he knew that he needed her help. He crossed his arms at his chest and regarded her with his best world-weary smile. "Okay. What do you want to know?"

Her lips tightened as she pressed one fisted hand against her side. "Why did you forget Stephanie?"

"She wasn't particularly memorable?"

Her opinion of that answer showed all over. In different circumstances, Neil would have found her body language a provocative challenge.

"This is ridiculous," she said. "I don't even know why I brought it up again. Except that it's an insult to women everywhere and you're making it into some big joke."

"I don't consider this a joke, Krista. And I certainly don't consider it an *insult* to all women. What do you expect me to do? Change my story? I don't remember and I fail to see how that would improve the situation."

"You're right." She clanked a can of formula into the upper basket. "Nothing you say will be an improvement. Let's just drop it."

"Fine, but before we do, why don't you be honest? The real reason you didn't like my answer, truthful or not, was because it wasn't what you wanted to hear."

"Oh, and what *did* I want to hear?"

"That I was fathoms deep in love with Stephanie. That I wanted to marry her and have children with her and live happily ever after." He shrugged. "You wanted to hear Cinderella."

She looked away, but not before he saw and wondered at the glint of hurt in her eyes. "Dr. Blanchard," she said after a minute. "You do not deserve to be the father of this or any other baby. You will only teach him a lack of respect for women."

Neil could feel his control deserting him. "I beg your pardon. I have tremendous respect for women. I like them. I enjoy their company and most of the time I admire the hell out of them. One mistake does not make me Henry the Eighth."

"No, it makes you Daddy the First."

He matched her impudent look with a stony glare. "Hartley," he said with supreme self-assurance. "Are you jealous because I slept with Stephanie?"

Her shoulders went back as her chin came up. "Every woman in the world is jealous, Neil. A woman *dreams* about being with a man who not only can't remember her name, he can't even remember whether or not he had sex with her."

"You're making too big a deal out of this, Hartley. It happened a year ago. And there were...extenuating circumstances."

"I'll just bet there were."

His lips tightened with a frown he hadn't intended to let her see. He grappled for a hold on his own temper. "I've already told you more than you have any right to know. Drop the subject."

"I'll do that," she said, her voice soft and taut with her annoyance. "I'll drop it right now." She spun around and marched down the aisle.

He didn't know how she managed to make nonsense out of so many words. What had he said? And where did she get the idea he had no respect for women? Hah. "Where are you going?"

"Don't worry about me. I'll get a cab from here."

"Damnation," he muttered under his breath, and the baby let out a wail that startled him and stalled Krista's exit. She hesitated, obviously debating the wisdom of returning. The night stretched before him like so much uncharted territory...and he wanted her company and counsel.

He bent over the basket, clucked his tongue as Suzan had done and stroked the baby's fat cheek. The crying diminished somewhat, and Neil felt like he'd climbed Mount Everest.

"All right." Krista spoke behind him. "I'll help you get him home."

A wave of relief swept over him. She wasn't deserting him and, while he knew she wasn't a willing companion in this adventure, at least she was going along for the ride. "Thanks, Hartley," he said. "I really appreciate this."

She looked up and into his eyes, and his relief changed to a sharp and sensual, uneasy awareness. His perspective on his assistant was undergoing a rapid and unexpected reassessment. She had changed. He had changed. *Something* had changed. The quickening in his pulse wasn't imagination and the evening ahead suddenly flirted with new dangers.

"I'm doing this for *him*." She snapped him back to reality. "I'll take him to the car while you check out." She lifted the carrier seat into her arms. "Make it the express lane."

With that impertinent order, she carried the baby down the aisle and disappeared. Neil looked over the items in the cart and wondered, not for the first time, what had happened to his quiet, agreeable, reasonable assistant.

"IT HAS TO BE WARM. Babies can't drink cold formula."

Neil looked at the bottle in his hand and felt frustration tighten his jaw. "It took me twenty minutes to figure out how to fill the little sack liner and four tries before I figured out that the liner should be in the bottle *before* I filled it. I burned my finger sterilizing the nipple and washed twelve dollars worth of baby formula down the sink. If he wants to eat, he can damn well take this cold."

Krista looked up from the floor where she sat beside the baby, who still sat in his carrier seat. "Then you give it to him."

Neil decided a challenge was a challenge. He knelt on one knee beside the baby and stuck the nipple of the bottle against the infant's lips. The baby opened his mouth eagerly and stopped the snuffling tears that had accompanied them on the journey home. He was hungry, no doubt about it. But in seconds, the look on his face had turned from eager anticipation to disgust. Formula began to dribble down his chin as he did his baby best to spit the nipple from his mouth.

Krista didn't say anything, but her entire demeanor was classic 'I told you so.'

Neil debated forcing the issue, but he was tired of hearing the baby cry. He wanted a stiff drink and fifteen minutes in the hot tub. Weren't babies supposed to take their bottles and go to sleep? He sank back on his foot and rested his arms on his upraised knee. A drop of formula ran down the side of the bottle, rolled over his thumb and dropped onto the carpet. "Why does it have to be warm?" he asked.

"Maybe it's easier to digest," Krista answered with a sigh.

"Temperature shouldn't make that much difference."

She looked at him, then transferred her attention to the baby. "Warm is the normal temperature," she said. "That's the way it comes from the mother's... breast."

"Oh." Neil felt a little embarrassed that hadn't occurred to him, and then a new thought made his chest tighten. "Stephanie wouldn't have left him if she were nursing...would she?"

"I don't know but he's getting upset with this delay in dinner. See how his forehead gets all wrinkled? He's going to start screaming any minute."

Neil pushed to his feet and promised himself *two* drinks as soon as the baby was asleep. "How do you warm this stuff?"

"The microwave?"

"Good idea. Five minutes ought to do it."

"YOU COULD HAVE burned him."

"You're the one who suggested the microwave."

"Anyone would have known better than to get it *that* hot."

"*Anyone* wasn't doing it. I was!"

"Well, he's taking it now."

"The ice cubes worked, then."

"He was starved."

"Shouldn't you hold him while he's eating? I thought babies liked to be held."

"Feel free to take over anytime."

"I have to clean the kitchen."

"IS HE ASLEEP?"

Krista looked up. The baby, who had laid his head on her shoulder just seconds before, bobbed up with bright, curious eyes. "Any other questions?" she asked.

"I thought he would go right to sleep." Neil thought Krista looked very contented holding the baby like that. "Did you burp him?"

"No," she said, advancing on his position by the living room doorway. "I didn't." She thrust the baby into his arms. "You burp him."

Neil found himself with an armful of infant and a heart full of panic. "How do I do that?"

Krista walked past without a word. "You're not leaving, are you?" he called after her retreating form.

"I helped you get him here, Neil. I helped buy the groceries. I fed him. I almost got him to sleep. Haven't I done enough?"

Neil felt like a heel for having asked her to help. He felt like an idiot for being afraid she might leave. But he was not fool enough to let her go. "You've been a brick, Hartley. But don't go yet. Stay just a while longer. Let me gain a little more confidence in handling him. Please?"

The hesitation was apparent in her dark eyes, and he adjusted his hold on the baby to demonstrate his awkwardness. The baby frowned.

Krista sighed. "All right, but thirty more minutes. No more. Then I'm going home."

"Thanks, Hartley. I—"

"I know," she interrupted. "You appreciate this."

NEIL LIFTED THE TELEPHONE with a terrible reluctance and weighed it in his hands. He did not want to make this call and if he'd been able to think of another alternative, he would have done so. But the situation was beginning to look desperate and he didn't think he had a choice.

With a glance over his shoulder, he confirmed that Krista hadn't followed him into his study and that she wasn't within hearing distance. He knew she was occupied with the baby. He'd left the two of them walking the living room floor. Actually, Krista had been walking. The baby had been looking around. Forty-five minutes since his bottle. Thirty since he'd been persuaded to release a larger-than-baby-size burp. And still the kid was wide awake.

Neil wondered if things like sleep habits were inherited. He himself had never needed more than a few hours of sleep in any twenty-four-hour period. Maybe the kid . . .

Whoa. Tricky train of thought. He didn't really believe the kid was his. Although his memory of that June night last year was admittedly fuzzy, he found it hard to imagine that he had made love to Stephanie and then forgotten about it. For one thing, she was too young, too giddy, and she'd talked incessantly. How could he have gotten her pregnant when she'd hadn't once stopped chattering about the predicaments of her life? He didn't believe it.

But he had to find her. And he knew only one person who might know how to go about doing that.

Neil inhaled a sharp, decisive breath, lifted the telephone receiver and dialed.

"Hello," he said. "Melinda?"

Chapter Four

Krista had been a guest in Neil's home on several occasions, always in the company of other Blanchard employees, and always under the canopy of polite good manners, which restricted her to the living room, dining room, a portion of the kitchen, and the first bathroom down the hall. But now, with the baby in her arms, she felt she could explore farther afield. In complete good conscience, too. He had brought her here for his own purpose. For that alone, she deserved a look at his bedroom.

Finding out about Stephanie should have squashed her curiosity about Neil's private life. *Should* have. Nothing about her feelings for him had ever been particularly logical or lucid. When she'd first met him, she'd been bowled over by his intelligence and charm.

Be honest, she thought. Her first impression had been a slack-jawed, weak-at-the-knee response to his looks. Face it. Intelligence and charm were great qualities, but they took time to appreciate. Neil's looks were just *there* and she had been as susceptible as the next woman. But she'd learned his ways and the attraction hadn't faded. Although he was often curt, always in charge, and completely arrogant, he was also possessed of the most dynamic personality she'd ever come in close contact with. And some silly feminine voice inside her head had whispered that *she* would be the one and only woman to win his heart.

It had been fantasy, of course, harmless for the most part, but enough to keep her from taking any other man seriously. She'd recognized the trap finally, had taken deliberate steps to eradicate any comparisons between Neil—Prince Charming—and the man she would eventually marry. She'd resigned. Today, in fact. So what was she doing carrying his baby down the hall to his bedroom?

The infant kicked contentedly in her arms as she pushed open first one door and then another. His room was the last door in the hallway and hardly resembled the bachelor pad she knew it to be. No heart-shaped bed. No jungle prints. No dim lights and soft music. No mirrors on the ceiling. It was just a room, tasteful and subdued like the rest of the house, with windows that made the most of an ocean view.

A set of open French doors led onto the walk-around deck and Neil stood, facing the beach, his hands pressed taut and tense on the railing.

Krista glanced at the baby in her arms and felt exasperation and a ridiculous sense of belonging. She had no business here, in this house, holding this baby. If she were smart...

"Still not asleep?" Neil turned his head, sensing her approach. "I'm beginning to think we've been misled about what babies are supposed to do."

"He's happy as long as I'm walking. Whenever I stop, he starts to fuss."

"Let's put him on the bed and see what happens," Neil suggested, leaving the deck to enter the bedroom.

The smell of ocean and faraway storm followed him, and Krista closed her eyes for a moment, shutting out the imaginary image of him coming through that door and reaching for her, as curtains and salt spray and desire enveloped them.

"We should have bought a pacifier. Maybe then he'd fall asleep." Krista moved around the king-size bed and reached far across to place the baby on his tummy in the center of the mattress. She sat, bracing her weight on one arm and keeping her body between the baby and the edge of the bed.

"I'm tired of baby-sitting," Neil admitted, sinking into a parallel position on the bed. "I'm tired of changing diapers and fixing bottles and walking him." At the quick arch of Krista's brow, he frowned. "I've taken my turns," he said in self-defense. "You haven't done it all."

"Considering I have no stake in this, I think my turns should count double."

"Didn't I say you were getting a raise?"

"Be sure and list that on my letter of recommendation. I did resign, you know."

"Why, Hartley? Why did you pick today, of all days?"

"I wanted you to remember." She moved away from the bed. "Honestly, Neil, you act as if everything happens as a matter of convenience or *in*convenience for you. I really struggled with my decision and all you can say is why did I pick today, of all days, to resign?"

Neil felt like a heel and realized he did not like the feeling at all. He was not an insensitive jerk and he did not treat every occurrence as a matter of convenience or inconvenience. No matter what she thought. "It's been a hell of a day, Hartley. Forgive me if I sound a bit self-absorbed. I'm ill at ease with the idea of parenthood and the loss of my assistant all in the same twenty-four-hour period."

She walked to the French doors and stood there a moment, looking out, looking dignified and lovely and maybe a little lonely. "I really should be going," she said.

"Why, Hartley?" His voice was surprisingly husky. "Why do you want to leave?"

She glanced at him, her eyes dark with answers he couldn't read. "It's late," she said. "I said I'd stay another thirty minutes and it's already past that. It's time for me to go."

"No, I meant the job. Why are you leaving your job?"

She turned back to the ocean view. "Because you're a workaholic, Neil. Because the lab is your family, your wife, your children. I'm going to be thirty this year. I want children of my own and I can't be your assistant and have a family, too. The job is demanding and it doesn't leave much time for a private life."

He was startled. "I've never intruded on your time off."

"No?" She smiled slightly. "It's after nine, Neil, and I'm still working. I even missed my date."

"But this isn't work. This is . . . different."

"This is different," she admitted. "But it's not unusual. You and I have worked a lot of evenings, a lot of weekends. I don't choose to do that anymore."

"That's ridiculous, Hartley. You don't just decide one day that you want a family, quit your job and then go to the mall and get one. It's slightly more complicated than that."

"Oh, I don't know. It appears that you've managed to have one delivered to you."

He got up and moved to her side, resisting the urge to give her a little shake. "That was not kind, Hartley. I know you're angry about the baby. You've hardly made that a secret."

"Maybe I'm angry for his sake, Neil." She gestured toward the baby on the bed, and then her eyes widened in surprise. "I think he's asleep."

"What?" Neil turned, his mind more occupied with the words he wanted to say than the words he'd just heard. "He's asleep," he repeated and started to renew the argument with Krista, then stopped for another look at the baby. "Great Scot, he's finally asleep."

"Shh." Krista's fingers were on his lips in a heartbeat; her whisper brushed the bottom of his chin. "Do you want to wake him?"

Her touch evoked a response he hadn't counted on. The bouquet of her perfume surrounded him, teased him with its blend of scents, tempted him to follow the line of her hand to her shoulder to her throat to her lips and identify each fragrance along the way. And over it all, he could distinguish the sweet, fresh scent of the baby, which clung also to her. "Hartley," he said, and she looked up.

"Be quiet." She mouthed the words and he watched her lips, fascinated that they should be so full, look so...kissable.

"He's got to be exhausted," Neil said, allowing himself a last assessment of her mouth before glancing again at the baby. "If he wakes up before noon tomorrow, I'll be surprised."

"He'll be awake and hungry long before then," Krista whispered. "We'd better fix two or three bottles so you'll be ready."

"We can't leave him like that." Neil moved to the foot of the bed and watched the sleeping infant. "What if he rolls in his sleep and falls off the bed?"

"Do three-month-old babies roll?"

"I'm not taking any chances." Neil walked into the hall and returned with an armload of pillows, which he piled in a soft rectangle around the perimeter of the bed. "Here…" He tossed a couple of pillows to Krista. "Put those on your side. Set them two deep. He might be able to roll, but I don't think he can climb."

Neil stepped back, pleased with his invention, thinking that, under the circumstances, he wasn't doing too badly. As Krista plumped pillows and completed the barricade, he wondered if this was what it would be like to be married and a new father… and found the prospect not without appeal.

"What do we do now?" Krista whispered across the goose-down barrier. "Are you sure he'll be all right?"

"We'll check on him every few minutes," Neil promised, already shifting his thoughts to the hot tub and a glass of wine. He wondered idly if he could persuade Krista to join him. "Would you like to—?"

The phone trilled across his suggestion and the baby jerked with the sound. Neil met Krista's dark eyes in a split second of shared panic before he made a dive for the receiver. Krista leaned across the bed and patted the baby, soothing with a touch and a murmur of reassurance.

Neil lowered his voice and spoke quietly into the mouthpiece. "Blanchard," he said.

"Neil? It's Melinda. Sorry it took so long to get back to you, but I think I have the information you wanted."

He frowned, wishing he didn't need to know whatever she was about to tell him. Cradling the receiver between shoulder and ear, he reached for a pen and paper. From the corner of his eye, he saw Krista slip from the room. The baby, thank God, slept on.

"Okay," he said. "I'm ready."

"Her name is Stephanie Starr and she's originally from Delaware or somewhere back East. She's an aspiring actress, works as a model when she can, has done a few commercials, and waitresses off and on at a place called Light Detectors."

His hope for a quick and easy solution to his problem suffered a setback, but he didn't let it die completely. "Do you have her address and phone number?"

Melinda laughed. "Why do you want to get in touch with her, Neil? She doesn't seem your type."

"Something has come up. I just need to find her."

"Why? What's wrong? I know she followed you out to the guest house that night after the party, but I never imagined you'd let her stay. Tell me the truth, she didn't give you some, uh, social disease, did she?"

He recalled how irritating Melinda could be. "No, Melinda, I don't have a *social disease*. For Pete's sake, I met her at your house and I want to locate her again. Is there something wrong with that?"

"No, no. Don't get upset. I know your reputation is much blacker than your exploits and I know you don't do stupid things. Still, she was such an odd little person. I didn't know her at all. She came with a friend of Doug's, and he'd never met her before the party, either. Doug, I mean. His friend had taken her out two or three times before. But when I called him just now—by the way, his name is Jon—he said he hadn't seen her since the night at our party. He'd heard she got a bit part in a play and had moved to New York, but that's all he knew."

"When?" Neil tried not to panic. "When did she move?"

"Jon didn't say. He hasn't seen her in nearly a year." Melinda paused. "What's going on, Neil? You can tell me. You know how discreet I can be."

"Yes, Melinda, I do know. You were so discreet I didn't even realize there was another man in your life until you were married to him."

"You weren't paying attention, Neil. But, really, it was just ... one of those things. And whether you admit it or not, I know I only wounded your vanity, not your heart."

She was right, but to admit it would only wound his vanity again. "So," he said, returning to the subject of Stephanie. "This Jon fellow doesn't have any idea where she is now?"

"No, and he didn't seem very interested in finding out, either. I'm afraid you've hit a dead end."

Neil looked at what he'd written on the notepad. *Starr. Actress. Model. Waitress. Light Detectors.* Not a hell of a lot of information about the mother of his son. *His son?* "Are you sure you can't think of anyone else who might know her?" he asked. "Someone who could give me a phone number? Address? Anything?"

"I'm sorry, Neil. That's it." Melinda's voice had a curious tone, as if she would have liked to spend the next hour or two playing catch-up on each other's lives and trying to find out why Neil wanted to find Stephanie. "If, by some chance, I hear any other juicy tidbits about your Stephanie, I'll be sure to let you know."

Neil decided not to bite on her obvious ploy. *Your* Stephanie. Sheesh. "How's married life, Melinda?"

"I always told you it was the best life, Neil. I'm happier than I've ever been and . . . we're expecting a baby. Doug and I are very happy about it."

"Congratulations," Neil said. "And thanks for your help."

The baby sighed in his sleep and Neil leaned across the pillows to pat the tiny back. Come to think of it, if it hadn't been for Melinda, he wouldn't be facing the disasterous situation he was in now. If she hadn't insisted he be their guest for the weekend and if he hadn't felt it was important to show her he was not heartbroken over her defection, he would never have met Stephanie and this little boy might not now exist.

Neil frowned. That would have been a shame. He was a good-looking kid. Had character, too. Considering that he'd been abandoned by his mother, thrust into the hands of an inept man who might or might not be his father, he had behaved quite well. Of course, much of the credit for that went to Hartley.

Hartley. If she'd slipped off and left him alone with the kid . . .

He found her in the kitchen, humming as she fixed more bottles. "You look very domestic," he said, leaning against the doorjamb to watch her. "Making a bottle for our kid's midnight feeding?"

She glanced up, blushed, and he was utterly charmed.

"I thought it would be a good idea," she said. "At midnight, you'll appreciate my foresight."

"I appreciate it now, Hartley." He'd always called her that. He liked the name and he liked the slight distance it kept between them. But it seemed strange to say it here, in his kitchen, with her jacket off, her blouse unbuttoned to an after-five level, and her hair mussed and alluring. "Do you mind if I call you Krista?" he asked.

She blinked, and he smiled at her surprise.

"Neil, I don't know what you want now, but, as I told you before, I am onto you." She pasted a hand to her hip, assuming a typically defensive pose. "I'm not going to be persuaded to do your dirty work because you smile and use my first name in that melt-in-your-mouth tone of voice."

He couldn't fight the tug at the corner of his lips. "Really? Melt in your mouth?"

She turned to the filled bottle and began maneuvering the nipple into place.

"What do you think I'm trying to persuade you to do, Hart—Kris—wait. What did we decide I should call you?"

"Hartley is fine," she snapped.

"All right . . . Hartley." He did his best to make the name melt in his mouth and rather liked the flavor of it. "What is the dirty work I'm trying to get you to do for me? Make bottles? Change diapers?"

"I shouldn't have said that," she said. "I am here of my own free will. I could have, and probably should have, left you to sink or swim. But I didn't, so I have no right to be mad at you."

"That's good to know. Why are you mad at me, then?"

She looked up, and he tried to appear somewhat indifferent about her answer. "The phone call," she said. "Was it Stephanie?"

"No." He crossed his arms at his chest and observed her curiously. "You're mad because you thought Stephanie called?"

"I'm only surprised you haven't gotten in touch with her already."

"If I knew how to get in touch with her, believe me, I'd have done so by now. The phone call was from Melinda. I thought she could tell me where to find Stephanie. That's where we met last June. Stephanie and I. At Melinda's house. Melinda and Doug's."

"Oh." Krista was beginning to wonder if she wanted to have this discussion. It was none of her business. And the baby needed his mother. And she needed to go home. "Did Melinda tell you how to find her... Stephanie, I mean?"

"Not exactly, but now, at least, I have her last name and a place where she once worked."

Krista snapped the nipple onto the bottle. "Someone had to tell you her last name." Shaking her head, Krista walked to the refrigerator and put the bottle inside. "I always knew you had the heart of a playboy, I just didn't think you took enough time away from work to behave like one."

He straightened, one slow inch at a time. "Hmm," he said. "I think we should get into the hot tub and talk about my life-style."

Hot tub. She had glimpsed it from the bedroom, a steamy barrel of invitation, of hot-blooded fantasy and imagined delights. She'd wondered if he brought his dates here and seduced them in the hot tub. She'd taken a moment—certainly no more than sixty seconds—to imagine herself in that tub, relaxed and lazy and sensual. And now he was dangling the fantasy in front of her nose like the apple before Eve. "Another time," she said, seeing the images crumple and fade in her mind's eye. "I really have to leave."

"I'd like to have your help in finding the baby's mother," he said. "I'm afraid this is going to be more difficult than I first thought."

"And what do you think I can do to help?"

"Lend moral support. A helping hand. A voice of reason. Wouldn't you enjoy watching my playboy heart get trampled by the consequences of a playboy life?"

Krista noted his droll tone and the amusement in his voice, but she wasn't up to the challenge. "I'd much rather see that baby in a secure place where he was loved and wanted and cared for."

"I don't think we've done too badly, Krista." He smiled slightly. "I mean . . . Hartley."

Damn him. She'd never minded his usage of her last name rather than her first. She understood the dynamics of a male/female working relationship. But now, suddenly, in one husky teasing moment, he'd made her name a term of intimacy and seduction. She turned away, trying to shake the feeling that she was in dangerous territory. "*We* can hardly take the place of his mother, Neil," she said.

"Someone will have to. She may have left town."

Krista whirled around. "But what about the baby?"

He moved across the room, and she was half-afraid he was coming for her. What he would do with her, she didn't know, but she stepped aside to be safe. Reaching behind her, he took two glasses from the cabinet and, taking the stems between his fingers, he carried them to the refrigerator. "There's a swimsuit in a closet in the guest bedroom. I think it will fit you." He set a wine bottle on the counter and began tearing off the protective wrap. "It belongs to my sister."

"You said you didn't have a sister."

He glanced at her before returning his attention to uncorking the wine. "I lied. Don't argue, Krista. You've already missed your date. It's too early to go to bed. Stay and have a glass of wine with me. Help me resolve this baby situation. I will be..." he paused as he worked with the corkscrew "... forever in your debt."

The cork came out with a soft pop and heightened the illusion that she was here for pleasure. She knew she'd be smart to turn tail and run, to beat a path for the door and not look back. She was here because he was her employer and he needed her help. She'd do well to weigh all invitations against that fact.

On the other hand, she *was* here and the hot tub was waiting and he'd already opened the wine and...she *had* turned in her resignation. So what if she indulged this one little fantasy? Wouldn't that be better than looking back in her old age and regretting that she hadn't given herself just five little minutes in a hot tub with the sexiest man she'd ever met?

"I'll meet you at the hot tub," she said as she walked to the door. "Bring the bottle."

Neil nearly dropped the bottle, he was so surprised. He'd expected an argument, ten reasonable excuses why she had to leave. He'd been prepared to be charming, persuasive, whatever it took to get her to stay. With a shake of his head, he congratulated himself on gaining the high ground without a fight. Then he grabbed the glasses, hefted the bottle and headed for some well-deserved relaxation.

THE HOT TUB had never felt so good. The water bubbled and frothed around him as he settled, chest-deep, in the corner seat. With his wineglass in easy reach, the steam caressing the underside of his chin, he was master of the universe, a man who knew life didn't get any better.

And then Krista stepped out onto the deck and he realized he'd been mistaken.

"He's still asleep," she said as she dropped the fluffy towel she carried and tested the water with her toes. "Did you check on him, too?"

"Yes." Neil appreciated his ringside seat as he watched her step down and into the tub. "I see you found the swimsuit."

She glanced his way, but didn't comment on the obvious.

"It seems to fit okay. You must be about the same size as . . . my sister."

"One of them, anyway," Krista said. "There was more than one suit in the closet. More than one size, too."

"Sis is a very versatile woman," Neil said, thinking that for an observant man he had certainly missed a few interesting angles when it came to his assistant. He was just now beginning to wish he'd paid her more attention sooner. Still, it didn't pay to blur the line between a professional relationship and a social one. He'd always known that. Melinda had only reinforced the idea.

"Hartley," he said after taking a thoughtful taste of wine. "Did I accept your resignation today?"

"You didn't have a choice." She slid into the water, up to her chin, and rested the back of her head against the molded side of the tub. "My decision is nonnegotiable."

"Hmm." That opened new possibilities, Neil thought. "Have some wine."

She eyed him suspiciously before accepting the glass he extended to her. "If you think you can get me drunk and sign me into slavery, you're mistaken. Three weeks, Neil, and I'm on my way."

"To the mall to shop for a marriage license, a birth certificate and a cottage in the country, if I remember correctly." He submerged one arm below the waterline and let the jet pulsate against his palm. "Stay with me, Hartley. I'll hire a deprogrammer and exorcise that demon Cinderella. Better than that, I'll let you take full charge of the baby. That will cure you of wanting kids of your own."

"Not to mention relieving you of responsibility?" She took a sip of wine and closed her eyes. "Thanks, but I have a job already. At least for the next three weeks."

"I'll give you time off."

"Has anyone ever told you that you can be rather self-serving?"

"No, and I take exception to that. I'm actually in my present predicament because of my overwhelming consideration for others' feelings."

Krista laughed, but didn't open her eyes. "You're good, Neil. Really good. But don't waste your time inventing good intentions for my benefit. I've decided you're right. It is none of my business how you became a pivotal player in this baby thing. The less I know about what actually happened, the better."

"I see," he said, closing his eyes, knowing curiosity would get the better of her eventually. For now, he was content to let the conversation lag. There were other, nonverbal topics floating in his consciousness. He wondered if she felt it, if she were debating, as he was, the wisdom of giving the tension a snap...just to see what would happen.

"Is the water too hot?" he asked.

"It's perfect," she answered.

"The wine? Do you like the wine?"

"Very much."

"It's not too dry?"

"It's perfect."

He allowed the silence to percolate for a moment. "Would you like to stay the night?"

The jets churned the water in a frenzied massage. The tension snapped taut and he knew, without opening his eyes, that she was now very much aware of him. Her laughter came three seconds too late to be her first response, and he noted the delay with a private pleasure.

"Nice try, Neil, but you're going to have to handle the midnight feeding on your own."

"What makes you think I'm only asking because of the baby?"

"Give me a break. For the past few hours you've done everything in your power, tried every trick in the book to keep me as a buffer between you and the realities of fatherhood."

"I have not tried every trick in the book," he murmured in halfhearted protest. "Not by a long shot."

"Save yourself the trouble. I'm not going to be seduced by a little wine, a little warm water and an invitation to stay the night."

"How are you going to be seduced, then?"

"Only in your dreams."

"Hmm." He opened his eyes and raised the wineglass to his lips. He really had no business pursuing this flirtation. He'd only end up making her mad and, if by some strange chance she surprised them both and responded to his overture, he'd be in a hell of a lot more trouble than he could handle at the moment. Still, she was tempting, lying there, her eyelashes a smudge of black against her ivory skin, one delicate hand curled around the stem of her glass, her whole demeanor relaxed and confident, sensual and serene. "I'll bet you don't accept many overnight invitations," he said, almost to himself.

"I don't have time," she answered. "I work too hard."

"Is that my fault?"

"Of course not. I take sole responsibility."

"And that's why you resigned."

She opened her eyes slowly and looked at the wine still left in her glass, swirling it slightly with a tap of one finger. "What are you going to do about the baby?"

He fought down a sigh. Flirting was more fun, but he supposed some decision would have to be made. Obviously, she wasn't going to talk about herself. "I don't know," he said. "While I was waiting for you, I called the supper club where Stephanie used to work, but it's gone out of business. I tried directory assistance and was told there was no listing in the L.A. area for anyone named Stephanie Starr. Wouldn't that have to be a stage name? No one could be named Stephanie Starr for real."

"Are you going to turn him over to the child welfare office?" There was a quiver of anxiety in the question, a hint of censure in the expression she held in profile. "Maybe they can find her."

"And in the meantime he'll be stuck in a foster home."

"What other choice is there, Neil?"

"I could keep him." The announcement surprised him nearly as much as it did her.

Her mouth dropped open and the wineglass tipped dangerously in her hand. "You wouldn't do that."

"Why not?"

"But you said you didn't...that you're not... I mean, he's not your responsibility."

"He doesn't have anyone else, Hartley." Neil liked the idea. He liked the thought that maybe, just maybe, the baby who now slept in the middle of his bed needed him. "I can afford to hire a private detective to find Stephanie. And I can hire someone to take care of him for a few days. That's got to be more than any foster home can offer."

She wasn't convinced, but Neil thought he saw respect in her eyes and a lessening of anxiety. "What if she can't be found?" Krista asked. "And what if she doesn't come back?"

He hadn't thought that far, but what were the odds a mother would simply abandon her child and never return? "She'll be back," he said confidently. "One way or another, she'll be back."

"You're sure you can do this, Neil? There's a lot more to taking care of a baby than hiring a nanny."

"I'll need your help." He said it simply and meant it more sincerely than any other statement he'd made.

"Neil, I... It's not that I don't want to help you, but—"

"Don't say no, Hartley." He broke into her protest, leaning toward her, forcing her to acknowledge and accept his command. She couldn't desert him now. He was just beginning to feel good about the situation. "It will only be for a few days. A week. Two at the most. He needs you. *I* need you. Don't let us down."

She knew his plea was not built entirely on selfishness. He did want the baby to be well taken care of. But he didn't understand what he was asking. Her emotions were already involved. She didn't want to form an attachment for the baby and then face the loss when Stephanie eventually returned to claim her rights.

"It won't work," she said. "Not even for a few days. You won't make it through tomorrow without crying uncle."

"Be optimistic. We've done all right, so far." He raised his glass toward her in a proposed toast. "To learning about babies," he said. "To you, Hartley, and to your generous heart."

It was a mistake to drink to that. She knew it to the marrow of her bones, but she drank. And when she lowered the glass from her lips, she admitted to herself that she had lost the battle the moment she'd walked into his house holding his baby. This was merely the ceremony marking her retreat into disaster.

"You know," he said with a totally guileless and devastating smile, "I feel good about this. In fact, I feel so good I think I'll kiss you. It's my playboy heart."

She had just enough time to realize *her* heart had stopped dead in its tracks before he was beside her and his lips were pressed to her cheek in a gesture of appreciation and good feelings. But she didn't want his gratitude and she didn't feel all that good. It was, she decided, time for him to understand she was a woman, and not just his overly helpful assistant.

Without further consideration of her action, she turned, tangled her fingers into the thick dark strands of his hair and pulled his head down until she could meet and command his lips.

Chapter Five

Of all the day's surprises, this was definitely the best. Neil didn't waste any time considering how or what had changed his mild-mannered assistant into this hot-lipped Mata Hari, he just let her have her way with him and surrendered wholly to the novelty.

She tasted of wine and flowers, water and wind, and sweeter dreams than he'd imagined. There was fire in her kiss...carefully banked at the moment, but fire, nonetheless. And there was challenge, along with a healthy curiosity. A curiosity which he matched, lip for lip. When she pulled back, he didn't make a move to stop her...but he didn't alter his own position, either.

She looked up at him, her eyes round and a little startled, her expression a mix of wariness and wonder. "I did that on purpose," she announced, catching him off-guard once again.

"I certainly hope so. I might not have enjoyed it so much if it had been an accident."

"I didn't mean for you to enjoy it." She paused, and a shade of her former blush returned. "I mean, I'm glad you did, but that was not the point."

He could not keep his sense of humor from lifting the corners of his mouth. "I can hardly wait to hear the rest of this."

She shifted in the water, but found there wasn't anywhere to go. He had her neatly cornered, thanks to the contours of the tub and some subtle maneuvering, and he thought he'd just maintain the status quo for a while.

"I'm very serious about this, Neil."

He nodded to prove he understood. "I consider kissing one of the most serious undertakings a man and woman can, uh, undertake."

Her quick frown didn't faze him. "Don't be patronizing."

"No, I'd much rather get back to the point of all this kissing," he suggested.

"*One* kiss," she said stiffly. "It was one kiss."

He leaned in and found her lips for a two-second, but very thorough repeat performance. "Two. Shall we go for three?"

Her glare was ferocious. "I'm sorry I ever started this." She placed her palm on his bare, wet chest and gave him a push.

He slid sideways an inch or so to accommodate her and to allow her the illusion of space. He wanted to cup his hand over hers and hold the warmth she emanated, but he didn't. He wanted to kiss her again, but he didn't do that either. "I still respect you," he said. "In case you were worried."

"Listen, Neil, you can turn off the charm. I know what you're trying to do. Ever since the baby arrived, you've been making little plays for my attention and passing out compliments like lollipops. The only reason you could have for suddenly treating me like a woman and not a fax machine, is because you want me to behave like a woman…in particular, a mother." She settled back, gazing directly at him, obviously of the belief that she had reduced him to splinters.

"If you kissed me to prove you're not a woman, Hartley, you made a grave miscalculation."

"Of course I didn't. I—" She turned aside, picked up her wine and took a sip. How could she explain that she'd wanted him to understand she was susceptible to his attentions? And vulnerable. How could she ask him to be careful with her emotions, to watch out for her heart? She couldn't. She had made the situation a thousand times worse by giving in to a stupid impulse and now she could only wish for a miraculous rescue from further embarrassment. Cupping the bowl of the wineglass in her hand, she waited, but no means of rescue appeared. With a sigh and some slight appreciation for his continued silence, she stared at the wine still in her glass. "It isn't necessary to seduce me in order to obtain my help with the baby, Neil. Our relationship has always been comfortable. Let's keep it that way."

"Don't be naive, Hartley. We just breached the comfort zone."

Her gaze flew to his, her breath caught in her throat. His expression was set, his eyes as blue as the Pacific, tinged with the threat of a storm. She swallowed hard as he stood abruptly and stepped out of the hot tub. Water sluiced from his body, raining over her in warm, wet droplets. He was lean and long, muscular and tan, and she ached to stroke his sinewy calves, his taut, intriguing thighs. With smooth, athletic grace, he bent, picked up the towel she'd dropped and ran it in swift, even strokes over his legs, his hips, his upper body. She watched, fascinated and mute, as he dried himself.

When he was through, he draped the damp towel around his neck, and bent down beside her. Placing his hand under her chin, he tipped her head back. "When I seduce a woman, Krista, I do it for only one reason. I have no ulterior motives and no hidden agendas."

Her lips parted on a breath of surprise, which never quite made it to open air as Neil leaned forward and kissed her again. Considering that this was the third time in less than ten minutes, she ought to have been prepared for the fever that raced like quicksilver through her body. It took an effort of will, but she did not let her arms creep around his neck. And she did not allow herself to lean into the kiss. But her lips responded like a thirsty earth to a nurturing rain and she couldn't bring herself to scold them. He was too good at this... too practiced, too polished, too altogether proficient. And she acted like a rank amateur and was totally devastated.

He pulled away slowly, letting his breath caress her, letting his gaze affirm his kiss in fair warning that their relationship would never again be 'comfortable.' "And, Hartley," he said, "I have never confused you with a fax machine."

She swallowed hard and summoned auxiliary composure. "Neil," she said in a voice that was steady, if not strong, "it's time you checked on the baby. And while you're at it, you should go ahead and call me a cab."

His mouth curved in a tantalizing smile. He released her chin, drew his fingertips along her jawline, across her cheek, and tapped her lightly on the nose. "Okay," he said. "You're a cab."

At the rueful lift of her eyebrow, he shrugged. "Sorry. Cheap joke. I'll phone for a taxi as soon as I've made sure the Kid is still asleep." He rose easily and looked down on her for a few seconds. A few, somewhat uncomfortably aware, seconds. "Are you sure you wouldn't rather stay?"

Krista answered him with a rueful smile. "Call the cab," she said.

HER TELEPHONE RANG at 6:00 a.m. and she groped for it through a haze of half-remembered dreams. "What?" she mumbled.

"Where did you put the other nipples?"

"Nipples?" She combed her fingers through her wayward hair. "Who is this?"

"Hartley, don't hang up. *Don't* hang up."

She vaguely recognized Neil's voice, but there was a distracting noise in the background . . . a loud squalling sound, like an angry baby. *Baby.* She sat up. "Neil? What's wrong with him?"

"He's hungry. And he's mad. Just tell me where you put the extra nipples."

"I don't—" She tried to recall. "I made up two extra bottles. What did you do with those?"

"He took one at midnight and one at three." Neil's voice was tight, but controlled. "And now he's ready for another one."

"He's not supposed to eat that often."

There was a small pause. "Here, let me put him on the phone so you can tell him that. Come on, Krista, just remember where you put the damn nipples."

"Look in the oven. I remember thinking they ought to be kept in a warm place."

There was a squeak, like a hinge. "Yes," he said. "Thank you, Hartley. I thank you. The Kid thanks you. My neighbors thank you."

"Have you had any sleep?" she asked, concerned by the weariness she heard in his voice and by the baby's continued crying.

"Sleep?" he echoed.

She rubbed one eye and yawned. "Do you want me to come over?"

The ensuing pause held a palpable hope. "I can't ask you to do that, Hartley."

"I'm volunteering."

"I'll call you a cab."

She smiled, despite herself. "Don't bother. This time I'll be a car."

"Two eggs or one?" Neil asked a couple of hours later, after a much-needed nap, a shower and a shave. "And no protests. You're having breakfast with me."

Krista looked up from the rocking chair, but continued the smooth pattern of rocking and patting the baby's back as he slept. "No protests," she said softly. "But no eggs, either. I'm more of a grain and granola person in the morning."

Neil smiled, revealing a refreshed and renewed outlook on life. "I would never have guessed that, Hartley. But grain and granola it is." He turned toward the kitchen, but stopped. "Have I thanked you?" he asked. "Because I think you may have saved my sanity."

"You've thanked me profusely," she said. "Now would you just get on with fixing me something to eat?"

"Just so you won't accuse me of dishonesty later, the housekeeper will be here in a few minutes and *she* will do the actual fixing. But don't worry. She turns out a mean bowl of cereal."

Krista felt the drip of disappointment ripple through her contentment. "The housekeeper," she said. "Then you have someone to watch after the baby today."

He laughed. "Magdalena does a great job with the house, but she wouldn't do well with the Kid. She's a hot-tempered woman who pretends she can't speak more than a dozen words of English. Most of her communication with me incorporates the words 'huh?,' 'uh-huh,' 'huh-uh' and 'payday.' She doesn't go out of her way to be friendly and or particularly accommodating. It would be a waste of time to expect her to take care of an infant."

"Still, she is in the house during the day," Krista persisted. "You have someone to help you with the baby."

"Yes. You."

"I still have a job, Neil. What about the lab?"

"Mary Nell can handle things today. It's Friday. We'll have everything settled by Monday. Where's the problem?"

Krista frowned and gave the baby a double-syncopated pat. "Mary Nell may not feel like coming in today."

"She doesn't get a choice," Neil said firmly. "If necessary, she can sit in my office with her feet up and an ice bag on her jaw. But she'll manage. You and I have things to do."

"Like what?"

"A shopping expedition for the Kid. He needs clothes and a basic set of baby equipment. And I'm going to talk to a detective."

"You're going to the police?"

"A private investigator," Neil corrected. "Someone who can track Stephanie to wherever she's now taken roost. Do you know anyone?"

Krista didn't want to think about finding Stephanie, although she knew, of course, it was necessary. "Sorry," she said. "Most of the people I know have normal jobs."

"Don't worry. We'll find one. How hard can it be to find a P.I. in southern California?"

"And you want me to go with you?" Krista asked, just to be sure of his intentions.

"Someone's got to baby-sit the Kid." He smiled and ducked out of the room before she could refuse.

"THREE HUNDRED DOLLARS a day plus expenses."

P. G. Madigan, Private Investigator, was not what Krista had expected. First of all, she was a woman. A wiry blonde, who greeted them with a formal handshake and an indifferent nod for the baby. Second, she didn't look particularly adventuresome. She looked bored, in fact, as she faced Neil and Krista across the expanse of an uncluttered desk. "I'm expensive," P.G. continued, "but worth every penny. What is it you want done?"

Neil cleared his throat and Krista wondered if he were having as many second thoughts as she was. She glanced down between their chairs, where the baby slept peacefully in his carrier seat, then let her gaze drift back to the woman behind the desk.

"I want you to locate a missing person," Neil said. "Can you do that?"

"With my eyes shut." P.G. tapped the eraser end of a pencil against the desk top. "How long since you last saw this person?"

"Approximately a year."

P.G. frowned. "Trail's a little cold, but I like tough cases. Tell me more."

Neil leaned back. "There isn't much. Her name is Stephanie Starr, but that's probably just a stage name. She's in her early to mid-twenties. She's an aspiring actress, has worked as a model and used to waitress at a place called Light Detectors."

P.G. gave a snort of laughter and Krista turned toward Neil. *Light Detectors?* she thought, surprised at this unexpected bit of information. Surely it wasn't as bad as it sounded.

"I know the place," P.G. said. "Not one of our city's better bars."

"It's closed now," Neil informed her.

"It'll reopen next week," P.G. said. "It seems like that place shuts down and opens under new management every few days. What relation is Ms. Starr to you?"

Neil barely hesitated. "An acquaintance. I met her last June at a party. She's blond, medium height, and I believe her eyes are blue. Or gray. Maybe green."

P.G. scribbled on a yellow legal pad, and Krista mentally sorted through the information, searching for some element of comfort in the list of known factors.

"Not much to go on." P.G. looked up and let her attention settle on Krista. Curiosity passed between them, but was allowed no opportunity for satisfaction as the private investigator turned again to Neil. "Do you have any idea where Ms. Starr might have gone?"

"New York is a possibility."

"Do you know when she left this area?"

"No."

"Do you know the last time she was seen in or near San Diego?"

"Yesterday, around noon, although I don't know anyone who actually saw her."

Madigan frowned. "You didn't see her yourself?"

"No."

"And you?" She looked at Krista.

"No. I have never met the . . . Ms. Starr."

"I see." P.G. scribbled more notes on her pad. "Any other information you can give me?"

Neil paused before answering. "She had a baby a few months ago. I believe he was born somewhere in this area."

P.G.'s focus turned to Krista. "How many months?" she asked. "Three, maybe? About the same age as . . . this baby?"

Krista didn't like the other woman's knowing look or the innuendo in the question, but she had to admit P. G. Madigan was quick. Of course, it didn't take a mathematician to add nine and three and come up with the 'year ago in June' that Neil had mentioned.

"Approximately three months," Neil said in a tone that indicated he, too, had noted the question's underlying assumption. "Can you find her?"

P.G. tapped the pencil once against the pad. "I have a forty-eight-hour minimum, payable in advance. Any expenses I incur will be fully documented and you'll receive copies of all receipts. I use a standard contract, which is legally binding upon both of us in a court of law. Once the contract is signed and I have your check, I'll start looking for your . . . acquaintance." P.G. smiled lazily. "I should have something for you within twenty-four hours, maybe less. At the risk of seeming over-confident, this will be a piece of cake."

"I hope so." Neil pulled out his checkbook, and within minutes the deal was done. Krista felt uncomfortable about the situation, but she wasn't sure if it was because she didn't particularly like P. G. Madigan or if she didn't like the idea that Stephanie's whereabouts would soon be discovered and the baby returned to her waiting arms.

And once that happened, Krista would have no choice except to take her own empty arms and go home.

"A CHARMING WOMAN." Neil strapped the baby in his carrier seat in the back of the car and gave the seat belt a last, unnecessary tug. "Why didn't you advise me to find someone with a genuine trench coat and a real private-detective-type name? Handgun Malone, maybe. Or Gumshoe Garrett. I'd have confidence in someone like that."

"What's wrong with P. G. Madigan? That sounds like a P.I. to me. And I'm sure, if you'd asked, she would have modeled her trench coat for you."

"P.G. can only stand for Peggy Gail, hardly a name that evokes my confidence. 'Piece of cake,' she said. As if I was just giving away my money. I'll bet you five dollars that any trench coat she's ever owned has a designer label."

"And you'd have more confidence in a seedy-looking detective with a grungy coat? Providing, of course, that he was a male and not a female?"

Neil tossed her an enigmatic look as he checked on the sleeping infant one last time and then closed the rear car door. Getting into the driver's seat, he frowned at Krista. "Don't get militant. This isn't a male-female thing. I'm as broad-minded as the next man—no pun intended—and I did hire her, didn't I?"

Krista smiled to herself. "You did sign the contract. I was a witness."

"So," he said, as if he'd made his point.

"So." Krista nodded agreeably, as if she believed him.

"Look, Hartley, you can't tell me P. G. Madigan looked the way you thought she would, either. Be honest—you expected a man."

"Maybe I did. But I'll bet you five dollars her initals don't stand for Peggy Gail."

"You're on."

"Now, what do we do?"

He started the car. "We shop."

"She said she should have something for you within twenty-four hours. Shouldn't we stay close to the phone in case she calls? The sooner she finds Stephanie, the sooner you can get rid of the baby." Krista offered the reminder without enthusiasm.

"Believe or not, Hartley, I am slightly more concerned than that. I may not be prime daddy material, but Stephanie isn't on the list of Super Moms, either."

"But she is his mother."

Neil looked at Krista with an expression she couldn't begin to interpret. "Merely a technicality. It takes more than bearing a child to be a mother."

"But if you don't want him and she doesn't want him . . ." The sentence trailed into its own dismal conclusion.

"For now, I've got him, and I'll keep him until I know he'll be okay." He shrugged. "We'll take this as it comes."

"And when you find her?"

"I'm sure Peggy Gail is hot on the trail even as we speak. I left her every phone number I own, including the mobile phone. As soon as Stephanie shows her nose, or any other part of her anatomy, in public, we'll know."

"I didn't realize she was so..." Krista hesitated "...young."

"I was surprised to find out she had worked at Light Detectors. Although she probably told me that the night we met. She never stopped talking."

"She must have stopped for a few minutes sometime during the evening." Krista felt a bit mean for pointing out the obvious, but it seemed to be her only defense against feeling a rising sympathy for Neil. "There is rather weighty evidence to support the idea. About thirteen pounds of evidence, I'd say."

"The baby might have been conceived another night, Hartley. A night when I wasn't around."

"I suppose Stephanie just chose your name out of a hat?"

Neil pursed his lips and stared out the windshield. "This sounds like a damn soap opera. I don't know, Hartley. I simply don't know. But I'm going to take care of the Kid until I do. Do you have a problem with that?"

Krista pressed back against the cushioned seat, feeling the weight of her own assumptions, feeling still that somehow, someway, Neil was not to blame. "No," she said. "No, I think you're doing all you can do at the moment."

His expression softened then and the slightest smile tapped his lips. "Thank you, Hartley. You know, I believe that know-it-all detective I hired thought I had fathered two babies—this one, which she obviously thought was yours and mine, and Stephanie's. I like

Peggy Gail better, just knowing she could make that kind of presumptive mistake.''

Privately, Krista thought P. G. Madigan had a fair grasp on the truth already, but she didn't want to say so. ''What are you going to do when she does find Stephanie?''

''I'm not sure. I told Madigan not to approach Stephanie or let her know that I'm looking for her. I don't want her disappearing again before I get a chance to talk to her.''

''And before you give the baby back.''

Neil gave the key in the ignition a rough twist and did not answer.

''DO YOU THINK THESE are his size?'' Neil held up a pair of red suspenders not much larger than his out-stretched hands. ''There's a bow tie to match.''

''He needs everyday clothes, Neil. Not a bunch of trendy doodads.''

''I don't want him to look like an orphan.''

''What does that mean?'' Krista took a soft, fleecy-knit, one-piece sleeper from the rack and held it up for Neil's inspection. ''Dressing him in suspenders and a tie is silly. He needs practical things, like this sleeper.''

''But he can't wear that when we go out. It looks like a union suit.''

''It *looks* comfortable, warm and easy to wash.''

''I'm buying the suspenders.''

''And a half dozen of these sleepers.''

His brows lifted in a challenge, which she met with a single determined look. ''Okay.'' He gave in, but added a condition. ''We're also getting him one of those San Diego Chargers outfits. I want him to have some civic pride.''

"You want him to look like a Fashion Babe."

Neil moved to her side, carrying the football suit and the suspenders with him. "If he's going to hang around with me, he will have to maintain a certain image."

"Hanging around with a baby isn't going to do much for your image, Neil, no matter what he's wearing."

The comment struck a nerve and made Neil wonder, again, what he had done to rate Krista's obviously erroneous opinion of him. "You're wrong, Hartley. Women are attracted to men who know how to handle an infant. Shows sensitivity or some such admirable and presumably atypical masculine trait."

He knew by the quick, upward slant of her gaze that she was surprised, even before her smile revealed it. "My goodness, Neil, you're beginning to sound as if you like being a father. Be careful or you'll have to throw out your little black book and replace it with baby pictures."

"You don't believe I would, do you?"

"What I believe is of no consequence." She turned aside, glancing protectively toward the clerk who was cooing over the baby and then returning her attention to a shelf of booties and socks.

Neil decided he wouldn't let her off so easily. Her opinion of him mattered, more than he really cared to admit. "When did you decide I was a womanizer, complete with little black book and a thousand shares of stock in 'Best in the West' condoms?"

Her smile faded, turned slightly cool. "I didn't call you a womanizer."

"No. You used the term 'playboy.' A more innocuous, but just as offensive title. Are my name and phone number listed on ladies' room walls across the city? Or did you come to this fascinating conclusion based on your own fantasies?''

She turned abruptly and thrust a handful of booties into his hands. ''The choices you've made are none of my business. I'm merely your hired hand. Why would you care what I think about your life-style?''

Her evasion made him angry and he wanted to shake her, right there in the store, although the impulse itself made him even angrier. And she was right. Why did it matter to him what she thought?

But he didn't want her to see him in that light, think the things she obviously thought, look at him in that judgmental way. She hadn't looked at him like that before the baby arrived, so her opinion had to be based on the night he'd spent—allegedly spent, he corrected himself—with Stephanie, an incident he hadn't been able to explain to his own satisfaction, much less to anyone else's. ''We'll talk about this later,'' he said. ''When I'm in a better position to defend myself.''

The swift arching of her brow made him think she didn't believe he could find such a position, but that only made him more determined to prove his point. Actually, that indicting lift of her brow made him want to kiss her, long and thoroughly, which would do nothing to add luster to his already tarnished image. Damn it all, he thought. How had one baby and a few unexpected kisses made so many changes in such a short time? He was no lothario, but he was no saint, either. Let Hartley think what she chose. He would kiss her whenever the opportunity arose. Image be damned.

''I think we probably are buying more clothes than he can wear in a month, much less a few days,'' Krista said, placing additional items on top of the ones Neil already held. "But I don't know know what to put back, either."

"We'll take everything. Are you sure we have the right sizes?" He looked at the pile of clothing in his arms and frowned. "Did you try these on him?"

"It says size three to six months." Krista pulled out a label to show him. "That has to be as close as we're going to get. What else do we need?"

We. Neil liked the sound of that. *We.* He and Hartley. And baby made three. "Toys," he said. "We need toys and a cage for him to sleep in, so we don't have to worry about him rolling off the bed."

She nodded, glanced around the baby department and then walked toward the clerk, who looked up at her approach. "He's so cute," the woman said. "What's his name?"

Krista stopped, and Neil had to step around her to place the baby clothes on the counter. As she turned, he could feel her tension, sense her question, discern the underlying accusation. *We don't even know his name.*

"Robert," he said, picking his grandfather's name at random. "His name is Robert."

The baby laughed, almost soundlessly, and Neil felt a curious warmth invade the area around his heart. Robert, he thought. Yes. His name would be Robert, even if he was a little small for the moniker at the moment. "We call him Robby, for short."

"Robby." The woman leaned over the baby and chirped his name in that high-pitched voice people seemed to use when speaking to an infant. "You're a doll, Robby. And your mommy and daddy are proud of you."

Krista's eyes were fathoms dark, and Neil grew a bit edgy under her direct regard, but he met her gaze and matched it. When she moved away from the counter, he followed. "Do you have a problem with calling the Kid 'Robby'?" he asked.

"Robert is a fine name. It happens to be my father's name."

"But . . . ?" Neil prodded for the source of her sudden chill in attitude.

"She didn't even bother to tell you the name of your son." Krista picked up a stuffed lamb and held it out to Neil. "It's not fair, Neil. There are people who want children, who wait and pray and hope for a child, and she just walked away. She left her son with a man she barely knows and didn't even tell you his name. It makes me mad. And it makes me madder that you're not even fazed by it. Someone asks you how old the baby is and you make up an age. Someone asks the baby's name and you give him one. Aren't you the slightest bit angry?"

"Hell, yes, I'm angry. If I could get my hands around Stephanie's throat right now, it would give me the utmost pleasure to choke her within an inch of her life. But emotions aren't going to resolve this situation. For Robby's sake, I have to take questions as they come and answer the best way I can. Obviously, he has an unstable, crazy person for a mother. I'm not going to do him any favors by going into hysterics because I don't know the name on his birth certificate."

"Birth certificate," Krista repeated. "That's probably on record somewhere by now. We could get a copy. Then we'd know his real name and his birthdate and maybe an address for Stephanie."

"That would take weeks, Hartley. We'd have to write to Sacramento and wait for a reply." Neil tossed the toy lamb into the air and caught it. "His name is Robert and, as to the rest, we don't really need to know. I hired Madigan and, if she's half as good as she thinks she is, she'll already have discovered whatever there is to know from a birth certificate. In the meantime, Hartley, we have a baby to take care of.''

We, she thought as he bent to examine some of the other toys on the shelves. What an awesome and ominous word. *We*. She and Neil and the baby. Her secret fantasy come to life. Except the baby wasn't hers. And Neil's interest in her was strictly self-serving. He needed her help. And when he didn't need help any longer, *we* would separate into three very separate pieces.

Krista sighed and tried to refocus her attention on stuffed animals and baby rattles. Robert. Her father's name. Robby. She liked the sound of it. She liked the feel of a cuddly, stuffed rabbit in her hands. She liked spending the day with Neil. And most of the night.

She was right in the middle of her particular fantasy and she liked it altogether too much for her own good.

Chapter Six

Prudence Gwendolyn Madigan, Private Investigator, struck pay dirt on her third phone call.

"Starr?" Alan Loney was a two-bit agent and a four-bit hustler. He ran a small talent agency in West L.A. On rare occasions he discovered an actor or actress with real potential. Prudence personally thought he could have made more money by channeling his phenomenal memory into another line of business. "Starr. Yeah, I know that name. What else goes with it?"

Pru felt the rush of adrenaline that always accompanied a possible 'find.' "Stephanie."

"Stephanie Starr." He mulled the name. "Blond? Blue eyes? A little old for this kind of work. Twenty-five? Twenty-six? Too short for modeling, too ditzy for acting. But I got her a couple of commercials. One of those vine-covered cottage things. Advertising apples, I think it was. She was perfect for the part. Yeah, I remember. How come you're looking for her?"

"Just trying to locate her, Al. Any ideas?"

"She in some kind of trouble?"

"Nothing important." Pru paused a moment before asking the next question. "Do you know anything about her personal life? Who she was dating? If she recently had a baby?''

Al laughed. "I'm a talent agent, Madigan. I try to steer clear of personal problems and I don't get many calls for a pregnant actress.''

"If she'd had a baby, would you have known about it?''

"Damn straight, I'd have known. Four months ago she came in to talk to me about a movie some penny-ante producer had promised her a part in. They were shooting in one of those states where everyone pretends to be a cowboy. Texas, I think. I advised her not to do it and I haven't heard from her since.''

Pru rapidly calculated four months ago into February and backtracked to January on the outside chance Al's memory for dates wasn't as great as his memory for names and other details. Stephanie would have been at least seven months pregnant at the time and unable to conceal it from anyone. "You're sure she wasn't pregnant the last time you saw her?''

"Hell, yes, I'm sure, Madigan. The last time I saw her, and that would have been the second—no, third—week in February, she was wearing a red leather mini-skirt and some kind of a bandanna top under a see-through shirt. If she had an ounce of surplus weight on her anytime during the last year, I need to have my eyes examined. And if she had a baby, I'll go out right now and buy myself a pair of dark glasses and a white cane.''

Al seemed positive of his information, and Pru kissed away any idea that this case would be a piece of cake. So much for easy money. Stephanie Starr, obviously operating under her stage name, had either never been pregnant or she had better camouflage techniques than the country's military forces. And if she hadn't had a baby, Neil Blanchard was either a liar or misinformed. Pru frowned. "Can you give me an address on her, Al? I know it's against agency policies, but this is an emergency."

"Every day's an emergency for you, P.G. Why don't you get a real job? Or get married? You need to settle down and quit playin' like you're Dick Tracy."

"I'd get married in a minute," Pru said with a smile. "But you're already spoken for, Al."

He laughed, as she'd known he would, and gave her the address.

"HE'S ASLEEP," Krista whispered, nodding at the baby in Neil's arms. "You can end the lullaby now."

Neil glanced up into Hartley's dark, smiling eyes and sang softly, "There was a young filly, named Mary McGilly, who walked kind of silly, and painted her grass." With a little shrug, he stopped singing. "No applause, please. It might wake the baby."

"I'm surprised he could sleep at all if that's the only lullaby you know."

"It's a little ditty left over from my college days. I cleaned up the lyrics some to make it suitable for Robby." He grinned as he levered himself out of the rocking chair, being careful not to jar the sleeping infant in his arms. "It's the only song I know, other than the national anthem and I can never hit the high notes in it."

"I finally got a sheet on the crib mattress," Krista said as she led the way from the living room to one of the extra bedrooms. "Those bumper pads are a nuisance."

"The clerk said he would bump his head on the slats if we didn't put the pads around the mattress."

"With all the toys and stuff we bought today, I don't think he'll be able to *move* anywhere in the room, much less bump his head." Krista switched on the soft, baby-size light in the colorful, baby-size lamp they'd placed beside the standard baby-size crib. "I think you and I were suckers for a good sales pitch, Neil, and that clerk went home with a pocketful of commission."

"She said we needed all this."

Krista looked at him, and he acknowledged to himself that perhaps they could have gotten by with a little less . . . stuff. But what did he know about babies and baby equipment? Suddenly his house was cluttered with diaper bags and diaper boxes, baby rattles and bottles and cans of formula. And now one whole bedroom was jammed full with a crib and blankets, stuffed animals and a changing table. Cute stuff seemed to be multiplying everywhere, and he was beginning to feel a few of the pressures of paternity.

"Lower the side of the crib," he directed.

"Where's the remote control?"

"Very funny." The baby stirred, and Neil rocked back and forth, silently commanding Robby not to wake up. "There's a manual lever somewhere on the crib. Remember? The clerk showed it to us. Weren't you paying attention?"

"Forgive me. I must have been taking care of the baby then." There was a hint of a snap in her voice, but Neil ignored it. He bent at the knees, cradling the baby in his arms, and looked at the crib railing. "There." He indicated the lever with a nod. "Do you see it? Push back on it and the side should slide down into a lower position."

"No wonder I had so much trouble with the sheet," Krista muttered as she pushed the lever and watched the

side of the crib lower. Neil maneuvered the baby out of
his arms and onto the mattress with hardly a bump. He
patted Robby's back, unfolded a blanket and covered
the baby with it. Then, with the barest whisper of noise,
he raised the side of the crib until it locked into position.

"You've been practicing behind my back," Krista
observed as they tiptoed from the room, leaving the
door half-open behind them. "I think you're ready for
the Daddy Olympics."

"I'm ready for a swim in the ocean," he said. "But
I'll settle for ten minutes in the hot tub. Get your swimsuit on and meet me there."

"No, thanks. Not tonight."

"Why not? Am I keeping you from another hot
date?"

"That is none of your business." She gave her head
a little toss, hoping to firm her resolve *not* to give
in...again. "You should not assume that I want to
spend the evening taking care of your baby and you."

He frowned, irritated by her refusal. "Did I forget to
say please, Hartley? Is that the problem? I thought you
liked the baby...and me. You're the one who said she
wanted a baby of her own. Well, here's a golden opportunity to try out the experience and find out if you
really like it."

"Before I commit myself to a lifetime of mother-
hood?" Krista moved ahead of him into the kitchen,
then whirled on him. "Is that what you mean, Neil? No
commitments? No responsibilities? I can take care of
Robby and then, when he goes back to Stephanie, I can
kiss your feet for giving me the opportunity—whoops,
make that *golden* opportunity—to experience mother-
hood without the hassle?"

Neil pressed his lips into one firm line. "You get angry about the stupidest things, Hartley."

"You should spend more time with intelligent women, Neil. You might actually learn something from the *stupid* ideas we take exception to."

"Really?" he said slowly, dangerously, as he reached out and clasped her shoulders. "What an interesting thought. Let's find out what I can learn from an intelligent woman like you, Hartley, shall we?"

He did not play fair. He asked the question, then prevented her from answering by the simple method of kissing her. Except that it wasn't a simple method. It was skilled and scintillating, sensual and so satisfying her arms looped around his neck without a whisper of invitation. Her knees trembled slightly and she moved closer, balancing her body against his, but throwing her equilibrium into a sudden, dizzying spin.

Her mouth opened on a gasp and he seized the opportunity, deepening the kiss with slow, sweet strokes of his tongue along the curve of her lips. It felt good. So desperately good. And she was ashamed of herself for not putting up a semblance of restraint. Not that restraint seemed to be an option for her at this point. No. She'd have to admit she was offering more encouragement than anything else.

He had to feel the terrific pounding her heart was delivering. He had to know her breathing was too quick, too uneven to be normal. And he was undoubtedly aware that she was clinging to him like a raft in a cascade of white water, that she was incapable of standing under her own power, that if he released her, she would simply melt at his feet. Her skin felt hot, her cheeks flushed, her whole body was in a fever of conflicting emotions.

She wanted this. But he was kissing her for all the wrong reasons. She was responding for all the right ones. He was good enough to do this for a living. She was a total idiot. And none of it made any difference.

Because if he was Prince Charming . . . then she must be Cinderella.

When the kiss drew to an aching end, Krista rallied her scattered senses and tried to think of something to say. Preferably something nonchalant and saucy. "I hope you meant to do that" was the best she could manage.

He drew back, still holding her in the heated circle of his arms. "If you have to ask, I must be out of practice. Let me try again."

Her hand slipped to his chest and wedged some small distance between them, showing a strength she had thought sadly depleted. Perhaps survival instinct had come to her rescue. Or perhaps it was merely pride. "Touch me again, Blanchard . . ." she said ". . . and you're asking for trouble."

He grinned, showing how dismayed he was by her threat. "I believe you. Now, will you join me in the hot tub?"

Hot water was exactly what she needed to stay out of. "Not even if you offer me a month's salary."

"Two months'?"

"Don't insult me."

He smiled lazily and allowed her to step just out of reach. "I rather thought it was a compliment, Hartley. I've never offered to pay for a woman's companionship before."

She tipped her head, and her lips parted in a sassy smile. "You're learning all sorts of things tonight, aren't you, Dr. Blanchard?"

He started to take advantage of her flirty challenge, but changed his mind and leaned against the kitchen counter instead, crossing his arms at his chest and regarding her with a keen and pleasurable interest. "Every time I turn around, you're surprising the hell out of me, Hartley."

When her lips curved into a smile this time, he was thoroughly enchanted. "Maybe you weren't paying attention before," she said. "Or maybe you're just trying to charm me into playing house with you."

"Beginning with a few minutes in the hot tub."

"Do you ever stop trying to get your way, Neil?"

He pretended to consider. "Why would I do that? Everyone tries to get their own way. I'm just straightforward about it."

She sighed, long and loudly. "How did I get mixed up with someone like you?"

"Tremendous luck," Neil said. "And a little boy named Robby."

"Be careful. I think you're beginning to like him."

The idea struck Neil as entirely possible. "That would be a disaster, wouldn't it?"

"For you, yes. For him, it might be a pleasant change."

Neil frowned. "He certainly hasn't gotten a fair shake. Age—unknown. Name—unknown. Father—unknown. Mother—whereabouts unknown."

"Will you stop that?" Krista's tone was suddenly laden with irritation. "Stop pretending you don't remember, Neil. I've worked with you for nearly two years and I know you don't do things without a good reason. And the only reason for Robby to be here with you is because you're 99 percent certain that you are his father."

Neil didn't like her logic, but he couldn't dispute it. He wasn't even sure he could explain his reasons to his own satisfaction, much less hers. "I'm not certain, Krista. I remember going to the party. I remember meeting Stephanie. I remember her coming out to the guest house. And I remember waking up in bed with her the next morning.

"It was a tense night for me. I hadn't been around Melinda since she broke our engagement and married someone else. I suppose I was trying to prove how un-affected I was by her obvious happiness. I don't really recall what I was feeling at the time. I was nervous and didn't eat much. The couple of drinks I had must have gone straight to my head. My memory is decidedly foggy after that." He lifted his hand to rub the taut line of his jaw... and knew the action somehow betrayed him, somehow conveyed to her how important it was to him that she should understand.

"Stephanie was—cute, funny. She talked a lot, which was okay because I didn't have much to say. I remember her telling me some incredible stories, unbelievable stories, really, about being an actress. She kept talking about how California was full of crazy people, and I remember her saying that her life was one long string of disasters."

"'My Life is an Udder Disaster.'" Krista quoted the epigram from the note which had been left with the baby in Neil's office. "She sounds very young."

"And unsophisticated," he added with some derision. "I don't know how I ended up in this situation, Hartley. I wasn't drunk that night and I wasn't over-come with a soul-destroying passion for her. The reason Robby is asleep in the bedroom is because my memory of that entire evening is fuzzy and no matter how hard I try, I can't get it to clear. And as long as there's a sliver of a chance that he is my son, I will take full responsibility for him.''

Krista backed up to the kitchen counter and leaned against it, crossing her arms at her waist in a replica of his stance. ''Maybe you slept with Stephanie to prove something to Melinda.''

''My reason wasn't that foggy. I went to the party to prove to Melinda that I held no hard feelings. I stayed over because it was simply too far to drive back the same night. I flirted with Stephanie because she flirted with me.'' He lifted his head and met Krista's dark, questioning gaze with a slight and serious smile. ''And, one more time, for your information, when I make love to a woman I don't do it with any ulterior motive.''

''I don't believe you.'' Krista smiled in return and pushed away from the countertop. ''But you can do your best to convince me some other time. Right now, I'm going home.''

''You issue an invitation like that and then announce that you're going home?'' He straightened, too, wondering how far he could carry this seduction before she would stop him. ''That isn't playing fair, Hartley.''

''I didn't break any rules, Neil. And, for your information, I didn't issue any invitation.''

''Which means you won't spend the night?''

She lifted her eyebrows in a smooth arc. ''See how quickly you're learning?''

He reached for her, but she evaded his grasp. The ringing of the telephone forestalled a second attempt. He looked at Krista. She looked at him. And he smiled. ''Saved by the bell,'' he said.

''I was never in any danger,'' she countered.

Neil didn't know how he had failed to notice this coquettish side of Hartley before now. Had she taken pains to disguise it? Or had he been too intent on thinking of her only as an assistant? "Hartley, I think I'm in trouble," he said.

"Yes," she agreed. "Especially if you're waiting for Robby to answer the phone."

The telephone, he realized, was still ringing and, although he thought about letting the machine answer, he decided he'd be better off to give himself a break. His interest in Krista Hartley needed a few minutes to cool to room temperature. "I'll get it." He walked to the wall phone and lifted the receiver. "Blanchard," he said.

Krista paused, there in the kitchen, giving her heart a moment to check its wicked, rhythmic beat. Neil Blanchard had just kissed her—very thoroughly and on purpose—and asked her to stay the night. Her fantasy was unfolding in front of her like so many yellow brick roads. Prince Charming was dancing her around the castle of Once Upon a Time. The glass slippers were snug and comfortable on her feet.

But the clock would strike twelve. Robby would wake up for his midnight bottle. And she would lose at least one of the slippers and any pretense that Neil did not have an ulterior motive.

"That's ridiculous." Neil nearly snapped at the receiver and Krista glanced his way. His jaw went tight as he listened to the person on the other end of the phone line. A moment later, he raked his fingers through his hair, leaving it attractively mussed and in need of a woman's touch. "Of course, I'm sure she was pregnant. Why else would I be looking for her?"

Krista pondered that bit of one-sided information and decided he must be talking to P. G. Madigan. Beyond that, she didn't have a clue.

"Very clever, Madigan." Neil's frown was more than evident in his tone of voice. "If I'd been going to lie to you, I'd have made more of an effort to negotiate your exorbitant rates. I told you all I know about Stephanie Starr and, of all the information I did give you, the one truth of which I am absolutely certain is that she had a baby sometime during the past few months. Now, you said finding her would be a piece of cake. The next time I hear from you, I expect that piece of cake on a silver platter." He hung up, and Krista jerked with the awareness that she had been blatantly eavesdropping.

"Where's Sam Spade when you need him?" Neil muttered with a last, frustrated glare at the phone. "Peggy Gail just called to inform me that she has reason to believe Stephanie wasn't, and has never been, pregnant. At least not in the past year."

"Where did she come up with that idea?"

"Apparently she knows some low-rent talent agent who worked with Stephanie. He said she wasn't pregnant, and Madigan believes him." Neil combed his fingers through his hair again. "I should have done the legwork on this myself. That's ridiculous. If Stephanie wasn't pregnant, where did she get the baby?"

"And if the baby doesn't belong to her, why did she leave him on your doorstep?" Krista couldn't begin to formulate all the questions such a situation posed, much less answer any of them. "I didn't think P.G. looked very interested when you were talking to her this afternoon. Do you suppose she's just trying to get more information from you and save herself some effort?"

"I don't know. She assured me she has several leads, but she thought I should know what she'd already found out."

"Which is?"

Neil raked his fingers through his hair again and gave a heavy sigh. "Stephanie worked with this agent. She did a fruit-salad commercial. She may be working on a movie somewhere in Texas. The agent has a phenomenal memory for details and he says Stephanie was not pregnant. Madigan was only passing along that tidbit for my information." Irritation formed a frown across his brow. "I believe she thought I'd lied to her about the baby."

"So what is she going to do now?"

"She's going to look for Stephanie. Hell, I'm already six-hundred dollars into this. I'll give her another twenty-four hours, and then, if she's still claiming misinformation, I'll find Stephanie, myself."

"What if she doesn't want to be found, Neil? What if she doesn't want Robby back?"

His blue eyes went dark with anger. "Then she'll have to answer to me. One way or the other, Hartley, she's going to have to answer."

Which might explain a few things, but wouldn't do much for the little boy asleep in the back bedroom. "What if she doesn't want him, Neil?" Krista pressed the question and tried to gauge his reaction. "What if she really doesn't want Robby?"

"We'll deal with that when, and if, we have to. It's only been a little more than a day, Hartley. Let's give her the benefit of the doubt." Neil pursed his lips as if considering the matter. "If she did land a role in a movie, it's possible she had nowhere else to leave Robby."

"So she left him with a man she'd only met one time?"

"She must believe I'm his father."

"Then her memory must be much clearer than yours."

That bothered him. She could see the distress imprint itself in the tight, set line of his lips, in the dark blue depths of his eyes, in the tenseness along his jawline. "Yes," he said slowly. "I guess it would have to be."

Krista had hoped for a contradiction, a quick, no-nonsense rejection of the idea, and her heart took a nosedive with his quiet acceptance.

"However," he continued, "not everything that appears to be true, is true."

"Well, regardless," Krista said. "Stephanie abandoned him. She didn't even leave so much as an extra diaper with him. She left him without any form of identification. It's only because of that cryptic note she left that he didn't end up in a foster home. She doesn't care about Robby, Neil, and when you find her, you can't just hand him over like a package you've been holding for her. He deserves better. He doesn't belong with a woman who has so little regard for his well-being. We can't let him down—he's depending on us." Krista realized the impact of her words as she saw the change in Neil's expression.

He met her eyes squarely, honestly, and acknowledged in silence that Robby had become, in some indefinable way, theirs...to give back...or to keep. "We'll take it as it comes, Krista," he said. "And the first thing we have to do is find Stephanie. Whether or not we think it's in Robby's best interests."

"You're right, of course." She turned her back to him, faced the sink, knowing she was beginning to care far too much what happened to Neil and his son. "I'll fix a couple of bottles for later."

"I did it already." Neil walked up behind her and put his hands on her shoulders, not as if he meant to pull her into his arms, not as if he intended to cover her neck with kisses, but as if he were offering friendship and comfort to her distress. "All we can do is take care of him through the night. Tomorrow's problems will have to wait."

She nodded, being careful not to dislodge the wonderful warmth of his palms against her cotton-covered skin. When he exerted a gentle pressure, she leaned against him with a sigh and relaxed for the space of a heartbeat or two. Beneath her resting place, she could feel the rhythmic beating of his heart and she wished she believed that spending the night was the right thing to do. But even Cinderella knew that on the stroke of twelve, she had to go home.

"If you're going home," Neil whispered in her ear, laying a path of warm chills across the back of her neck, "you'd better go now. Another few minutes and I might not let you leave."

Krista drew in a deep breath, trying valiantly to rally her good sense, her better judgment. "Now, that would be a disaster, wouldn't it?" she said in a voice that was none too strong, but steady enough. She moved away from his touch and away from temptation.

And as she did, Robby began to wail.

Chapter Seven

Robby cried most of the night.

"I'll walk with him for a while," Krista said around midnight, as she took the baby from Neil's arms. "Why don't you get some sleep?"

With a weary smile, Neil relinquished the floor. "Should I fix another bottle?"

"There are two still in the fridge. Besides, I can't imagine how he could hold another drop. You lie down. I'll take this shift."

"Thanks, Hartley." He turned, then glanced back. "Do you know the lullaby?"

"I went to college, too," she answered. "Go on, I've got this under control."

Brave words, she thought, as she watched Neil walk from the living room. She shifted Robby to her shoulder and began a slow stroll in front of the window, grateful that he'd stopped crying for a few minutes. "You're causing a lot of trouble," she told the infant.

He bobbed his head, yawned, and waved his fist at the ocean view. Trouble could be his middle name, for all he cared.

Krista patted his back and fought back a yawn of her own. "When you get ready to go to bed, just let me know." She thought of her own bed, unmade and awaiting her return to her apartment. Oddly enough, it didn't seem too appealing.

Robby made a soft baby sound, a cross between a gurgle and a sniff, as he grabbed a fistful of her hair. "Hey," she warned quietly as she untangled her hair from his grasp. "You'd better be nice to me. I can leave anytime I want, you know."

With a couple of jumpy kicks, Robby indicated his lack of concern at her threat and his desire to continue their walk. "Okay. Okay. I didn't say I was going to leave. I was only reminding you that I can, if I want to." Krista kissed his fuzzy little head and resumed the midnight stroll.

"MY TURN." Neil entered the kitchen around 2:00 a.m., on the heels of Robby's latest crying spell. He wore the bottom half of a jogging suit, no shirt and no shoes. Krista looked from the sleepy disarray of his hair, past the wide, tanned expanse of his chest to his bare feet and thought all kinds of thoughts she had no business thinking. How could he look seductive after staying awake for most of the past twenty-four hours and just now getting up from a brief nap? Why didn't he have pillow creases in his cheek? Why did his hair look attractively mussed and not wild and uncontrolled? Why, after practically living in his lap for the past day and a half, did she still find his sexy, "kiss me if you will, love me if you dare" attitude intriguing?

"Are you giving him another bottle?" Neil asked, coming to stand beside her, and reaching for the baby at the same time. His arms brushed against her breast and she felt her nipple pout with disappointment as the touch moved on, leaving her to imagine the contact under a different set of circumstances. The warmth of a blush crept into her cheeks and she busied herself with the baby's bottle.

"I don't think he'll take it," she said. "But I don't know what else to do for him. If only he'd go to sleep...."

Neil positioned the baby in the crook of one arm and placed his free hand on Krista's chin, tipping her head back until he could see her eyes. "You look dead on your feet, Hartley. I'll handle things from here. You lie down for a while."

"Are you sure?" she asked. "Can you manage if he keeps crying like this?"

Neil jostled his arm, rocking Robby slightly and achieving a lull in the seemingly constant wailing. "Go lie down," he ordered. "You're too tired to drive home. If this keeps up, I'm calling my doctor and finding out if something is really wrong. Babies aren't supposed to cry all night. They're supposed to sleep, like normal people."

"I'm not sure they are normal," Krista said with a shake of her head. "We should have bought a how-to manual at the store. How the clerk let us get away without some sort of instruction booklet, I'll never know."

Neil's lips curved in a smile, despite Robby's continuing distress. "She missed a sale, for sure. Go on, Hartley. Sleep for a while. It will do us all good."

She was too tired to argue. "Where?" she asked. "The couch? In the living room?"

"Don't be ridiculous. That's too close to the racket. Use my bed. I just got out of it and left a warm place for you."

The idea nestled pleasantly inside her. His bed. His body heat. A warm place for her. A new fantasy bloomed, unbidden. "You'll wake me if you need me?" she asked.

"You can count sheep on it." He leaned close and kissed her, lightly, firmly on the lips. "Now, hand me that bottle and get out of here before I change my mind."

Krista released the bottle and the baby into his hands, but she paused in the doorway for one more glimpse of the new men in her life. They belonged to her in some small way. She was the one woman each of them had turned to in the middle of this long night. They might not belong to her come morning, but for now she laid claim to them with a gentle smile.

Neil glanced up and caught her watching. "Go to bed, Hartley, and dream sweet dreams. That's an order."

Krista didn't see how she could refuse.

ROBBY TOOK ALMOST HALF of the formula in the bottle in greedy gulps, before he spit the nipple out of his mouth. He lay quietly, regarding Neil with a wide, blue-eyed and unblinking gaze. "About time you quit crying," Neil said, shifting in the chair and positioning Robby more comfortably in his arms. "You have a new crib and a whole roomful of stuff. What do you have to cry about?"

The baby only stared. Neil stared back. "I'm doing the best I can, Kid. If you didn't like the stuff I bought, you should have let me know before we left the store."

Robby moved his lips, but his eyes didn't waver from Neil's face.

"I don't think you've made out too badly, Kid. I haven't turned out to be such a disaster. Your mother, now, that's another story. You're better off here with me and Hartley. You like her, don't you? I'd have probably sent you off to the orphan's home if she hadn't been around to help, so you'd better treat her nicely."

With a low gurgle, Robby waved his fist and Neil captured it in his larger hand. "You know, Kid," he said, "I think I'd make an okay daddy. What do you think?"

The baby smiled, and a languid pressure squeezed Neil's heart. He was a fool to get emotionally involved with this kid, but somehow the past twenty-four-plus hours had changed him, made him think about a family of his own, a son, a woman who smiled when she saw him and filled the empty places in his life.

As Robby's fingers curled around one of his, Neil knew he was at a crossroads he'd never meant to reach. He hadn't thought he was cut out to be a family man, especially after his experience with Melinda and her twins. But suddenly he had another opportunity to prove he could handle relationships . . . if he chose.

"Hey, Kid," he said. "Would you like to stay here with me? We might not find your mother, you know. And if she doesn't come back, I may be your only option."

Robby's forehead creased in the frown which usually preceded a round of crying. Neil sighed and levered himself out of the chair. "It was only a suggestion," he said as he carried the baby back and forth in front of the window. "And a bad suggestion at that. The last thing I need is a brat like you making changes for me. Listen, forget I mentioned it. Hartley would have laughed herself silly if she'd heard it. She doesn't think I'd make much of a father, either. So don't tell her what I said. Understand?''

Robby kicked one foot, but Neil didn't know if it was an agreement or a signal to start walking.

KRISTA AWAKENED GRADUALLY, soothed by the calming sound of the ocean beyond the windows, as warm as a cinnamon bun heated in a slow oven. She arched one foot in a small circle beneath the covers, then stretched her leg, seeking a cool spot in the sheets. She encountered more warmth... and a hairy leg.

Her eyes flew open without further prompting and she drew in a sharp breath. Moving her foot up along the curve of the leg behind her, she made a series of rapid assessments. One, she was not in her own bed. Two, she was not in this bed alone. Three, there was a man's arm draped comfortably over her shoulder. And four, the person who was curled around her like a sleepy kitten was Neil Blanchard, her employer.

Her first clear thought was that she should get out of the bed, as quickly as possible.

"Lie still," he commanded in a voice no less authoritative because it carried an edge of sleepiness.

She lay still, giving her mind a few seconds to catch up to reality and pinpoint the highlights of the preceding evening. The baby. Robby had kept crying. She had stayed to help. Neil had told her to go to bed. A warm place. She'd fallen asleep with her head on Neil's pillow, her heart full of the fantasy of being in his bed. And now he was in it with her. Wasn't this what had happened to Stephanie? Krista inched her leg toward the edge of the mattress.

"Where do you think you're going?" he asked.

She inhaled sharply and, drawing the covers around her, she rolled over to face him. "What do you think you're doing?"

"Trying to sleep . . . if you'll be still."

"You startled me," she said.

"How did I do that?" He kept his head on his pillow, his arm around her, and didn't even open his eyes. "I was asleep until you started all the thrashing about."

"I didn't know you were going to sleep in this bed."

"I finally put Robby in his crib a little after three. Getting a little sleep myself seemed the natural thing to do. Do you have a problem with that?"

"You could have slept somewhere else."

"This is my bed."

"But you told me to get in it."

"Hmm. A delightful bit of forethought on my part, wasn't it?"

"You might have mentioned that you intended to share the bed with me."

"I didn't *intend* anything, Hartley. I thought Robby would stay awake all night. Look, this is really not a big deal. We're only sleeping together."

"You probably said the same thing to Stephanie, and look what happened to her."

He opened his eyes at that point . . . and looked down at her. "Worried, Hartley?"

"Well, at least you still remember my name."

"It's early yet."

She sighed, admitting to herself that she was no match for him, especially not when they were lying face to face in bed, looking at each other across the slight distance between two pillows. "I'm getting out of here," she said, making her move as she spoke.

"I don't think so. Not yet, anyway." His arm remained draped over her shoulder and the pressure increased to hold her still. "We have things to discuss."

"Not in bed, we don't."

His lips curved in a wicked smile. "What do you suggest we do. . . in bed?"

"How about a game of solitaire?"

"Too stimulating for this hour of the morning. I have a better idea."

Just in case his idea involved getting closer together in the bed, she managed a couple of quick maneuvers and wedged her palms against his chest. . . his *bare* chest. A ripple of genuine concern rolled through her. If his chest was bare and his leg was bare. . . what in sweet heaven was he wearing? "Do you have any clothes on?" she demanded.

His smile widened. His blue eyes shone with mischief. And her heart began to pound like a kettledrum. "Good question, Hartley. I like it. Shows that you're alert and paying attention. That's good, because I want you to be fully awake for what is about to happen to you."

She gulped. If he made a move, any move, she would. . . do something. She wasn't quite sure what. "I am not one of your bimbettes, Neil. You can't scare me with these meaningless innuendos. Besides, I have the ultimate weapon. Make me mad and you can find yourself another baby-sitter."

"Hmm, blackmail. You must be worried, Hartley. I merely wanted you to be awake when I brought you a cup of coffee and a Danish. Breakfast in bed. No tricks. The truth is, I hardly ever ravish women before breakfast." His lips curved with new mischief. "But let's go back to your original question. What *am* I wearing beneath these covers?" He moved his arm and covered one of her hands as it lay pressed against the wiry cover of hair on his chest. "Why don't you find out for yourself, Hartley? Take your hand and run it down—"

"In your dreams," Krista snapped, jerking her hand from his grasp and wiggling backward to the edge of the bed. She was on her feet an instant later, breathing far more quickly and visibly than she wanted. "I told you before, Neil, I am not going to play house with you."

He propped his head on one hand and regarded her lazily. "What are *you* wearing, Hartley?"

She glanced down. The white undershirt hung halfway to her knees and was, in daylight, a little more seethrough than she would have liked. "A T-shirt. I found it in the bathroom." She brought her gaze up slowly. "I suppose it's yours."

His gaze traveled from the hem of the garment to the neck, from the top of her head to the tip of her toes. "Mine," he confirmed. "You put it on backward. The V goes in front."

The V dipped unusually low in back. If she'd put it on correctly, she'd be facing true disaster at this very moment. "I like it better this way." She shrugged and then had to yank the cotton T back into place before it drooped on her shoulder and revealed too much of her chest. "It's more my style."

"Could I see it the other way, with the V in front? So I can form my own opinion?"

"Wake up, Neil. You're dreaming again."

His eyes held a sleepy desire, a soft, biding-my-time kind of gleam. "Are you sure you don't want to get back in bed with me and catch an extra hour's... sleep?"

As if sleep were even a remote possibility. "Are you trying to seduce me, Neil?"

"If I were, I'd never have let you get out of bed. I'm simply concerned about you, Hartley. It was a long night and I'm inviting you to get a little more rest. That's all." He patted her pillow, then held up his hand in a lazy pledge. "Scout's honor."

"You were never a Boy Scout."

"Don't be too sure of that." He raised up, pushed back the covers, and Krista clapped her hands over her eyes and spun away, sure in her imagination that he would be completely naked.

Neil's laugh did not lessen her embarrassment. "Dr. Hartley," he said. "I'm surprised at you. Now who's dreaming? Did you actually think I got into bed without a stitch of clothing on?"

She wasn't taking any chances and maintained her see-no-evil stance as he got out of bed and walked to her.

He reached up and took her hands, easing them slowly, but surely, away from her face. "I have on a perfectly respectable pair of jogging shorts which I was wearing under my sweats, which I took off before I got into bed. Normally, I would have taken off the shorts, too, but out of my great respect for your tender sensibilities, I left them on."

"Are you saying that the only reason you're dressed at all is out of courtesy to me?"

"Actually, the truth is, I was too tired when I crawled into bed this morning to think about what I was wearing, what you were wearing or what might happen if we weren't wearing anything. Walking the floor with a crying baby is not my idea of an aphrodisiac." He tipped up her chin with his index finger and arched one eyebrow in delicious provocation. "On the other hand, I'm rested now, and what you're wearing is rather... exciting. It is early, but if you need to be ravished, perhaps I could be persuaded...?"

He was flirting with her. Outrageously flirting and thoroughly enjoying her discomfiture. Well, even at this hour of the morning, she could handle one overconfident male. She invented a soft, shy smile as she placed her hand over his. "Does that mean your invitation to get back into bed still stands?" she asked.

"I wouldn't be much of a gentleman if I withdrew it now, would I? And shorts and T-shirt would be optional."

"Hmm. Well, Rip Van Winkle, I think I have a better idea. I'm going to take off your shirt and give it back to you."

"Now? Here?" He sounded more than a little disbelieving.

"Follow me," she said. "In here." Leading him into the adjoining bathroom was easy, getting him into the shower stall took a little more maneuvering. "I think an early morning shower is terribly romantic, Neil. I know I always... rest... much better afterward."

He pursed his lips, followed her into the glassed-in cubicle, then used his body to press her against the tiled wall. Bending his head, he toyed with her, scattering kisses behind her ears, reigning havoc on the delicate nerve endings that curved to her shoulders, nibbling at her resistance from a dozen different angles. She had nearly forgotten her plan by the time he got around to kissing her on the mouth. But when his hand came up to cup her breast, she decided the time to move was now or never. Despite the trembling which had begun in her stomach and was working its way down her legs, she managed to reach behind her and grasp the cold water tap.

"Don't even think of turning that on," he growled against her lips. "I promise you'll regret it."

She considered that. Her original plan had not included her presence during the cold shower, but she decided that at this point a little chill wouldn't do her any harm, either. She gave the knob a twist and shivered as water streamed over the two of them in a frigid torrent.

"Hartley! You're going to pay for this."

She laughed, even though her teeth were chattering. "Take it out of my baby-sitting fees."

He reached behind her and turned on the hot water, adjusting the flow to a comfortable, even temperature. Then he smoothed his wet hair away from his face and looked down at her. "Upon further consideration, I think the show is well worth the price of admission."

Krista followed the direction of his gaze, realizing too late the effect of water on the thin cotton T-shirt. The material was soaked and clung to her skin like Super Glue, revealing every wet inch of her, from the mole above her left breast to the fact that she was still—thank goodness—wearing bikini panties. She raised her head and met Neil's appreciative gaze for the space of a panicked heartbeat. Then, with a gasp at her own idiocy, she pushed open the glass door and grabbed a towel from the rack. In ten seconds she was on the opposite side of the shower door, shivering, but amply covered. "Neil Blanchard," she said. "I quit. I resign. I am going home."

His laughter was warm and self-assured as a pair of sodden jogging shorts sailed over the shower door and landed with a splat on the tile floor. "Be sure and take off my shirt before you leave."

Cheeks blazing with an embarrassment she could only blame on herself, she grabbed her own clothes and headed for the door.

"Hartley?" His voice stopped her just as she crossed the threshold into his bedroom.

"What?" she snapped, maintaining her death grip on the towel.

"Does this mean you don't want breakfast in bed?"

She marched out of the bedroom and gave him her answer in one quick, efficient jerk of the door. It slammed shut with a satisfying pop.

And Robby let out a howl.

"HARTLEY?" Neil's voice carried, confident and friendly, through the phone wires to Krista's ear. "I was calling to make sure you made it home okay."

"Safe and sound." She glanced at the alarm clock in her bedroom. "I've been home now for fifteen, maybe twenty, minutes. It doesn't take long to drive from your house." She was still annoyed with him, still embarrassed that she had let his silly flirtation catch her in an awkward situation. Even if the shower bit *HAD* been her idea, he shouldn't have gone along with it. He should have behaved with a little more propriety, a little more concern for appearances. He was, after all, still her employer. And he should have thought of Robby, too. "Did you get Robby to stop crying?" she asked.

"He's in the lull before the storm."

"Then you should probably spend this time making up more formula for his bottle."

"Hartley." His voice softened on the name, making her stomach drop at the tender sound. "I called to apologize. I shouldn't have teased you."

"You shouldn't have gotten into bed with me," she said.

"Scout's honor, Hartley, I had no intention of doing anything except sleeping. I swear it."

She believed him. Unfortunately, that did not make her feel any better. "Forget it, Neil."

"Good," he said too easily. "Because I really need your help this afternoon. If you could come over and sit with Robby for a couple of—"

Krista hung up on him.

"HARTLEY." Neil clipped out the word with authority. "Do not hang up this time, I need some assis—"

The line went dead. Damn. What had gotten into that woman? He'd apologized. He'd said he needed her help. Women always fell for that. Had he been too abrupt? Maybe that was it. He hadn't sounded sincere. Women were real sticklers about sincerity.

"Robby." Neil turned to the baby, who was sitting in his carrier seat, kicking contentedly. "Why don't you start screaming again and I'll dial Krista. When she hears you crying, she won't hang up. What do you say, buddy?"

Robby yawned.

"You cried most of the night. I know you haven't forgotten how."

Robby gurgled.

"We need her over here, Kid. I've got to go into the office for a while and I can't leave you here by yourself. Who else am I going to find to stay with you? Magdalena doesn't come in on Saturdays. My mother lives in Florida and I damn sure don't want her up here cooing over you, anyway. You're used to Hartley. *I'm* used to her. I can't leave you with just anyone, now can I?''

Robby boxed at a sunbeam making its way through the window.

"Maybe Mary Nell wouldn't mind a couple of hours of baby-sitting. Is she okay with you?"

Robby didn't seem to have an opinion, so Neil dialed his secretary's home number. But Mary Nell wasn't there. Or else Krista had called ahead and warned her not to answer her phone. Neil decided there was only one thing left to do.

Unfortunately, Krista wouldn't answer her door, either.

P. G. MADIGAN hadn't realized Texas would be so hot.

"First trip to San Antonio, ma'am?" The man standing next to Pru looked like a cowboy, but then so did nine out of ten men on the movie set.

She cut him a sharp glance. "First trip to Texas," she said. "Is it obvious?"

He pushed back the rim of his ten-gallon hat and grinned. "I was just guessing. The leather jacket sort of tipped me off."

Prudence glanced at the jacket hanging limply over her arm. "I heard it sometimes gets cold at night."

"Yes, ma'am. Sometimes it does."

She frowned at the jacket. "But not in the summer."

"No, ma'am, but that ain't to say that one of these nights we won't break eighty."

She nodded, reminding herself that with just a stroke of luck, she could be out of this place by nightfall. "Do you know Stephanie Starr? She's one of the actresses, I believe."

"That's her, over there. The one talking to the wranglers. You see her? The blond ponytail sitting on the corral gate. You want me to call her over?"

"Uh, no. She looks... involved."

The cowboy chuckled. "Yeah. Steph is nearly always involved in somethin' or other. Sure you don't want me to call her over?"

"No, this is supposed to be a surprise." She wondered if she should "mosey on over," as they said here in Texas, for a better look at Ms. Starr. Neil Blanchard had said not to alert Stephanie to the fact that he was looking for her. Pru's first impression was that it would take something a little larger than a Patriot Missile to alert Stephanie Starr to any fact other than the location of the nearest available male.

After a slight hesitation, Pru skirted the movie set, tossed her jacket over the fence rail and hoisted herself up onto the corral gate beside Stephanie. "Hi," she said, then decided she should try to sound more like a Texan. "Howdy."

The wranglers nodded, tipped their hats and moved on. Stephanie turned and blinked big blue eyes. "Hello," she said brightly. "Are you new on the set?"

Pru nodded. "Just got here. Flew in from San Diego this afternoon."

"Really? I live in L.A." Stephanie giggled. "I guess most of the people working on this movie live there, huh? The extras might be local people, but the real stars live in California. I mean, there is only one Hollywood."

Pru smiled because that seemed like the only possible response. "Do you have family there?" she asked. "My family all live back East."

Stephanie blinked twice. "So does mine. New Jersey. I came out to L.A. three years ago. To be discovered." She nudged Pru with her elbow. "You know…to become a star. Starr, with an extra *r*. That's my stage name. Well, really, it's my real name. I had it changed. It sounds so much more like a…well, like a celebrity, than Walsh. That's my real name. Sally Walsh." Stephanie Starr, a.k.a. Sally Walsh, made a face. "Ugh. Isn't that awful? What name are you using?"

"Prudence," Pru answered. "Do you think I should change it?"

Stephanie looked horrified. "Oh, I would. I mean, it's hard enough to get a break without having a name like Prudence. That just has no star quality, at all."

"Some people use my initials. P.G."

"Ooh, that's worse. You should try Pamela. Or Patricia. Something normal sounding."

"I'll think about it," Pru said politely. "Didn't your family get mad when you changed your name? I'm afraid mine would disown me."

"Don't tell them," Stephanie advised. "My parents still don't know. They probably won't even figure it out when I'm famous. I told my sister, though. That way, if I'm ever in a terrible plane crash or something, someone will know it's me."

That made a certain illogical logic, Pru decided. "But what if you have kids? Will they be Starr or Walsh or what? Won't that be confusing?"

Stephanie gave her head a toss, sending the blond ponytail swishing from shoulder to shoulder. "They'll use their father's name, silly. But I'm not going to have children. At least not until my acting career is established and I'm very famous. Having a baby ruins your figure, you know, and plastic surgery can't fix everything, no matter what those ads on television say." She adjusted the strap of a halter top which covered—just barely—the ample attributes of her figure. "I had these done," she said matter-of-factly as she tugged on the material which harnessed her breasts. "Cost of doing business, as they say. You might want to consider it yourself." She cast a pitying glance at Pru's chest. "It couldn't hurt."

"I've always felt that less is more," Pru said with a vague smile. There was no sense, she decided, in trying to compete with a live Barbie doll. "When are you going back to California?" she asked.

"I really can't say. Hi, there, Slim." Stephanie offered a wave and a sparkling smile to a passing cowboy. "I have other offers which I'm considering. I've been asked to audition for a role in 'Days of Our Tomorrows,' but I'm not sure I want to commit my time to a daytime soap opera just now. Soaps are so limiting, if you know what I mean. On the other hand, it would be a steady paycheck."

"Tough decision." Pru wanted to tell her companion to accept the first offer of steady money that came down the wire, but she kept her advice to herself and hopped off the gate instead. "Hey, Stephanie," she said. "What part do you play in this picture? The Indian Princess?"

Stephanie Starr had a laugh like a dozen tinkling cowbells. "No, silly. I'm the farmer's daughter."

"What a coup for the casting department." Prudence dusted her hands on the seat of her slacks, lifted her leather jacket from the fence and walked away. Now that she'd satisfied her curiosity, she supposed she'd better let Dr. Blanchard know that his piece of cake was on the platter.

Chapter Eight

"Hartley? Pick up the phone." Neil's voice on the answering machine was demanding, sharp and urgent. She reached for the receiver automatically and then stopped. If she answered this call, she'd be right back where she started—vice president in charge of day care. The chief baby-sitter. True, he'd stopped calling after she refused to answer her door. That had been yesterday afternoon. It was now Sunday afternoon and he did sound serious. And, much as she hated to admit it, she really wanted to talk to him.

"Hartley, please. I know you're there. I need help. Madigan has found Stephanie."

Krista grabbed the phone. "Neil?"

There was a moment's pause as relief filtered through the connection. "She called a little while ago from Texas. Somewhere close to San Antonio. A ranch, I think, where the movie is being filmed. I'm going to fly down there and talk to Stephanie, try to find out what she plans to do about Robby. Can you take care of him while I'm gone?"

"Of course," Krista agreed without hesitation. "I'll come right over."

"Thanks, Hartley. Robby will be glad to see you."

"It's been barely twenty-four hours. I doubt he's had time to miss me."

"Trust me, Hartley. He's missed you."

"It will take me a few minutes to get my things together," she said. "How soon do you have to leave?"

Neil cleared his throat. "As a matter of fact, I'm calling from the mobile phone. Could I just drop Robby off on my way to the airport?"

Krista sighed. The man was incorrigible. "I'll be watching for you."

There was a pregnant pause. "You can go ahead and open the door. I'm parked right outside."

NEIL ARRIVED in San Antonio late Sunday night and phoned Madigan from the airport. "I've got a rental car. I'll pick you up in fifteen minutes," he said after she answered the phone in her hotel room. "How long does it take to get to this movie set?"

"Look, Blanchard," she said. "You're on Central Daylight Saving Time. People here have been asleep for a couple of hours already. You can't go out to the set until tomorrow. Get a room. Get some sleep. Call me in the morning. And take two aspirins, whether you need them or not."

She hung up, and Neil was left holding the phone. What was it with women? Didn't they know it was rude to hang up without so much as a cursory goodbye? He dialed her hotel again.

A male clerk answered. "I'm sorry, sir. Ms. Madigan has asked that she not be disturbed before 8:00 a.m."

"Ring through," Neil snapped. "This is an emergency."

"She said you'd say that, sir. I'm very sorry, but I can't disturb her. Would you like to leave a message?"

"Yes. Tell her I'm out of aspirins." He slapped the receiver into its cradle and frowned. He'd hoped to see Stephanie and get home by morning. But it looked as if he was stuck in Texas for the night. Well, he would just deduct the cost of his hotel room from Madigan's fee. At the rate things were going, this baby caper was going to cost him a fortune.

A room at the Four Seasons on Riverwalk took the edge off his frustration. A shower and room service improved his attitude even further. The thought of calling Krista even made him smile. But as he picked up the phone to dial out, he decided it wasn't a good idea. If Robby was asleep, the ringing of the phone might wake him. And if the baby was awake and screaming, Hartley would not be pleased to hear, long distance, from his absent father.

With a return of his black mood, Neil hung up the phone and went to bed.

WHILE ROBBY SLEPT like an angel in his crib, Krista walked the floor, waiting for Neil's call. Her stomach churned as she contemplated the outcome of his meeting with Stephanie. Would she demand Robby's immediate return? Would she have some perfectly reasonable excuse for leaving her baby on Neil's desk? Would Neil even *ask* for an explanation before he made arrangements to transfer possession of one small boy back to his mother?

She walked out onto the deck, trailing her hand along the edge of the hot tub as she passed. She was staying at Neil's house, obstensibly for Robby's sake. Neil had left her his key and the code to his security alarm. She'd

brought Robby here almost as soon as Neil left. He'd
sleep better in his own crib, she had reasoned. He was
accustomed to the sound of the ocean. He wouldn't be
as comfortable staying in her apartment.

But in reality, she'd chosen to stay here because it
made the fantasy seem real. In Neil's house, she could
walk through the rooms and imagine herself belonging
there. She could take care of Robby and make believe
that he was hers. She could touch Neil's things and
pretend that she had every right to do so. She could
sleep in his bed and dream sweet dreams. She could wait
for the phone to ring and believe that he was calling because he missed her. In Neil's house, she was Cinderella living happily ever after.

Krista leaned against the railing and searched the
night sky for a falling star. A wish made on a falling star
always came true. Or so she'd heard.

She stood outside for a long time, but no star fell.
And the telephone never rang.

"THAT'S HER." P. G. Madigan pointed. "The ponytail
standing behind the guy on the hay bale."

Neil narrowed his eyes on the buxom blonde and
summoned every single memory cell he had to attention. Her? he thought. *Her?* "You're sure," he said to
P.G. "There's no doubt in your mind that she is Stephanie?"

"In the flesh." P.G. stuck her hands in her hip
pockets. "Ask anyone on the set. Excuse me. I meant
to say ask any *male* on the set."

He frowned at P. G. Madigan. She had no reason to
be smug about the whole thing. "Thanks, Madigan,"
he said. "I'll handle things from here. You can wait for
me in the rental car."

"I'll just hang around the set." She gave him a cocky grin. "So many 501 Levi's. So little time." She turned her head to follow the passage of a denim-clad cowboy. "Honk the horn when you're ready to leave and I'll come a'runnin', as they say here in Texas."

Neil didn't care much for his companion's flippant attitude, but he wished fervently that he could insist she be a witness to the upcoming confrontation. However, he didn't really want an audience. It would have been different, if Krista could have come with him....

Inhaling sharply, he squared his shoulders and walked to where Stephanie was standing. "Stephanie?" he said quietly to the back of her head. "Ms. Starr?"

She turned toward him and her smile went from amateur to professional status in a split second. "Yes?" she said as she gave him the once-over and then went back for a second look. "Yes, I'm Stephanie Starr. Were you looking for me?"

Neil had expected immediate recognition...on her part, if not on his. But she registered no hint, gave no indication that she had ever seen him before. And as he looked at her, he felt nothing. No bits of memory clicking into place. No sense that he had ever been closer to this woman that he was at this moment. "You're Stephanie." He said it slowly, gingerly, hoping that this was just a simple mistake.

She laughed. "Yeah. I'm Stephanie Starr. And I hope to heaven you're looking for me, because it's going to break my heart, honey, if you're not."

This woman was Robby's mother? "Is there someplace we could talk? In private?"

The expression in her eyes grew thoughtful and maybe a little calculating. "Sure. Over here." She took his arm, and Neil decided he could tolerate the familiarity for a minute or two.

"Hey, Bill," she called to the man who was straddling a hay bale and poring over a thick set of papers. "I'm going for some coffee. Call me if you need me."

Bill didn't even turn around, and Neil envied the man's indifference. Stephanie was not what he remembered. He had had vague recollections of a small woman with a nervous giggle and a stream of giddy conversation. He could understand how he might have blocked their first and only previous meeting from his memory. She definitely was not his type. It was, however, hard for him to believe he could have forgotten the size of her breasts.

"In here." She pulled open the door of a trailer that had seen better days. Neil looked around for a place to sit and decided he'd rather stand.

Stephanie perched on the edge of a table and crossed her legs. "Now, sugar," she said with an affected Texas drawl. "What can I do for you?"

Neil regarded her—and what he had to do—with distaste. "We've met before, Stephanie."

"Men say that to me all the time." She challenged him with a saucy toss of her head. "It's a pickup line."

"This time it's not. We met a year ago. At a house party in San Luis Obispo. Melinda and Douglas Battles were the hosts. Does that ring a bell?"

Her forehead and her nose wrinkled in a studied frown. Then her concentration cleared with a smile and a shake of her head. "Sorry, not a single ringy-dingy." She leaned forward, revealing more clevage than good taste. "I would have remembered meeting you, darlin'. Trust me, I have quite a memory for male . . . faces."

Neil wished he had a picture of Robby's face to test her memory. "How about baby faces?" he asked.

"I prefer men with a more mature look." She adjusted the hem of her skirt...what there was of it. "But you don't need to worry. No one would ever mistake you as a 'baby face.'"

"Stop acting, you little idiot." Neil snapped the words like a commando. "Quit pretending you don't know who I am and why I'm here."

Her eyes widened and she uncrossed her legs. "You're a crazed fan," she said. "I've read about men like you. Men who become obsessed with a famous person. I think you're obsessed with me. You'd better get out of here before I call Bill."

Neil struggled with his temper. "Stephanie. I'm Dr. Neil Blanchard. We met last June at the Battles' home and we spent the night together in their guest house."

Her eyes got even rounder and she nervously rubbed her hands up and down on her bare thighs. "You are crazy. I may be blond, but I'm not stupid. I have never seen you before in my life and if you don't leave right now, I'm going to start screaming."

Her vehemence took Neil aback. But only for a moment. "Are you going to pretend you don't know anything about the baby, either?"

"Baby?" she whispered. "What baby?"

Neil was angry enough to shake the living daylights out of her and so he buried his hands, and the temptation, in his pockets. "Your baby, Stephanie." He narrowed his eyes on her. "A three-month-old baby boy. That's *b-a-b-y b-o-y*. *Your* son. The one you abandoned in my office. The one you left on my desk with a cryptic note that said *you* didn't need the responsibility."

Stephanie gulped. "Oh," she said. "That baby."

"DON'T ASK any questions." Krista walked through the front door, past her mother and into her parents' Coronado condominium. She placed Robby, in his carrier seat, in the middle of the carpeted living room. Shrugging the strap of the diaper bag from her shoulder, she dropped it beside the baby and then turned toward her mother. "Just answer yes or no. Can you keep an eye on him for a few hours?"

Phyllis Hartley closed the door and advanced on the baby like a mother hen after a truant chick. "Where did you find him? Oh, he's precious. Is it all right if I hold him?" She had Robby in her arms faster than Krista could process the questions. "What on earth are you doing with a baby and how long do I get to keep him?"

As she sank onto the nearest chair, Krista pushed back a strand of unruly hair and tried to capture it behind her ear. "Hello, mother," she said. "How are you?"

Phyllis smiled over Robby's round head. "I'm fine, dear. How are you and where did you get this baby?"

"I'm exhausted, Mom, and he followed me home." Krista waved a hand in defeat. "Does that answer all of your questions?"

"Not yet, but it's a start." Phyllis patted Robby and spoke to Krista. "Do you want a cup of coffee? Or some breakfast?"

"No. I'm on my way to the office. I have a ton of work to do and I knew I wouldn't get anything done if I took him with me." Krista lifted her shoulder in a weary shrug. "So I brought him here."

"Good idea," her mother said. "Your daddy and I will enjoy having a baby around the house. Especially since you've been so slow to make us grandparents."

Krista rolled her head against the cushioned back of the chair. "For years you told me to concentrate on school, concentrate on getting my career established, and then suddenly, the moment I land a job, you start singing a different tune and wanting to know when I'm going to start producing babies. Honestly, Mom, you and Dad could be a little more patient. It's not a simple matter of changing directions in midstream, you know."

"I know, dear, but none of us is getting any younger and you have to realize that your biological clock is ticking like a time bomb."

"Oh, that's a cheerful thought, Mom. Thanks for pointing it out to me."

"You're welcome, dear. I hope it helps." Phyllis turned Robby in her arms so she could look at him. "You're just the sweetest thing." She clicked her tongue and Krista stifled a groan. Robby hadn't been too sweet a few hours ago. He'd slept from early evening until early morning without making a single sound. Then, about twelve-thirty, he'd let out a squall that could have doubled as a train whistle for its startle effect. Krista had sat bolt upright in bed and muttered a few choice epitaphs with Neil's name on them.

"He reminds me of you," Phyllis said. "Such a happy baby."

"Oh, yes. He's so happy he cries almost all night every night."

"Just how many nights have you had him?" her mother inquired.

"Four. A friend of mine is . . . keeping him while the mother is out of town. My friend had to take an unexpected trip and so I'm stuck with the kid."

Phyllis clicked her tongue, tossing guilt Krista's way. "Shame on you. Taking care of an infant is such a sweet experience. You should be enjoying it."

Krista pushed up from the chair. "I've got to go. Are you sure you don't mind watching Robby for a while? I'll finish up as soon as I can."

"Robby? That's his name?" Her mother smiled at the baby as Krista nodded. "Hello, Robby. We're going to have a wonderful time together. Dad and I might teach you to play golf."

"Don't let him get sunburned," Krista warned. "And make sure he's not too hot or too cold. Really, Mom, it would probably be better not to take him outside at all."

Phyllis waved her hand in dismissal. "Goodbye, sweetheart. Have a nice day at work. Don't worry. We'll be fine."

Krista was suddenly very worried. "Mom?"

"Go on. Go on." Phyllis motioned toward the door. "I know your office number in case of an emergency."

Which, Krista couldn't help thinking, was more information than she herself had about the whereabouts of Robby's parents. Neil was going to pay for this. In spades. "Be careful with him, Mom."

"You're being awfully protective for someone who is 'stuck' with a kid."

"It's my nature to be responsible. You know that." Krista walked slowly to the door, wondering if she ought to write down the phone numbers of the police, hospital and fire departments before she left. "Call me if . . ." The words dwindled into an aching sensation somewhere near her heart. What if Robby missed her?

What if he didn't like being left with strangers? What if *she* missed *him?* "Maybe I should just take him with me."

"Maybe you should just go on to work."

"You're right." She headed for the door, glancing back once and then wishing she hadn't. Robby was smiling. Phyllis was smiling. As soon as her dad saw the baby, he'd start smiling, too.

Krista left . . . because she couldn't think of a single thing to smile about.

"I'LL GET AN ITEMIZED statement to you by the end of the week." Prudence fastened her seat belt with a snap and a pull to tighten the excess. "Expenses were a little heavy on this case, so I hope you won't have a heart attack when you see the final figure. Of course, this upgrade to a first-class seat didn't help your cause. But you did insist."

Neil turned to look at her. He'd been thinking long and hard since his interview with Stephanie and, until this moment, he'd been only vaguely conscious that he had a traveling companion. "What time is it, Madigan?" he asked.

She shoved back her shirt cuff. "Two-thirty, San Antonio time. Twelve-thirty in San Diego. You'll be home in time for dinner, with a couple of hours to spare."

Home. What a pleasant thought. Hartley would be there. With Robby. Waiting for him. What was it Hartley had said she wanted? Babies of her own and a husband who came home with a contented look in his eyes? Neil gazed out the window at the ground activity, preparatory to takeoff. "Madigan," he said without diverting his attention from the window. "There are going to be a few more days and several more entries on your expense sheet before this is over."

"Don't tell me there's another missing person in your life." She paused, and he knew if he turned around he would see her cocky know-it-all smile. "Is it possible that Stephanie wasn't the woman you were looking for, after all?"

"Have you ever been to the Caribbean, Madigan?" Neil asked, giving the question a pensive twist. "It's a popular honeymoon spot for newlyweds."

"Sorry, but I make it a rule never to get romantically involved with a client. You'll have to take someone else on your honeymoon."

Neil's lips curved. With a little effort, he might get to like P. G. Madigan. "You're breaking my heart, Peggy Gail, but I was planning to *send* you, not take you."

"The name is P.G." She corrected him firmly. "The initials do not stand for Peggy or Gail."

He turned toward her then and asked a silent question with a lift of his eyebrows.

She sighed. "Okay. They stand for Prudence Gwendolyn, but if you tell anyone, you're a dead man."

"Why do you go by your initials?"

"Would you let your fingers walk through the yellow pages of the telephone directory and land on a private investigator named Prudence?"

"I see your point."

The engines whined and the plane moved slowly backward. Forty minutes to Dallas. Three hours from Dallas to San Diego. Neil didn't think he'd ever been so anxious to get home. It had been a long time since anyone had been waiting for him. A long time since he'd had a good reason to want to be home.

"So, Blanchard..." Madigan—it was hard to think of her as Prudence—made another adjustment to her seat belt. "When do I get to go cruising through the Caribbean? And whose honeymoon am I going to crash?"

"I'll give you all the information I have before we reach Dallas. You can get a connecting flight there and be on the beach at Barbados by dawn tomorrow."

"You realize that if you expect me to do any sleuthing on the beach, I'll have to buy a new bikini."

"It will be my pleasure to okay that particular item on your expense sheet."

"You bet it will." Prudence glanced at the leather jacket she had slung over the arm of the seat and frowned. "Good thing I brought my coat. I've heard it sometimes gets cold on the beach at night."

Neil turned back to the window as they taxied toward the runway. It promised to be a long flight...even in first class.

KRISTA DROPPED THE BOTTLE. "Now, look what you've done," she told Robby, who was crying like a banshee in her arms. "You were a perfect *angel* for my mother and dad. You didn't cry. You didn't fuss. You were a *precious* baby for them. The minute I get you home, you start screaming."

She shifted his position and bent to pick up the bottle with its now contaminated nipple. With a twinge of guilt and a heavy dose of desperation, she turned on the hot-water tap and held the nipple under the faucet, hoping the temperature was high enough to kill any germs. There were parts of this baby business that were not so enjoyable, she decided, as she cooled the nipple with a burst of cold water and then stuck it into Robby's open mouth. He looked startled, and then peace descended like manna from heaven. Only the sounds of his sucking and an occasional sniff broke the blessedly sweet silence.

With a sigh, Krista carried him through the house and out onto the back deck. She sank onto the top step of a set of stairs which led down to a terrace and, eventually, to the beach farther on. The ocean serenaded her. The occasional cry of a sea gull added a minor note with a certain harmony of sound. The breeze from the water carried the soothing rhythms to her ears and touched her with gentle caresses. Robby closed his eyes and sighed in her arms. Krista sighed, too, and wished she could make the sunset linger until she tired of it, wished she could will her fantasy into a reality that would last the rest of her life.

Neil found her there, her head resting against the wood brace of the stairs, her arms wrapped around Robby, an empty baby bottle on the deck next to her elbow, her dusky hair glinting with the waning rays of the sunset. He was surprised, but not startled by the desire that wound through him. She was a desirable woman, and the sight of her holding his son in her arms touched him. He had missed her. "Is this performance sold-out?" he asked quietly.

She turned her head and her smile made his heart stop beating. "Shh. The show's almost over, but there is one good seat still available. Do you want it?"

He moved forward and eased down beside her, brushing her arm with his shirtsleeve and experiencing a nearly painful longing to kiss her long and hard. "Glad I made it before the final curtain," he said. "I'd have hated to miss this."

"It is lovely, isn't it? You have such a great place here, Neil. I didn't realize how quiet and peaceful it is."

"Since Robby arrived, there's been considerably more noise."

She smiled . . . and he had to swallow hard. "True," she said. "In fact, he's been crying, screaming really, since I brought him home this evening. He stopped just a little while before you got here."

"Probably saving his strength for the middle of the night." Neil watched the remaining arc of sunlight sink into the ocean, flinging arrows of light against the coming dusk. "Did he give you a lot of trouble?"

"More than I bargained for." Krista looked down at the sleeping infant and caressed his baby cheek with a stroke of her finger. "But, now, it feels like he was really no trouble at all."

A feeling of intimacy circled the three of them and settled like a warm fluffy blanket around them. *Family is written all over this picture,* Neil thought. *A man, a woman, a child. Family.* Something he had believed he'd be happier without. Neil knew he should shrug the feeling aside, shatter the too-cosy picture, reestablish his independence from this woman and this child. He ought to make some sort of statement that no heart could misinterpret. But instead, he leaned forward, rested his arms on his knees, clasped his hands and waited for something else to break the spell.

"I took Robby to my parents' house and went in to work for a while today." Krista continued to look at the baby, but Neil sensed that she was focused, now, on him.

"I know. Mary Nell told me."

"When did you talk to her?"

"Yesterday. This morning. This afternoon. Didn't she tell you I called?"

A second's irritation tightened Krista's lips, then moved on. "I was so busy the whole time I was at the office, there wasn't any time for chitchat. And I didn't think you'd want me to discuss Robby with anyone, even Mary Nell." The pause lasted a moment, maybe more. "You might have called me at least once."

Obligation settled around him like dusk, and the intimacy began to feel cumbersome. He had wanted to call, but there didn't seem any point in telling her that. "I had complete confidence in your ability, Hartley. I didn't want you to think I was checking up on you."

The quick tilt of her lips held no warmth and no humor. It didn't take a mind reader to know she believed he hadn't given her or Robby a thought while he was gone.

"Of course not," she said.

"I talked to Stephanie this morning," he said casually, as if the subject wasn't racing back and forth between them in silent loops of reluctance.

Krista nodded and kept staring at the sleeping infant in her arms. She had prayed that this moment would never arrive. But suddenly, too soon, it was here. And Neil seemed so cool about it. So unconcerned. Within hours, Robby would be gone. "How soon does she want Robby back?"

"She doesn't want him at all."

Krista lifted her head to meet Neil's dark blue eyes. A band of terrible hope squeezed her heart. "She doesn't want him?" she repeated in a whisper.

Neil cleared his throat. "As it turns out, Stephanie is not Robby's mother."

The ensuing silence ticked like a time bomb. "What?" Krista went tense all over and the baby stirred in his sleep. "If this is a joke, Neil, it isn't funny."

"It isn't a joke, Krista. Stephanie Starr is not Robby's mother. She is also not the Stephanie I met last June at Melinda's house party."

"Is she the Stephanie you *slept* with?" Krista couldn't prevent her agitation from bleeding into her voice.

Neil was more than a little agitated himself. "Then?" He snapped the words at her. "Or... since then?"

She rose from the step like an undine rising from the ocean. Grace and anger coupled with the dusk to lend her an untouchable dignity. "Here." She thrust the baby toward him. "You do whatever you want with him. Sleep with whomever you please. But don't expect me to play 'What's My Secret?' when you're through."

Neil rose, too, bringing his superior height into play and wanting, more than anything, to pick her up and carry her to his bed. He reached out, placing his hands on her shoulders and capturing her gaze with his own. "This has been a difficult day, Hartley. I have a lot of things on my mind. Can we please discuss this like adults and not let emotions get in the way of reason? I need your assistance, Hartley. But I do not need your accusations."

Robby stirred, whimpering in his sleep. Krista drew him close against her body and continued to meet Neil's gaze, stare for stare. "I'll try to keep my emotions in check, but I'm not making any promises. Look, Neil, you dumped your problems in my lap. You put Robby in my arms and said, 'Help me take care of him until his mother is found.' And now that she's found, you're giving me a song and dance about her not really being his mother. Forgive me if I find that just a little bit upsetting.''

"Has it been such a burden to take care of him, Krista?''

The question was unfair. Completely unfair. "That is hardly the point,'' she said. "This baby didn't just appear, Neil. He has two parents somewhere. So, if she's not the mother and you're not the father, how did he end up here?''

Neil glanced away, a brief but telling movement, and Krista's heartbeat shifted into an erratic, staccato rhythm.

"My name is on the birth certificate, Hartley. Under the heading Father of Child.''

Chapter Nine

Father of the child.

The words hung suspended in the evening air, ripe with significence. Krista instinctively hugged Robby closer. Neil turned away.

"Did you see the birth certificate?" she asked finally.

"Stephanie told me about it," he answered, without turning around. "That's the reason she brought him to the office. She'd seen my name on the document and decided I should have to bear the responsibility for him."

"But she couldn't explain this to you at the time? She had to abandon Robby without so much as an introduction?"

Neil shrugged. "She said she was in a hurry."

Krista sighed, long and sadly. "I'm going to take Robby inside and put him in his crib. Do you want me to bring you anything from the kitchen? A drink or something to eat?"

"Nothing, thanks."

She turned and carried Robby to the door leading into the house.

"Krista?"

She stopped. "Yes?"

"All this time, I didn't believe it was true. I didn't believe I *could* be his father."

She knew that. She hadn't truly believed it herself. But now, well, this changed things. "I'll be back in a minute." Turning, she carried Robby into the house.

Once he was settled in his crib, she hesitated. Before pulling the side rail into position, she leaned over and pressed a kiss to his fuzzy head. He was precious . . . and dear to her in a way she knew better than to analyze. Because, regardless of who or where his mother was, regardless of what else Neil had to say, sooner or later Krista would have to say goodbye. Perhaps she was the only one who could hear the mournful notes of a clock tolling twelve.

Outside, Neil drummed his fingertips on the deck railing. The resulting thuds were hollow echoes of his own restlessness. The ocean-drenched air offered no balm for his anxiety. This, the one spot where he had always found tranquillity, denied him tonight and he drummed the railing in frustration. What was taking Hartley so long? How in sweet hell was he going to explain? And what was he going to do?

"Who is his mother?"

He froze into stillness at the sound of Krista's voice behind him, feeling a little like an errant husband about to confess an infidelity to his wife.

He did a slow turn, coming around to face her and feeling, again, that rush of desire when he saw her. Did she know? he wondered. Could she feel the electricity that had arced into life, full-blown and exciting, when their eyes met? He could hardly breathe for the vivid images that were racing through his mind. "Come here,

Hartley," he said softly, urgently. "Beside me. You're too far away."

"I'm fine right here." She knew. Every instinct told him that she was very much aware of his thoughts, his feelings . . . and reluctantly receptive to them. "Who is his mother, Neil?" She repeated the words with quiet self-control, but he noticed the subtle fidgeting of her hands, and a sudden gentle longing blended into his desire.

"Robby's mother is Carrie Walsh, Stephanie's sister." Neil leaned back against the deck rail, prepared to give what information he had uncovered. "Carrie is the woman I met at Melinda's last June. She was masquerading as Stephanie, pretending to be someone she wasn't presumably so she could do things that she, as Carrie, would never do."

Like sleep with you. Krista didn't say the words aloud, but Neil heard them all the same. He wondered if she might be a little jealous.

"Carrie had been engaged to her high school sweetheart, but when he left her at the altar, she came out to stay with her older sister and . . . recuperate."

"And that's where you came in." Krista stopped fidgeting and put her hands in her skirt pockets. "A sure cure for a broken heart."

Neil frowned, experiencing a pang of resentment at the description. "Stephanie was gone most of last summer, working on a movie or a commercial or something. Carrie was on her own for the first time in her life and . . . apparently, decided that the best way to have a wonderful time was to shed her own identity for a while and become someone entirely different. Voilà—Stephanie, who is really Carrie, arrives at Melinda's party and spends the night in my bed."

"And then voilà—Robby."

Neil decided there was no point in responding to that. "After that, I don't know what happened. All Stephanie, the real one, could tell me was that when she came home in late August, Carrie was gone. She left Stephanie a note giving an address in L.A. and an emergency phone number for a data-processing company where she would be working. She called every week, but was vague about where she was staying and what she was doing. Finally, in October, she told Stephanie she was pregnant and that she didn't want anyone to know. She especially didn't want her parents or the former fiancé to find out."

"Stephanie went along with all the secrecy?" Krista shook her head. "And neither one of them ever tried to contact you, to inform you that you were going to be a father?"

He made a dismissing gesture with his hand. "That, at least, is self-evident. I don't know *why* any of this happened, Hartley. I'm merely telling you what I've been able to piece together. Carrie had the baby in March and, after telling Stephanie all along that she didn't intend to keep him, she changed her mind. Stephanie didn't think it was such a good idea, but she had problems of her own.

"Then, one day in early May, Carrie brought the baby to Stephanie's apartment and asked her to baby-sit for a few days, which turned into a week and then two. Finally Carrie called, told her sister that she had reconciled with the fiancé and that, as soon as she had a chance to explain about the baby, she'd be back to get him."

Krista's mouth tightened. "And when she didn't come back, Stephanie decided it was your turn."

"Something like that. Carrie had supplied my name as the only possible candidate for paternity, and I'm listed on the birth certificate. Stephanie had to go to Texas. Since she couldn't keep Robby, I was the logical choice. She knew Carrie had used her name, so she wrote the note and left it in the carrier seat for me to find. She figured I'd recognize the name and the baby, and that when Carrie *did* return, she'd know where to find me. Then, with a clear conscience, Stephanie took off for San Antonio."

"Where's Carrie now?"

"Stephanie thinks she's somewhere in the Caribbean, on her honeymoon. Madigan is on the trail, so maybe we'll hear something soon."

Krista moistened her lips as she finger-brushed a strand of dark hair and anchored it behind her ear. "What are you going to do?"

That was the $64,000 question. And Neil didn't have a clue to the answer. "Soak in the hot tub and go to bed. What else can I do tonight?"

"I don't know. Nothing, I guess."

He regarded her for a long moment, holding her gaze by the sheer force of his will. "Join me?"

Her quick, indrawn breath told him that she understood. The upward tilt of her chin made it clear that she was marshaling her defenses. "No," she said. "Now that you're here, I can go home."

"Can? Or should?" He advanced a couple of steps from the deck railing. "You're always trying to leave me, Hartley. Do you dislike my companionship so much that you have to run home the minute Robby isn't awake to chaperon? Are you afraid of me, Hartley? Is that the problem?"

"No," she said. "No, of course not. It's just that...I don't need to be here, Neil. You're tired. I'm tired. It will be better if I leave now."

He closed the remaining distance between them. "You're not tired, Hartley. You're scared. Scared stiff of what's going to happen if you stay."

Her lips parted, as if she was about to protest, but no protest came out. And Neil took full advantage of that one moment's hesitation and covered her mouth with his own. The kiss was rich with emotion, brimming with a hunger he hadn't known he possessed until then. She tensed as his arms went around her, trembled as he crushed her close. He gave her no quarter, demanding her response, insisting on her participation. And she didn't disappoint him.

Gradually, her hands slipped from a defensive position against his chest to a power hold around his neck. Her lips slowly softened beneath his, became inviting and more tempting than he had thought possible. Desire coursed through his veins with increasing heat, from the steady flame of first longing to the consuming blaze of a full fire. He needed her, more than he had needed anything for a long time. He wanted her with a desperation which felt both alarming and exciting. Her kisses lured him. The pressure of her hips pressed to his thighs invoked his most erotic thoughts. He lifted his hand to cup her breast and ran the pad of his thumb across the tip, testing her willingness through the silk of her blouse.

She stiffened against his touch and then, with visible effort, she pulled back from his kiss. "Neil," she whispered. "I don't think this is a good idea."

"You're right." He bent again toward her upturned face. "It's a great idea . . . and it is long overdue." For a second time, he claimed her lips. He showed no mercy, turned a deaf inner ear to any reservations she might be harboring and exulted in the sweet, satisfying taste of her. Her mouth opened at the insistence of his tongue and he probed the soft, sensuous lining of her lips. The hot, eager ache of desire permeated his senses. A sharp, scintillating need twisted the first threads of passion through his reason. For the longest time, he had kept Hartley at a distance because it was necessary to maintain a successful working relationship. But suddenly everything was changed and he could not get close enough, could not delay any longer.

He lifted her in his arms and ignored her quivery sigh which blew warmly across his cheek. "I'm going to make love to you, Hartley. If you have any objections, you should probably state them now."

She swallowed hard, closed her eyes and clung to him like a lost and frightened kitten. "I have a thousand," she said in a voice too low, too unsteady to be assertive.

"Good." Neil kissed her, drawing her lips into a sweet and reluctant parting. "That was the first of a thousand answers. Next?"

She couldn't talk, couldn't grasp the words to refute his sudden, compelling claim on her. This was madness. Dulcet, agreeable madness. Fantasy bordering on a reality; fairy tale blending with misty dreams. She made another attempt at salvation, a second try for sanity. "You don't really want me, Neil."

The low sound that escaped his throat was laughter, soft and ever so slightly mocking. "Oh, Hartley. Let me show you how very wrong you are."

He carried her into the house, stopping every few steps to kiss her, to demonstrate the hunger that was still building inside him. Standing at the foot of his bed, he released her, forcing her to slide the length of his body in gradual, wanton degrees. Her clothes caught and pulled upward as she traveled inexorably downward, creating an expanse of nylon-stockinged leg that rubbed too easily against the fabric of his slacks. The sensation of silk and cotton meshed, creating a swirl of restless commotion inside her.

As if that weren't enough to set her nerve endings reeling, his body was tightly muscled beneath her hands and hardened by the exertion of supporting her weight. His arms, his chest, his thighs, the sinewy strength of his torso all gave mute testimony to his statement. And there was no denying the evidence of his arousal ... or of her own immediate response.

She pressed closer, seducing her reason with the knowledge that, for whatever purpose, Neil wanted her. She might be a momentary distraction, a soothing way to bury his problems for one night, a warm body to hold. It did not matter. He wanted her ... and she had wanted him for oh, so very long. When she lifted her face to his, he lowered his mouth to hers. "This is a mistake," she breathed against his lips.

"I disagree." He proceeded to prove his theory. He moved his hands down her back in imperative circles, urging her to mold herself to his contours, cupping her hips and demonstrating the raw hunger of his need in unmistakable terms.

Krista felt a tug on her zipper and then the fabric of her short, straight skirt loosened and began a slow descent to the floor. He was good, she realized anew, and very practiced at seduction. When he eased her blouse off her shoulders, she decided his fingers should be registered as lethal weapons, capable of decimating a row of buttons in ten seconds or less. She, on the other hand, felt dreadfully awkward when she tried to pull his shirt from the waistband of his slacks. What should have been an easy, sensual task tangled in her hands and finally, she simply gave up on removing the shirt and sent her fingers exploring beneath it.

Neil exhaled a sigh of pleasure and Krista experienced a sudden, electrifying sense of control. As she touched the wiry mat of hair that covered his chest, new sensations ran unrestrained, communicating a frenzy of impulses throughout her body. She wanted to touch him everywhere, kiss him everywhere, caress him until he cried out for her to stop... or go on. She wanted to exercise this feeling of power, bring his will around her finger, and make him want her as he had never wanted anyone else.

And then, her sense of power was gone, vanished along with her bra which he'd eased from her body with hardly a warning brush of silk against skin. How had he done that? And did she really care? Her breasts ached to know the cradle of his hands. She felt heavy with need and desperate to take him inside of herself. When he stopped kissing her and raised his head, she was bereft. And when he reclaimed lost territory, her heart soared to her throat with unanticipated appreciation.

She hadn't thought she could feel so wanton, so careless of possible consequences. Neil was a fantasy she'd nurtured too long, she supposed, because now that he was kissing her for real, preparing her for a very real seduction, she couldn't dredge up a single argument against this all-out assault on her senses. All she could do was follow the dream to its conclusion and try to savor each and every honeyed moment.

With a hungry groan, Neil pushed her onto the bed and followed her down. Her practical, no-nonsense panty hose became an instrument of exquisite torture as he massaged and rolled, kissed and manipulated them from her body. She was burning by the time he pulled the hose over her toes and tossed them carelessly aside. He took possession of her, one slow inch at a time, making his way from the foot of the bed, kissing his way from her ankles to her knees, to her thighs, to the weeping center of her body, to the throbbing peaks of her breasts, to the hollows of her throat and the sensitive skin just below her jaw. He found every pleasure point and discovered a few she hadn't known existed.

Her sense of power had disappeared entirely and she knew she was completely helpless to do any more than take what he offered and cherish it for the rest of her life. When he stripped off his shirt, shucked off his pants and briefs, she held her arms open and ready. And when he came to her, fully aroused and hot with desire, she accepted the moment as complete. Fantasy would never be so good.

Neil tried to be gentle, but his control was badly strained and he settled for a random tenderness within the boundaries of the passion that consumed him. Krista was so tempting, so beautiful, so damnably seductive. And he couldn't contain his burgeoning desire. His need for her was like a thick, aching pain inside of him and, even when he thrust deeply into her, it did not ease. The last thing he wanted was to rush her and yet he couldn't seem to delay his own dizzying plunge toward fulfillment.

He felt her tension, and then the world spun into a shattering, spectacular release. Her shuddering sigh and soft, almost inaudible "Oh" stripped away his last tenuous thread of restraint and sent him thrusting deep and finally within her.

As he rolled to his side, he took her with him, cupping her and cradling her against him. He turned his head and kissed her, recklessly, easily soothing her warm and swollen lips with a now infinitely gentle pressure. Life, he thought, could not get any better than this one most beautiful moment.

Krista kept her eyes closed, willing the pleasurable sensations to stay and not fade into oblivion. But already they were slipping away, moving beyond her reach. Tomorrow she would probably wonder if this had all really happened. Tomorrow, Neil would probably have forgotten her name.

A sobering thought.

She moved in his embrace, maneuvering a small distance between them, but he shifted closer, canceling any gain. "Don't even think about leaving." He stroked her cheek with the side of his hand. "I want you to stay."

It was more of a command than a request, but Krista acquiesced with good grace. After all, what else did she have to lose?

ROBBY'S WAKE-UP CALLS started around two o'clock. Krista was still mostly asleep as she swung her feet toward the edge of the bed. And then, from some heavenly dream, a hand reached out to stop her, and a husky voice said, "Go back to sleep. I'll take care of him."

If she'd been able to get her eyelids open, she might have made a token protest. Instead, she curled into a warm bump beneath the covers and slept on, blissfully free of responsibility. At one point in the intervening hours, she arose at Robby's cry. But Neil was already up and tempting the baby with a warm bottle and the rocking chair. He waved Krista back to bed, and with a baby-size blanket of guilt, she went. By the time she was settled back in bed, the guilt had shrunk to a manageable size and she had no trouble drifting back to dreamland.

She awakened slowly, sensing the arrival of morning by the slight lightening of the dark. She was alone in the bed and the house was quiet, except for the continuous rhythm of the Pacific Ocean. There were other noises, too—the hum of civilization a very few miles away in any direction, an occasional creak within the structure wall—but the house and its residents slumbered on.

Krista yawned once as she got out of bed. Grabbing a silk robe from inside the closet, she cinched the belt and padded down the hallway to the baby's room. The door was open and his crib was empty. Her heart fluttered with a momentary panic and then she scolded herself for worrying. Robby was with Neil. Safe, secure and obviously not crying. She continued down the hall, pausing in the living room.

Neil was asleep on the couch, lying on his back, his arms curled protectively around the infant who lay, also asleep, on his chest. A rush of pure and innocent longing flooded her at the sight. She framed the picture in her mind, titled it "Late Night Date" and stored it away in her memory. She felt the wistful slant of her lips, the slow, inexorable squeeze on her heart, and knew she had fallen in love with this man and his tiny son.

"TELL ME WHAT is going on." Mary Nell entered Krista's office and closed the door with a determined click.

Krista looked up from her desk. She had known Mary Nell would demand an explanation sooner rather than later, but she gathered an innocent smile to her lips, just the same.

The older woman didn't give her a chance to come up with an excuse. "And don't pretend that you don't know what I'm talking about." She pressed her back to the door and crossed her arms in a manner which reminded Krista of her mother.

"I assume you're referring to the baby."

Mary Nell dropped her chin a notch, realigning her no-nonsense stance. "Of course I'm referring to the baby. Where is he? Who is he? And why in tarnation is he still with Dr. Blanchard?"

"How did you find that out?"

"Aha. I'm right, aren't I? I just put together a little piece here and a slip of the tongue there and the frazzled way you look and the way he yawned on the phone and came up with 'and baby makes three.' Now, answer my question and put me out of my misery before I die of curiosity."

"Neil is keeping him for a while." Krista chose her words and her inflection carefully. "Until the mother returns."

"So he *is* the father."

"I didn't say that, Mary Nell."

"And I wasn't born yesterday. The only reason—and I repeat, *only* reason—Dr. Blanchard would tolerate the presence of a baby in his house is if he believed—and I mean, *believed* as in *was convinced*—that that baby was the fruit of his loins."

Krista cringed. "Mary Nell, you sound like a tele-evangelist."

"I just call it as I see it. So, where is this mother? This *Stephanie* person?"

"I'm not sure." Krista put down the pen she had been holding and reached for her cup of coffee. "There seems to be some uncertainty about who she is and where she is and when, if ever, she's coming back."

That bit of information silenced Mary Nell for a moment. "You mean he might have to *keep* the baby?"

It was an idea Krista had struggled to avoid all morning. She'd slipped out of Neil's house early, leaving father and baby still asleep on the couch. She'd gone home, showered, changed clothes, and had come in early to the office. There had been no sign of Neil, no indication that he realized she had spent the night with him, become his lover, but hadn't stayed to confront the morning after, no indication that he might decide to keep *her*. "I can't answer that, Mary Nell," she said, evading the mental issue. "I have no idea what he plans to do."

"Hmph. He is not cut out to be a father, I can tell you that much. He works too hard. He plays too hard. He doesn't have the patience for children. You should have seen him with Melinda's twins. A disaster." Mary Nell shook her head sadly, as if he were far beyond redemption. "I've worked for Dr. Blanchard for a number of years and I have the greatest respect for him. But I'm telling you that, if by some fluke he ends up with this baby, he'll get someone else to take care of it."

"I think you're wrong." Krista set down her coffee cup and jumped to his defense. "He's been very good with Robby. Very good."

"Of course, honey. You've been there to make it easy for him, haven't you?"

"But he's done as much as I have. More, even." It sounded like a desperate attempt to vote him Father of the Year. Krista tried again. "Look, he hasn't come into the office today. That makes two days that he's put Robby's welfare above the company. Doesn't that say something for his sense of responsibility?''

Mary Nell pursed her lips in a grandmotherly and sympathetic frown. "Don't fool yourself, Krista. It has nothing to do with responsibility. He's just not cut out to be a family man. Period. End of story.''

"But, Mary Nell—''

"Save your breath.'' Mary Nell held up a quelling finger. "And save yourself some heartache. You know there is no one who thinks more highly of Neil Blanchard than I do, but I'm telling you the truth, Krista, he isn't going to change just because some silly woman left a baby on his desk. If he'd been the one to find the baby, he'd have stamped it 'Return to sender' and put it in his out-basket and he probably would not have been able to remember later that there had been anything different about his day.''

"You're exaggerating.'' Krista didn't want to continue this, but whether it was because she believed Mary Nell or because she didn't *want* to believe her, she couldn't tell. "And it is none of our business, anyway. The baby certainly doesn't belong to you...or to me.''

Mary Nell sniffed and then stiffened at the sound of heavy footsteps approaching the doorway.

"Hartley? Where the hell are you?'' Neil's voice preceded his entrance. The door flew open and Mary Nell hopped out of the way, barely avoiding getting hit. Neil crossed the threshold, his expression set and solemn, the carrier seat and sleeping baby in his arms.

Krista rose automatically, as if he were royalty or the President or something. Her gaze dropped to the baby and then returned to Neil's face and frown. "Were you looking for me?'' she asked.

"I was looking for my secretary."

Mary Nell snapped to attention at his tone. "Krista and I were talking. Is there something you need?"

"Yes. Here." He handed over the baby like he was a stack of paperwork. "Take care of him. I've got to get some work done."

Mary Nell thrust out her hands just in time to find them full of baby. "But... ?"

"I left his stuff with the receptionist. If he cries, give him a bottle, change his diaper or carry him up and down the halls. Dr. Hartley will spell you if you need a break." Neil turned and walked out of the office.

Krista blinked. What was the matter with him?

"I'm not usually one to say I told you so," Mary Nell said, "but I *did* tell you so."

Krista answered with a frown. Neil had just shot holes through her attempt to defend him. Worse, he hadn't said good morning to her. She had lain naked in his arms not twelve hours before, and he hadn't even seen fit to say good morning. "I'll take care of Robby," she said to Mary Nell. "He really shouldn't have dumped the responsibility onto you. Baby-sitting isn't your job."

With a shrug, Mary Nell turned toward the door. "Actually, I would much rather take care of this little fella than of that big one down the hall. Trust me, honey. My mama didn't raise any fools." At the doorway, she turned back. "Krista, take my advice. Develop a splitting headache and go home. This day is not going to get better."

The splitting headache was already in place, but Krista wasn't about to turn tail and run. If Neil could pretend nothing had happened between them last night, then by God, so could she. "I have an appointment with one of our distributors in about ten minutes," she said. "But if you need help with Robby, interrupt me. Understand? Interrupt me."

"Don't worry. If I have any trouble, you'll be the first person I call. That way, you'll be the one who has to deal with Papa Bear. Not me." Mary Nell left with the baby, and Krista sank into her chair.

She had just begun to massage her forehead when her intercom buzzed.

"Hartley?" Neil's voice clipped through the call box. "In my office, please."

The "please" was clearly rhetorical in nature because his tone left no doubt that this was a command appearance. Through force of habit, she pushed to her feet. Wait a minute. She had resigned. She didn't have to jump every time he snapped his fingers. Besides, she had slept with him and, whether he liked it or not, that put their relationship on a slightly altered footing. She sat back down.

Two minutes later he stood in her doorway. "I wanted to see you," he said, none too nicely.

She waved a hand. "Well, here I am. Take a good look."

He came into the room and shut the door. "Is there something on your mind?"

Krista knew that was her opening, but she wasn't about to let him pick a fight with her. If he had come in here to disabuse her of any perceived fantasies about their relationship, he was going to have to come right out and say so. She wasn't going to make it easy for him. "What was it you wanted to see me about, Neil?" she asked with supreme composure, even though her heart was beating like a drumroll.

He frowned, paced to the window, paced back and stopped in front of her desk. "What time did you leave this morning?"

"I don't remember." She shrugged. "Early."

"You could have left a note."

"Why? You already knew I would still respect you in the morning."

His jaw tightened, clearly stating his annoyance. "Hartley—" he began just as the phone buzzed an incoming call. Before Krista could pick up the receiver, Neil had it in his hand.

"Yes?" He clipped the word into the mouthpiece. "Who? Well, tell him to wait." Slapping the phone into place, he lifted a cynical eyebrow. "You have a visitor, Hartley. Is it the guy you're involved with?"

Irritation undermined her effort at outward composure. "Well, I don't know. Who is here?"

"He told the receptionist his name was Gentry."

If she hadn't been so aggravated with him, Krista might have smiled. "*Bill* Gentry?" she asked to annoy him.

Neil's expression darkened. "I think that was the name. He seems to think he has an appointment."

"At ten-thirty." She glanced at her watch. "Punctual, isn't he?"

"Who is he, Hartley?"

She stood, straightening some papers on her desk as she rose. "Bill Gentry?" she repeated. "He's our distributor in the Northwest region. I thought you knew him."

Neil's scowl relaxed a bit. "Right," he said. "I do. And he can wait. Are you involved with anyone, Hartley?"

That took her by surprise and she raised her eyes to his. A mistake, she realized, when awareness flared into a thousand points of longing inside her. "What kind of question is that?"

"A legitimate one. Please answer."

She hesitated, not at all sure what he wanted to know. "That is really none of your business."

"After last night, I think I have a right to ask. It's a simple question and I'd like a simple yes-or-no answer."

Last night? Was he worried about her prior lovers? Did he think she had some disease? "No," she said with an audible degree of tension. "No, I'm not involved with anyone."

"What about the guy you have dates with? The guy you stood up so you could help with Robby."

Pride wouldn't allow her to admit that that guy was a name on a bottle of shampoo. "Nothing to worry about. I assure you that my health card reads like a church hymnal."

Neil paused, obviously processing that information with some surprise. "Health card? Hartley, I was not insinuating that I thought you were—I didn't mean for you to think that I was worried about—" He looked toward the window, pursed his lips, then turned again to her. "Would you sit down? You're making me nervous."

"Then we're even. Why don't *you* sit down?"

"I can't." He ran his hand through his hair and then adjusted the knot of his tie. "I've been thinking." His pause was pregnant and nearly stretched into next week. "I've decided to get custody of Robby."

She really intended to stay standing, but his announcement stripped the stiffening from her knees and she sank, grateful the chair was there to catch her. "What did you say?"

His scowl was gone; his lips no longer pulled into a tight and unhappy line; the set of his jaw eased. He looked eager and . . . yes, excited. "I'm going to go to court and get custody of my son. My name is on the birth certificate and that gives me the legal right to be his father. His mother abandoned him, and that gives me the moral right to keep him. I'm not going to give him back to her."

Krista was shocked, but somewhere in the back of her mind, she taunted Mary Nell, *I told you so. I told you so.* "But, Neil," she said. "Are you sure you want to do this? I mean, babies take time and money . . . and love and time and . . . are you sure?"

"Yes." He smiled then . . . and Krista went limp. "There's something else you should know. I've decided to get married."

Her heart took a nosedive. *Married?* Oh, God, she thought, don't let him know that I care. Please don't let it show. "Married?" she whispered. "Oh . . . well, congratulations."

He placed both hands on the top of her desk and leaned across, coming uncomfortably close to her weakened defenses. "I don't think you understand, Hartley. I'm going to marry you."

Chapter Ten

"By the power vested in me by the state of California, I now prounounce you husband and wife." The minister flashed a toothy smile. "You may kiss your bride."

As Neil bent toward her, Krista decided that if she were dreaming, this was the moment she would awaken. But the pressure of his lips on hers was firm and warm and very real. And the sound of her mother crying in the background was a little too authentic to be a figment of her imagination. There were also the small noises of the close friends and relatives who had been invited to the ceremony...the sighs and sniffles, coughs and throat clearings, not to mention Robby's occasional gurgles. As the kiss ended, Krista decided she was not asleep, she was not dreaming and she had just made the worst mistake of her entire life.

"Congratulations." Mary Nell, with her husband in tow, was the first to step forward and kiss the bride. "I still can't imagine how you both were able to keep this a secret from me. But no one is happier about your marriage than I am. And it was such a beautiful wedding."

That much was true. Neil had chosen his home as the setting and sunset as the time for the ceremony. On the deck, against the golden sky, accompanied by the rhythmic sighs of the Pacific, the wedding had taken place. In a dressy suit of candlelight linen, holding a bouquet of exotic flowers, Krista had become Mrs. Neil Blanchard. In her sweetest dreams, she couldn't have imagined changing one single detail of this fairy-tale wedding. If she'd planned it herself, she couldn't have done as well at fulfilling her own fantasy.

Except, of course, she would have insisted that the bridegroom be at least a little bit in love with her.

"Oh, honey." Phyllis Hartley pressed her tear-streaked cheek against Krista's. "You look so lovely, I could just cry. Now, be sure the photographer gets a picture of the two of you before the sunset is completely gone." She turned to her new son-in-law and gave him a tentative hug. "I can't tell you how happy this makes me," she said to him. "I was beginning to think I'd never have a son-in-law, much less a grandchild. And now I've acquired both in less than twenty minutes."

"Believe me, Mrs. Hartley, it is my pleasure. Robby and I are very pleased to be a part of your family."

Krista had never seen her mother's smile stretch so wide. Phyllis was going to be terribly upset when this was all over but, of course, at the moment, she had no inkling that this marriage wasn't going to last forever.

"You are more than welcome." Phyllis grasped his hand and shared her smile equally between Neil and her daughter. "Are you sure you won't change your mind and let me keep Robby while you and Krista are on your honeymoon? Her father and I would be delighted."

"Thanks, but I feel Robby should be with us. We'll only be gone a few days."

This was something new. Krista arched an eyebrow in his direction. "Honeymoon?" she gritted as her mother stepped away. "You didn't tell me anything about a honeymoon."

"Oh, I'm sure I mentioned it." He motioned for the photographer to move in and snap the requested picture against the sunset. "Smile for posterity, sweetheart," he said as the man framed the shot and snapped the shutter, not once, but half a dozen times.

"Are you sure a honeymoon is necessary?" she asked when the picture taking was over.

He shot her a patient look. "Don't be ridiculous. Of course, a honeymoon is necessary. We want to do this right, don't we?" He encouraged the return of congratulatory guests as the photographer slipped back into the crowd. "Look out," he leaned in to whisper in her ear. "Your mother-in-law is approaching. If you don't mind, act like you're thrilled to be married to me. She is my mother and I'm afraid she will expect a certain amount of adoration from my bride."

Krista watched the tall, distinguished-looking woman come toward her. Marian Blanchard looked exactly like Krista had imagined her. They had met for the first time the preceding evening, but Krista felt as if she had known Neil's mother for much longer. "I like your mother, Neil. But I'm not sure I can fool her into thinking I adore her."

He pinched her arm. "Adore *me*," he said. "For her sake, act as if you adore *me*."

Krista smiled as she offered her hand to Marian. "Thank you for coming all this way to be with us. I know Neil wouldn't have been happy if you couldn't have been here for the wedding."

Marian laughed. "Are you kidding? I would have walked from Florida before I'd have missed this. I have to tell you, Krista, I never thought I'd live to see him married. And I'm not quite comfortable yet with the idea of being a grandmother. Frankly, I always thought I'd have at least nine months to get accustomed to the idea." She smiled easily and with inherent grace. "But Robby is changing my mind about a lot of preconceived notions." She released Krista's hand and grasped Neil's. "Congratulations, dear. You have achieved quite a coup. A beautiful bride and a darling son. Handle them with care." With a kiss on his cheek, she moved on.

Krista glanced up at Neil. "You did explain to her that I am not Robby's mother, didn't you?"

"I'm sure I mentioned that." Neil reached past Krista to shake another hand and receive another round of congratulations.

The tangled web was tightening around her, and Krista was beginning to feel the sting of her deceit. But she had done this for Robby, because she sincerely believed it was in his best interests. Neil had been convincing in his pleas for her help. If he were married, he'd have a better chance of getting custody. If he were married, he'd be on equal ground if Carrie decided to fight. If he were married before a custody battle was launched, it wouldn't look like a last-ditch attempt to provide a stable home for Robby.

At first, Krista had been the devil's advocate, but she'd known from the beginning that she would agree. Who wouldn't reach out to grab the brass ring? Especially when the whole carousel ride was just a crazy dream, anyway.

"Krista," Neil took her hand and squeezed it as he drew her attention to a man and woman who she hadn't met before. "I'd like to introduce you to Melinda and Doug Battles. Melinda, Doug, this is Krista Hartley, my wife."

My wife. Her heart gave a little jump of pleasure. Life came and went in sweet moments like this one, she thought. Maybe he didn't love her, but this was their wedding day and she wasn't going to look back on it with sadness. She smiled as she turned to meet Melinda, the woman who, however inadvertently, had made this moment possible.

THE HOTEL WAS FULL of tourists. In fact, Prudence thought there were probably more Americans in Jamaica in June than there were politicians at the Democratic and Republican national conventions in election years. If she'd been on vacation, like almost every person she'd met so far, she'd have been on her way to the beach. There was some sort of luau-type party going on, courtesy of the hotel she'd checked into just that morning. But she was working, depleting her expense account with amazing speed and amazingly little effort. A trip to the Caribbean wasn't cheap. And tracking down Carrie Walsh and her new husband hadn't been simple.

"Hey, little darlin', aren't you goin' to the luau?" Tex, the man of her worst nightmares, clapped a hand on her shoulder and gave it a hefty squeeze. "Come on, I'll walk ya down to the beach."

She had met him on the plane going from Florida to Nassau and he'd been hitting on her in every port of call since. The man did not understand the word *no,* in any language. "Thanks, but I'm meeting someone."

"But everyone's goin' to be there, sugar. You'd best come on along with me." He chuckled to show, she supposed, that he meant no harm.

"No. I've made other plans." She was actually planning exactly how to inflict bodily harm on his shin if he persisted, when her sixth sense kicked into overdrive. She glanced toward the elevator bay in time to see Mrs. Jason James, née Carrie Walsh, step into the lobby. The game was afoot.

"Excuse me." She left Tex standing there with his hand squeezing the air where her shoulder had been. It had taken four full days, a couple of dozen phone calls, commercial hops between islands and a considerable amount of loitering in hotel lobbies to locate the honeymooning Carrie. But this morning, she'd followed a thin trail to this Americanized resort in Jamaica and found her quarry... a woman who looked enough like Stephanie Starr to be her sister. Prudence had spent most of the afternoon in the lobby, waiting for Carrie to make an appearance. She wasn't about to lose her now.

When Carrie entered the restaurant, Prudence was hot on her heels. "I'm with her," she told the maître d' and brushed past him to follow Carrie to a table for two.

"Do you mind if I join you?" She pulled out the chair opposite Carrie and was in it before there was time for protest. "There's a man who has been annoying me and I told him I was meeting someone, so please don't give me away. Are you here alone, too?" She flashed her best ingenue smile and took advantage of Carrie's momentary surprise to study her. She looked a great deal like her sister, only packaged in a softer, cuter style. Her blue eyes were wide and held a certain vacant sparkle, although that might mean nothing more than too much honeymoon and too little sleep. The diamond on her third finger, left hand, was plain but pretty and the wedding band beneath it was thin and gold. She was dressed in a conservative style that, while attractive, was a far cry from Stephanie's flamboyant halter top.

Carrie continued to stare at Prudence for an uncomfortable moment and then she turned to look over her shoulder. "What man?" she asked. "That big one over there?"

Prudence nodded, although she didn't even glance up. "He's been following me around, trying to get me to go places with him. His name is Tex. Honestly, men can be such *toads*."

Carrie laughed, as if in perfect agreement, and suddenly came alive. "I'm Carrie Walsh. I mean, Carrie James. I've only been married a week. Well, not even quite a week. We're on our honeymoon, but it's been just one disaster after another. My fiancé, I mean, my husband, Jason—he should be here any minute—has been sick. He's been throwing up everywhere and we don't understand why, but I guess it could be a touch of the flu. I didn't think people could get the flu in the summer, especially not in this climate, but there you have it. If anything is going around, Jason will get it. And on our honeymoon, too."

She smiled, and Prudence took a deep breath, but missed her opportunity to insert a word by a split second. "And would you believe it? The airline lost our luggage. Can you imagine? We arrived without a stitch of clothes to wear, except what we had, of course, and we've bought a few things since. I mean, we *had* to have at least a change of underwear. And Jason has this special pair of shoes that he wears almost everywhere. I was even surprised that he didn't wear them in our wedding, but he wore this nice pair of black leather, which looked much better with the tux. Anyway, his shoes are lost and he's been mad about that. And then he's sick on top of it. They misfiled our reservations at the hotel and we waited simply *hours* to get a room the first night. The second night wasn't a lot better because there was a fire drill in the middle of the night, and there we were, without our clothes or Jason's shoes. And it started raining and Jason couldn't find the bathrobe he bought in Bermuda. It was *just* miserable.''

Prudence nodded, wondering if Neil Blanchard had actually slept with this woman. She certainly did not seem his type. Actually, it was hard to imagine any man with this Kewpie doll, although to give Carrie the benefit of the doubt, she might be the next in line if Barbie ever dumped Ken. Pru began to look forward to meeting the absent and flu-struck Jason. "Where are you and your husband from?" she asked, wedging the question in between the arrival of a waiter and Carrie's short pause for breath. "The East Coast?"

"How did you know? My New Jersey accent, right?" Carrie was off and running again, and in a drawn-out and roundabout manner gave Pru more information than she probably intended to give. The discourse on the pros and cons of living "back east" ended with a question. "Where are you from? I can't quite place your accent."

Probably because she hadn't had a chance to give it much of a workout, Pru thought. "California," she said, watching Carrie for a reaction. "I'm a private investigator from San Diego, California."

Carrie's smile went slack. "Oh," she said. "I've never been there."

"You don't have to lie to me, Carrie. I know all about the time you spent there last summer. I know you masqueraded as your sister, Stephanie. And I know about the baby you abandoned on Dr. Blanchard's doorstep."

"Baby?" She went pale and the one word came out in three shaky syllables.

Prudence was sorry she had to do this. "Dr. Blanchard wants to know what you intend to do about the baby."

Carrie gulped. "I left him with my sister."

"And she left him with Dr. Blanchard. But the question is still, what do you intend to do now?"

"I don't know." With a nervous glance toward the front of the restaurant, Carrie began biting her lower lip. "Please don't say anything to Jason. I was going to tell him. I was going to tell everyone, but somehow, the subject just never came up. And then, with the wedding being so last minute and so many things to do... I'm going to tell him about the baby, though, really I am, but everything's been such a disaster and I thought the baby was with Stephanie and oh, it's just a mess. Jason is never going to understand. I mean, he will *eventually,* of course. But now, well, I don't know. He's just gotten his first teaching assignment at the college, you know. And he's very ambitious. I know he loves me, but I should have told him sooner, I guess. What with the wedding and all, the truth just got pushed aside and—"

Prudence wished she could feel some sympathy for the other woman's distress, but frankly her emotions weighed in heavily for Neil Blanchard and the baby. "Here's my business card." She flipped the card onto Carrie's plate. "Dr. Blanchard's phone number is writ-

ten on the back. I suggest you get in touch with him before he takes legal action. This situation is a real
disaster, Carrie, and I hope you'll do something to set
it right before it gets any worse. For your baby's sake.''
Pru pushed back from the table and rose. ''I hope I
haven't ruined your dinner.''

Carrie picked up the card and bent down. Pru
watched as she glanced furtively at the entrance before
slipping the card inside her shoe. ''That's okay,'' Carrie said. ''Jason would probably have ruined it, anyway. He's got some kind of stomach flu, you know.''

Tex was beginning to look better and better, Pru
thought. ''I'll tell Dr. Blanchard that he can expect to
hear from you very soon.''

''Oh.'' Carrie looked as miserable as if *she* had the
flu. ''Okay. I'll take care of everything. Tell him . . . tell
him that I'll be in touch.''

''See that you are.'' Pru walked away, wondering if
Carrie realized that she hadn't come anywhere close to
asking about the health and welfare of her baby.

''HE'S ASLEEP.'' Krista walked from the bedroom onto
the deck, her nerves tense and jumpy, despite her outward calm.

''I think all the activity this evening tired him.'' Neil
turned his head to watch her approach. ''Being passed
from one grandparent to another must be exhausting.
He was very good during the ceremony, though. I didn't
hear him cry once.''

''Are you kidding? My mother and your mother gave
him so much attention he couldn't have gotten out a cry
if he'd wanted to.'' She stopped and leaned against the
railing a short distance from where Neil stood. Wishing she knew what he expected her to say, she watched

the shadow-drenched shoreline, listened to the rush of the ocean onto the sand and waited for the bubble to burst.

"I thought everything went very smoothly," Neil said after a while. "Especially considering the short amount of time in which we had to make the arrangements."

"It was a lovely wedding."

"You were the loveliest thing about it."

Krista wished he wouldn't say things like that. Not tonight, when honesty was so important. "Personally, I thought Robby was the center of attention."

"Babies always do steal the show." Neil laughed softly as he braced his forearms on the railing. "One week with Robby and I'm talking like an expert. I hope you don't mind that I want him with us when we leave on our trip tomorrow. I know children aren't usually invited on the honeymoon."

"Since he's the only reason we're taking one, I think it's appropriate that he come along." She tapped her fingernail against the solid redwood under her hand. "But I think the whole idea of a honeymoon is a little ridiculous, considering that our marriage is merely one of convenience."

The subtle tension snapped taut and the air began to vibrate with new energy. "Don't say that again, Krista. Not to me. Not to anyone. When we go into the attorney's office, when we go before the judge, I intend for this marriage to be real in every respect. I don't want anyone to question its authenticity."

"And you believe a honeymoon will make it authentic?" She didn't know why her tone sounded argumentative. She knew he was right. It was just that the reality of what she had done, of the terrible risk she was taking, made her nervous and edgy. But of course, she couldn't tell him that. "Where are we going on this *authentic* honeymoon? Niagara Falls? Hawaii? Lovers' Paradise, North Dakota?"

He was silent for the space of too many anxious heartbeats and when he straightened and turned toward her, she trembled. "I know this week hasn't been easy for you," he said. "But let's not start our marriage with an argument. I've arranged for us to spend a few days at a private resort up the coast. With Robby along, I didn't want to fly anywhere. Driving seemed the better option. We'll have a house all to ourselves and we don't have to see another soul if we choose not to. We can cook our own meals, have meals delivered or go up to the main lodge for dinner if we want. I think Robby will be content there. I hope you'll enjoy it. But like it or not, we're going on a honeymoon. You may as well reconcile yourself to the idea."

"What if I refuse to go?"

"I'll carry you kicking and screaming."

"Wouldn't that tend to contradict the 'authentic' claim?"

"Krista, I don't want to make this situation any more difficult than it already is. I know you did this for Robby and I appreciate your sacrifice. But damn it, let's not let marriage ruin our relationship."

"Oh, our relationship hasn't changed, Neil. Last week I was your assistant, paid to help you manage your business. Today I'm your wife, hired to help you obtain custody of your child. Don't confuse the issue. I'm still nothing more than your employee."

His sudden frown conveyed his loss of control even before the tension in his voice confirmed it. "In that case, let me go over your new duties with you."

Krista froze in place, seared by the anger she had provoked, chilled by the threat in his words and movements. Why had she pushed him? Had she expected him to say he was madly in love with her and would have married her even if there had been no Robby? She knew better. She knew *him* better than that. "Leave me alone, Neil." The cold snap in her voice belied her own inner struggle for control. "I'm tired and I'm going to bed."

"You've got that right." He reached her in two strides and picked her up in his arms, without gentleness or consideration. "You're going to bed with me—your *employer*—and you're going to stay there until I'm satisfied that I'm getting all the benefits I'm paying for."

"Sex is not a part of our deal."

"The hell it isn't." He strode across the deck, holding her securely against his chest. The rhythm of his angry heartbeat pulsed through him and into her.

"Don't do this, Neil."

"Shut up, Krista. And that is an order."

She couldn't have said another word, anyway. His displeasure was a little frightening, but it was also inherently exciting. As he carried her into the bedroom and dropped her uncermoniously onto the bed, she wondered if this reaction had been her aim all along. Had she aroused his temper because she wanted him to feel some kind of passion on their wedding night? Even if it sprang from anger rather than from love?

He leaned across her, bracing his arms on the mattress and devouring the remnants of her pride in a kiss that probed and searched and demanded her acceptance. She knew she should fight him, put up a show of resistance, if only to support the accusations she had just tossed at him. But his touch, just the pressure of his

mouth on hers, set her head spinning and made her
body pull tight with desire. With a supreme effort of
mind over body, she managed to turn her head. Her
action didn't faze him. His lips slid from her mouth to
trace a pattern of titillating kisses across her cheek and
he dipped his tongue into the sensitive hollow below her
ear, sending shivers through her like the quicksilver trail
of escaping mercury.

He brought one hand to her throat and stroked
downward, returning again and again to repeat the
rough but stimulating massage, moving a little lower
each time, until he was pushing at the neckline of her
blouse. The one she'd worn all afternoon. The silk and
lace confection that had peeked from beneath the linen
jacket she'd worn when she became his wife.

The blouse buttoned in the front, a neat row of tiny,
cream-colored pearls looped by a twist of fabric. It was
as delicate and as seductive as any bit of clothing she'd
ever worn. Neil had chosen it, just as he'd chosen her,
because it suited his needs at the time. It looked bridal,
it was her size and it didn't need any alterations.

But now, as he pushed his fingers beneath the scal-
loped lace, she felt certain the blouse was going to need
major alterations very soon. He was impatient, and the
hands stroking her throat and shoulders were becoming more insistent. So, too, was the hot, heavy ache of
her own need. She wanted him to rip the blouse, to
scatter the buttons across the bedroom like a broken
necklace. She wasn't going to wear it again, anyway. It
was as symbolic to her as Cinderella's glass slipper, and
at the stroke of midnight it would be forever shattered.

A tiny moan escaped her throat, a moan of dreams
lost and passion found, a little cry for a lovely dress and
a beautiful wedding, and for all the moments that were

slipping away from her so fast she couldn't count them. Neil reclaimed her lips then and she couldn't think clearly any longer. He was seducing her, taking her in his own way, in his own good time, because she suited his need of the moment. She had taunted him and he was repaying her for each and every word. Employer. She had called him her employer and he was demonstrating the myriad of powers he had over her.

And she didn't care. God help her, she just did not care.

The neckline eased as, one by one, the buttons surrendered to pressure. One button hit the headboard and clattered over onto the bedside table, rocking there like a clock ticking the hour. Neil pushed a rough and reckless path to her breast, laying open the barriers of clothing and rewarding himself with the fullness of her flesh in his hand. Her nipple puckered beneath his touch, revealing her weak display of resistance as the lie that it was. She wanted him. What was the point in pretending otherwise?

Neil moved his hand from her breast and cupped her chin, turning her head so that she had to face him. He swooped in to kiss her...forehead, eyelids, her nose, her mouth, the corners of her lips...and there was such hunger in him that Krista had to respond, had no choice but to bring up her hands and wrap them around his neck, open her mouth to his plunder, open her heart to take him in.

But he escaped, shifting his weight onto the mattress, straddling her body with his legs and grinding against her with the hard, delicious, powerful force of his arousal. He bent his head and captured her one exposed breast with his lips, pulling and teasing and drawing it into an aching peak of desire. Bracing his upper body with one arm, he explored the curve of her waist and the swell of her hip with his free hand. And then, like the rush of an incoming tide, he rolled her to one side and unfastened the zipper of her skirt. It was gone in a matter of seconds, removed with a deft motion and the combined effort of a mutual will.

Neil made a noise, a throaty sound of pleasure as he let his fingers glide over the length of her leg, from her ankle to the back of her knee and upward to the middle of her thigh where a lace-and-ribbon garter caught and held the band of her silky hose.

"Nice touch," he said hoarsely. "I didn't know women wore these anymore."

Krista swallowed hard. "It came with the dress."

"No, it didn't." He denied her attempt to pretend. "You wore this for me, Hartley. Only for me."

Just the way he said her name sent tremors of longing coursing through her. He hadn't called her Hartley all week. And oddly, she'd missed the sound of it. "I didn't," she whispered and knew it was the least convincing phrase she'd ever uttered. "Not for you."

"Well, if you made another date for tonight, Mrs. Blanchard, you're going to miss it. And some unlucky guy is going to sleep alone, because I'm not letting you leave...with or without your garter belt." He bent to kiss the skin above the garter, deftly unhooked the snap, and then, with hardly a pause, he was exploring a greater expanse of her thigh. His lips were as silky as the hose he rolled down and out of the way, then peeled off in one sensual pull. He kissed his way from her instep back to where he'd started in the middle of her thigh and then repeated the entire process on the other leg.

By the time he unfastened the clasp of the garter belt itself, she was shivering with the tension of waiting.

When he tossed it aside and turned his attention to the triangle of lace-and-silk panties, she thought she might die of the ache inside her. She reached for him, barely aware of her intentions, but he evaded her grasp and began a slow, tortuous return to her lips. In short nibbles and long, slow, wet strokes, he kissed her in places no one else had ever touched, places no other lover had bothered to discover.

And when he finally, ultimately, returned to her lips, she was starving for him, ravenous to take him within her and yield the only power she would ever have over him. But still he was elusive, finding again the tip of her breast and manipulating it into an almost painful longing. The remaining buttons of her blouse were undone, slowly this time, with painstaking commitment, and as he pushed the lace from her shoulders and eased it down and off her arms, he kissed the unexplored territory and teased the underside of her elbow with soft strokes of his tongue.

She trembled, and in one urgent moment of exertion, she pushed him and he rolled onto his back beside her. In a heartbeat, she reversed their positions and, unmindful of power plays or any hidden significance in her actions, she began the arduous process of undressing him. She couldn't begin to display the patience he had shown and so she settled for pulling at his shirt and managing to separate the buttons, one by one, from the buttonholes that held the fabric together.

As soon as she had an opening, she ran her hands inside the shirt, bringing all her senses to bear on the exquisite pleasure of touching him. His chest was muscled and covered with a thin, tingly mat of wiry dark hair. When she kissed it, the hair lent a springy and tantalizing texture that her tongue seemed to delight in exploring. When she discovered the hard nub of a nipple hiding there, she circled it with her tongue, enjoying the way it knotted with response.

His groan might have been hers. She didn't know. The sound was just there, between them, longing and need bound within a futile silence. Her hand slid over his flat, taut stomach and pressed against the insistent bulge below. He wanted her. She was his wife and he wanted her. And for tonight, she thought, that was enough. Want wasn't need and need wasn't love, but sometimes it was a passable substitute.

She fumbled with his belt buckle, and with the first sign of impatience, he moved beneath her, grasping the buckle with his hands and flipping it loose. Then he pushed her aside, pulled into a sitting position and removed his shirt, tossing it across the room with careless abandon. His shoes and socks went on the floor next, joining the dressy heels Krista had lost some long time ago. He rolled to the edge of the bed and slid to his feet, shucking his pants in one clean movement and then moving toward her again with an abundance of clear and breathtaking purpose.

Fascinated, she watched him come to her. She drank in the passion-tightened features of his face, the fire of desire in his dark eyes, the determined set of his lips— not a smile, not a frown, but somewhere in between— the sheen of moisture just beginning to caress his skin, the hard straight lines of his body. He would never want her this badly again, Krista thought. They would make love again, probably many times before the marriage deal was ended, but it wouldn't be like this. Maybe she would never want him this badly again, either. But somehow, she thought this might only be the beginning for her. She might live the rest of her life, knowing the sweet demand of such urgent wanting and regretting that it could not last for more than one night.

But this was that night. And she was going to live every minute of it.

Bold with the intensity of her desire, Krista reached for him, stroked him, kissed him and drew him down, down and into her. She tangled her legs around his hips, clasped her arms around his shoulders and sank into a storm of new sensations. Like a special gift wrapped in a series of ribbon-bedecked packages, she unwrapped each moment and savored it. His possession was demanding. He required her full participation and wouldn't allow her to drift into a secret fantasy. She matched his gaze as she rose to meet the thrust of his hips, and the love she felt seemed more powerful than any emotion she'd ever experienced.

Husband. Employer. What did it matter what she called him? He was her lover, the one man she wanted above all others. And he was hers. Now. In this moment. "Neil," she cried out on a sigh of surrender. "Neil."

He moved faster, responding to her call, and her body shivered in hot, delicious waves of release that tumbled and rolled through her like the rush of sand through an hourglass. And then Neil was flowing into her, filling all the empty spaces inside her, claiming her like the tide claimed the sunbaked beach at evening. And when it was ended, a single tear slipped from the corner of one eye and trickled past her temple.

He rolled away from her and lay, staring at the ceiling, no longer touching her, his breath coming in short, shallow rasps. Krista felt as if the whole room were throbbing with the sound of her pounding heart. And the silence . . . the thick, deafening silence that should have been full of sweet nothings and an eternity of promises.

But she had nothing to say to this man who was, but really wasn't, her husband. What was it he'd said to Suzan that day in the supermarket? *Ceremonies are often meaningless. Nothing more than rituals for the benefit of a society that's overburdened with traditions.* Well, she'd gone through the ceremony for Robby's benefit, but she didn't have to sacrifice her pride by letting Neil know she had done the unthinkable and fallen in love with him.

She sighed and moved to the edge of the bed. Shifting her feet to the floor, she stood and started toward the bathroom.

"Krista?"

Reluctantly, she stopped. "Yes?"

"If you don't want to go, I'll cancel the honeymoon. Maybe you're right. Maybe it is too much of a sham."

As if anything that had happened between them was honest. "If you think a honeymoon trip is in Robby's best interest, then I have no objection. But, Neil, this marriage is a business arrangement. That's the way you put it to me in the beginning and that's the way I expect it to stay. Honeymoon or no honeymoon."

With that, she walked into the adjoining bath and closed the door with a firm and decisive click.

THE PHONE RANG early the next morning, an annoying jangle in the midst of a too-polite tension. Krista continued mixing formula to fill the baby bottles lined up on the counter. The trip was still on as far as she could determine, and she was preparing all the necessary items Robby would need for a few days away from home. No wonder people didn't do much traveling once they had children.

"Blanchard." Neil turned away from her as he answered the phone, and she wondered how in hell he thought she would enjoy this little 'vacation' when he exuded a chill to rival any Frigidaire. Of course, it had been her stupid idea to mention "business arrangement." Right after he had made wonderful love to her, too. Krista couldn't help believing that if she had had a little more experience and a little less principle, this morning wouldn't have started off on such an awkward footing. The night, too, probably would have had a different ending. Instead of sleeping alone in the guest room, she could have stayed in Neil's warm embrace and pretended that they both thought she belonged there.

"And what did she say when you told her?"

Neil braced a hand against the door casing and leaned his head on the curve of his arm as he listened. Krista would have liked to approach him, to massage the back of his neck and brush her fingers through his hair. But, of course, she didn't. It was clear he was getting impatient with the person on the other end of the phone line, and she didn't want to be in his line of fire when the conversation ended.

"Damn it to hell, Madigan. Didn't she give you any indication of what she plans to do?"

Madigan. Krista knocked over a bottle, and formula spilled like runny glue across the counter and dribbled onto the floor. In his room, Robby began to cry in earnest as he did anytime he'd been left alone for too long.

"It certainly took long enough," Neil snapped at the phone. "What have you been doing for an entire week?

And then you let her go without getting an answer? You were supposed to scare the living daylights out of her.''

Krista knew very little about P. G. Madigan and what she was supposed to find out. What she did know was that Madigan was to search through the islands of the Caribbean until she located Robby's mother. This phone call could only mean that the woman had been found. And that meant that she was real. Until this moment, Krista realized, she had thought, hoped, that somehow there wasn't really a Stephanie. Until now, she'd been able to pretend that somehow, some day in the future, *she* herself could be Robby's mom.

''Yes. That is exactly what I want you to do. I don't care what kind of hornet's nest you have to stir up, I want her to know I mean business.'' He hung up with a clatter and slapped the woodcasing with the palm of his hand. ''Damn,'' he said forcefully. ''Madigan found her.''

''Robby's mother?'' Krista had to ask, had to put the reality into words. ''Stephanie.''

''Carrie is her real name. She's on her honeymoon and apparently is still waiting for the appropriate moment to tell her new husband about Robby.''

''She hasn't told him?''

Neil gestured with clear cynicism. ''She's an idiot.''

''So where does that leave you? Is she coming back for him or not?''

''Madigan didn't ask. She said I hired her to find the woman, not interrogate her.'' He ran a hand through his hair. ''I suppose she's right. It's just that now that I've decided I want to keep Robby, I want the red tape sliced and the legal documents signed. I don't want to have to think about her picking him up and then leaving him somewhere else when he doesn't fit in with her schedule.''

''She doesn't seem like much of a mother.''

''But the law is on her side. She left him with her sister while she went on her honeymoon. What judge is going to find that unreasonable?''

''But she abandoned him, Neil.''

''I know, Krista.''

Suddenly, from Robby's room, there was a furor of crying. Loud, walloping wails that turned into spasms of hacking cough. Krista went cold all over as the cough turned to a strangled gurgle. She couldn't move, just stood there, terrified that the baby was choking. Neil pushed past her in a panicked run as the noise stopped abruptly and turned into a horrifying silence.

Chapter Eleven

"Is he breathing?" Krista paused in the doorway of Robby's room as Neil bent over the crib. She tried to calm down enough to remember everything she'd ever heard about infant CPR. It was different from doing it on an adult. You had to cover the baby's nose and mouth. That was it. And how many seconds were you supposed to count? She should call a doctor. No, she should call for an ambulance. 911. Emergency. Someone there would know what to do. She twisted her hands and helplessly watched Neil lift the baby out of the bed.

An immediate and healthy cry split the air with relief. Krista sagged against the doorframe. "I thought he'd stopped breathing."

"No," Neil said. "No, he's breathing." Robby's cries became a steady, rhythmic wail, and Neil closed his eyes for a few seconds. "Apparently, the kid just got mad. He seems to be fine now." With a sudden frown, Neil thrust Robby into her arms, then turned and strode from the room as if the incident hadn't happened, as if he hadn't been scared witless, too, as if he had other more important things to do.

Robby kept crying, but he was already calmer. Krista held him against the terrific pounding of her heart and kissed his sweaty little head. "Shh. There, now. You're all right. Did you think we'd left you all by yourself? Hmm? You scared me, fella. Did you know that? I thought something was really wrong with you."

She had never been so frightened in her life, Krista thought. Was this what it meant to be a parent? This heart-stopping, total terror at the thought of anything happening to Robby? Had Neil felt it? she wondered. Was that the reason he'd left the room so abruptly? Because he'd been so scared?

As the baby's wailing subsided to an aftermath of dry sobs, Krista carried him into the kitchen. The bottle she'd spilled was still there, a gooey mess across the cabinet and floor, the sweet, gummy smell of formula soaking the air. Neil was nowhere to be seen, and she followed her instincts to the bedroom. He was standing outside on the deck, his arms resting on the railing, shoulders bent as he stared at the ocean view.

She hesitated and then walked out to join him. Robby forgot all about crying and began kicking with delight when she propped him against the rail and held him so he, too, could enjoy the view. "He's okay," she said. "I didn't know a baby could get mad enough to hold his breath like that, but I think that must be what he did."

Neil didn't even glance around.

"He really scared me. I didn't know my heart could beat so fast." She gave a little laugh, hoping he would join her.

He didn't.

"Come on, Neil. It's over. Everything's all right."

"Everything is *not* all right, Hartley. What in hell am I trying to prove? The things I don't know about babies would make a list long enough to circle the globe a hundred times. Two weeks ago that was just fine with me.'' He shook his head. ''I am not cut out for this.''

''Cut out for what? Being a parent? Or being married?'' Robby gave a big kick, and she steadied him with her hands. ''A little late to think of that...now that you're stuck with a wife and a kid.''

The silence stretched too long without disagreement and, Krista's heart picked up another awkward rhythm. That was it, she realized. That was the problem. He was already regretting their hastily struck bargain, their marriage of convenience, his decision to keep Robby. Her throat tightened and a desperate ache settled in her chest.

He straightened and flexed his shoulder muscles. ''Let's get going,'' he said.

''Where?''

The ghost of a smile appeared on his lips and then vanished. ''Where else, Krista? On our honeymoon.''

''PSST! HEY!''

Careful not to knock over the bottle of suntan lotion wedged against her thigh, Prudence pushed up from her prone position and looked around.

''Psst! Miss Madigan!''

Miss Madigan? No one called her that. Narrowing her eyes in a squint, she scanned the sun-worshipers on the beach. Everyone was either bronze, red or a pink color somewhere in between the two. A few sunbathers were toasting only their lower extremities and were partially shaded by colorful beach umbrellas. No one seemed to want her attention. She must have imagined someone calling her name.

Good. She didn't want to be disturbed. For the past week, she had hopped from one Caribbean island to another and, now that it was time to go home, she intended to spend at least a couple of hours enjoying herself. Prudence dropped back onto her blanket and repositioned her sunglasses.

"Shh. Pretend you don't see me."

Prudence opened one eye and turned her head—just slightly, so it would look as if she wasn't actually looking at the woman who was arranging a bulky umbrella in the plot of sand next door. "What is this? Did I win the beach-blanket lottery?"

"Shh!" The hiss nearly vibrated the umbrella off its shaky foundation. "It's me. Carrie James. Do you remember me? We talked last night . . . in the restaurant? I told you about—"

"I remember." Prudence closed her eyes and pretended she was alone.

"I've got to talk to you." Carrie got the shade anchored precariously in the sand and plopped down with a sigh. "But I can't get sunburned. You do realize that you could get skin cancer and die just from this one exposure to the sun, don't you? The sun's rays come right through the hole in the ozone and target people lying on the beach. It has something to do with reflecting off the white sand and the water."

Incredible, Prudence thought. Carrie *looked* like a normal person, but when she opened her mouth . . . "If you're trying to tell me that there's a solar ray out there with my name on it, I just want you to know I'm ready." She lifted the lotion bottle with a lackadaisical motion of her wrist. "SPF 15. Better protection than a body condom and much more comfortable."

Carrie shook her head.

Prudence didn't see her, but she knew that's what happened.

"Blondes are more at risk, too," Carrie continued. "Has something to do with the lack of pigment in our skin."

"I knew I was lacking something, but I thought it was peace and quiet."

"It's a scientific fact that blondes are more likely to get skin cancer. I'm just telling you what my dermatologist told me, and I had to pay him to get the information. You're getting it for free."

"I'm forever in your debt. So tell me, Mrs. James, why are you sneaking around on the beach? Are you the official doomsayer? Or perhaps you're a sunscreen salesman in disguise? Or maybe you're just trying to escape from your husband, the flu bug?"

"Oh, none of those things," Carrie said with a giggle. "Jason is feeling much better, thank you. In fact, he's probably looking for me right now. I didn't know it would take so long to find you. But I don't want him to catch me talking to you—no offense, Miss Madigan, you seem very nice. It's just one of those situations. You understand, I'm sure. And I had to talk to you and find out if he's mad."

Prudence considered that bit of rambling. "I have no idea. But if *you* think he's mad, you probably should go find him right now and ask him."

"I can't do that. I'm on my honeymoon."

"The very best time to stay close to your husband."

"No, no, no. I didn't mean Jason. He's my husband. I know *he's* not mad. Not yet, anyway. I'm talking about Dr. Blanchard."

"Ah. Dr. Blanchard. You want to know if *he's* mad. Yes, I think it's safe to describe his state of mind as angry. You might even say that he'd be all too happy to wring your little neck."

"Oh, dear. And it seemed like such a brilliant idea to put his name on the birth certificate. I never thought he'd find out and I certainly never thought Stephanie would give the baby to him. Oh, dear. This is such a disaster. My whole life has been a disaster, you know. Just one big screwup after another. Except for Jason, and there's no telling what he's going to say about this. I mean, he broke our engagement once because he thought I was too much trouble. But then, he did kind of miss me and everything has been going so well. Except for this trip and losing our luggage and him being sick and all. But none of that was really *my* fault, unless he caught the flu from me. But I just don't know what he's going to say about this."

Prudence tried to imagine herself on a deserted beach. Alone on a deserted beach. Completely alone on a deserted beach. Imagining was hard when Carrie kept talking.

"You have to believe I never meant for this to happen. Actually, I never intended to get pregnant. Of course, I guess most women don't. Well, maybe married women do. Or some of them do, anyway, I guess. I don't really know quite how *I* got pregnant. Well, of course I *know*, but I didn't mean to and there I was, pretending to be Stephanie, and you can't even guess what she would have said if she'd known. And then, I'm throwing up every morning and the doctor says the rabbit died and I didn't know what to do. So I ran off to have the baby, but I came back. Then Jason called and I *couldn't* tell him over the phone, and I was watching a show on television about this woman who—"

"Carrie!" Prudence put all the authority and aggravation at her command into that one word. "I'm not interested in any of this. Dr. Blanchard is the person you should be talking to, not me. Take my advice. Call him and make arrangements to get your baby back. Surprise Jason with the news that, voilà, he's become a daddy in less time than it takes for most people to lose five pounds. Tell him all you have to do is go to California and pick up the kid. Do it now, Carrie. Don't wait until this disaster multiplies.''

"But that's the reason I had to talk to you." Carrie leaned toward Prudence, coming very close to exposing her fair skin to the deadly sun rays. "I couldn't sleep last night, I worried about this so much. And at five o'clock this morning, I came to the conclusion that you were right. Jason has to be told. But he'd take it a lot better if it came from you."

At that point, Prudence stopped trying to pretend she didn't see the woman sitting next to her. She opened her eyes, removed her sunglasses and stared at pretty Carrie James, who sat innocently in the shade of the umbrella, the epitome of 'dumb blonde' jokes around the world. "Carrie," she said. "You have a baby and sooner or later, your husband is going to find out. It will be better if he hears it from you, but either way, *I* am not going to be the one to tell him. Now, if you don't mind, I have some serious suntanning to do."

"But, Miss Madigan. What am I going to do?"

Prudence sighed as she put the sunglasses on again. "Grow up, Carrie. Grow up and take the responsibility for your mistakes."

Carrie sank back under the umbrella's canopy, and her voice came out muffled and melancholy. "Responsibility," she repeated. "I don't even know how to spell that."

TIMMERLEA RESORT SAT on a narrow strip of land like a giant sand crab that had crawled out of the tide and got stuck too far from shore. The resort's rustic theme had become a reality over the years and now it was little more than a clump of weathered clapboard cottages clustered on each side of a central lodge which sat as close to the beach as the law allowed. Time, however, had granted Timmerlea a certain provincial charm. The cottages themselves were simple to the point of being plain and yet their very simplicity gave the whole resort a relaxed and easy atmosphere. The lodge was more modern with long panels of square-paned glass and an occasional touch of old-world elegance.

On first glance, Krista thought Timmerlea Resort belonged anywhere but Southern California. It didn't match the hurry-up world that existed a very short distance away. It didn't jibe with the glamorous image of West Coast spas. It catered to retirees and vacationers who preferred strolling on the beach to jogging in the sand. It was not at all the sort of place Krista would have thought Neil would choose for a honeymoon.

But then, this wasn't a real honeymoon.

"I'll get the portable crib set up," Neil said as he set the last of the bags on the hardwood floor of their assigned cottage. "In case he decides to take a nap."

An unlikely happening, but Krista decided not to say so. Neil wanted to be busy. He had had little to say on the trip to Timmerlea, and she didn't expect the amount of conversation to increase during their stay. Clearly, he was having second thoughts about the course of action he'd chosen, and he was a man who was unaccustomed to even a hint of regret. She had seen him make split-second decisions and forge ahead, regardless of the repercussions. She knew he ran his business with a cut-throat determination to do whatever it took to achieve his goal. He'd approached the situation with Robby in the same manner. He decided he was the father. He decided Robby was his responsibility. He decided the way to get custody was to present a complete family unit before the ruling judge. But now, suddenly, his decisions were bringing unexpected repercussions. Emotional consequences he hadn't foreseen. And Krista didn't know why she had allowed him to put her dead in the center of his no-win situation.

"I think Robby and I will take a little walk outside," she said as if she didn't know anything was wrong. "We'll be back in fifteen or twenty minutes."

"Sure. Take all the time you want."

Would he notice if they didn't come back at all? Krista wondered. *New bride and new baby disappear on honeymoon.* She could see the headlines now. Of course he'd notice. He would never admit he'd made the wrong decisions, even if he knew he had.

"Maybe I'll stop and get something to drink at the lodge."

"Sure," he said. "Charge it to the cottage."

"Of course." She left in a mood that was rapidly deteriorating. And it hadn't started off with far to fall. "I don't know about you, Robby," she said to the baby who bounced with utter contentment on her shoulder, "but I'm beginning to wish I'd resigned one day and left the next. The more I do to help him, the more tangled up I get in his problems. He is going to break my heart, you know, and I have no one to blame but myself."

Robby jumped in her arms, kicking and tossing his fists in general delight at being outdoors and moving.

"Okay, okay." Krista gave his padded rear a series of affectionate pats. "I'll shift the blame to you. If you didn't have such big blue eyes and a killer smile, I wouldn't be in this mess. And don't try to deny it. You're going to break my heart, too. When your mamma comes back, you'll throw me over for her so fast my head will spin.''

"YES, OPERATOR, I'll hold." Neil carried the phone with him as he walked out onto the porch. Krista and Robby hadn't been gone ten minutes, yet, but he found himself scanning the beach for signs of them. Not that they'd be anxious to return to his company. He hadn't been exactly pleasant to either one of them. The fact that he was feeling particularly vulnerable at the moment didn't help. He didn't have a lot of experience with 'vulnerable' and he did not like what he'd had of it so far.

He shouldn't have persuaded Krista to marry him. He shouldn't have listened to the lawyer who'd told him a stable family environment was essential to getting custody of a child. What was he doing with Robby, anyway? Two weeks of taking care of a baby—especially since Krista had done most of the 'taking care of'—did not qualify him for full-time daddyhood. Why had he been so eager to tackle the role in the first place? It wasn't as if his life was short on challenge. It wasn't as if he had to go looking for a child to give meaning to his existence.

The call to Jamaica went through, and he requested a connection to Madigan's room.

"I am sorry, sir." A crisp, Jamaican accent came on all too quickly and made a staccato echo across the phone lines. "Ms. Madigan is not in her room."

Neil felt like tossing the phone into the ocean out of general frustration. Of course, at this distance there wasn't a chance he could get it anywhere near the water. "Send someone to look for her," he snapped. "I'll hold."

"I can leave a message for her, sir. I am positive she will check at the desk upon her return."

"Can you page her? She could be still in the hotel."

"That is possible, sir. Do you wish to leave a message?"

"No. I wish to hold while you find out where she is."

"Very well, sir."

Neil was losing all patience with Madigan, the hotel clerk and himself. Why hadn't he told Madigan to call him back? Why hadn't he insisted she wear a beeper so he could find her when he wanted her? Why had he sent her there in the first place? If he'd wanted to find Carrie, why hadn't he gone himself?

The voice came back on the line. "I am sorry, sir. Ms. Madigan does not answer the page."

"Take down this number," Neil instructed. "Have her call me the minute she comes in."

"The minute she comes in. Yes, sir." The clerk took the number Neil gave him and was courteously and continuously apologetic. Neil finally hung up on him.

A swim. With a determined look around the "honeymoon suite," Neil decided he definitely needed a swim. Madigan was not likely to return his call anytime soon, and he needed to let the surf beat up on him for a while. Maybe then he could stop all the mental beatings he was giving himself. He had not handled this well, and that upset him more than anything else.

Business arrangement, Krista had reminded him last night. Right after he'd forced her into his bed. Neil frowned. Actually, there had been no force involved. If she'd resisted . . .

Still, that was no excuse. She clearly thought their marriage was one of convenience. Hell, why wouldn't she? At his request, she'd signed the prenuptial agreement his lawyer had drawn up. What did he expect? Enthusiasm because he had *hired* her to pose as his wife for a few weeks until he got what he wanted?

Honeymoon. Damn it. He should have had better sense.

WHEN KRISTA RETURNED to the cottage, it was empty. Neil had unpacked his bag, staked a claim on one side of the bathroom sink and disappeared.

"I wouldn't worry about him," she advised Robby as she strapped him into his carrier seat and set him safely on the floor in the bedroom. He kicked vigorously and made bubbly noises as she lifted her bag onto the bed and began to unpack. "He'll be back. He's probably checking out the golf course for tomorrow."

Robby gurgled excitedly.

"I know you think you're a pro, but take it easy. Your father will not be happy if you whip him on the front nine. Save your birdies for Grandpa Hartley."

Krista tucked her lingerie in the middle drawer of the chest, thinking that she should have left the dainty stuff behind and brought sturdier, more practical underwear. What use was the lace teddy going to be? And why had she brought the scrap of filmy nylon her mother had slyly called "a nightgown"?

"Here, honey," Phyllis had said. "Here's a little something every bride should have for her wedding night."

Ha, Krista thought as she held the black netting to the light. "Little nothing" was more like it. There was more light pouring through the gown than the curtains let in.

"Don't look at this, Robby," she said. "You're too young. Your grandmother is a sick woman."

The phone rang, and Krista dropped the bit of fabric on Robby's feet as she picked him up and hurried into the other room. "Hello," she said into the receiver.

"Is this—?" A set of numbers were rattled off and Krista had to switch everything in her arms in order to lean down and verify the phone number.

"Yes," she confirmed.

"This is Madigan. Where's the man?"

"Do you mean Dr. Blanchard?"

"Who else would send half the bellboys in Jamaica looking for me? Where is he?"

"I don't know." Krista stooped down and placed Robby's carrier on the floor. She took the nightgown and stuffed it into her shorts pocket. "Have you talked with, um, the baby's mother?"

"I've done a lot of *listening* to her, but talking? No, I haven't actually talked with her. And if he wants me to get anywhere near her again, my fee is going up. I'm telling you, the woman is a board-certified space cadet."

Krista glanced at Robby. "Is she . . . crazy?"

Madigan's laugh was not funny. "Beats the heck out of me. All I know is that her mouth hasn't figured out that there's nothing between her ears but rooms for rent."

"Did she mention the baby at all?"

"Only that she didn't know how she got pregnant. She certainly didn't intend to."

"Oh." Krista's stomach churned. "Is she coming back for him?"

"I couldn't tell you. I advised her to call Dr. Blanchard and at least talk to him about what she plans to do. Whether or not she will is anyone's guess. I have more information about her than the government has, so if she doesn't show up to get the kid, it won't be hard to locate her again." Madigan paused. "Listen, I'm scheduled to fly out of here in about two hours. I'll be in my office tomorrow morning. Tell Blanchard he can call me there anytime after nine."

"Madigan? Is she nice?" Krista felt stupid for asking, but she had to know. "Does she seem—well, basically—like a nice person?"

There was a pause, and when the answer came, Madigan's voice had changed to a softer, more sincere tone. "Basically? Yeah, I'd say she's nice. Naive, immature, no common sense, bubbles for brains, self-focused and a textbook case of arrested development, but overall, a *nice* person."

"Okay, thanks." Krista wasn't sure that knowing made her feel any better. "I'll tell Neil you called and ask him to get in touch with you tomorrow at your office. Call this number if anything else comes up. We'll be staying here for a couple of days."

"A little vacation?" Madigan asked.

Krista sighed. "Our honeymoon."

"Honeymoon! It's an epidemic. What did you do with the little nipper?"

"He's here with us."

"Well," Madigan said. "I'll be damned."

"How long ago did she call?" Neil bent at the waist and used a towel stamped Timmerlea to brush the sand from his bare feet.

"Twenty, thirty minutes." Krista stood on the porch, holding Robby and wishing Neil didn't look so devastatingly attractive with the sun in his hair and the sheen of an ocean swim covering his body. "She said you could call her at the office tomorrow."

"If I'd wanted to talk to her tomorrow, I'd have waited until then to call her." He flicked the towel once more across his ankles then straightened and crossed the porch. Brushing past Krista and Robby, he entered the house and went straight to the phone.

Obviously, Krista thought, a swim hadn't improved his mood. Robby kicked, indicating that he was tired of standing still and ready to move on. With a sigh, she walked down the short set of stairs and settled herself on the bottom step. She turned Robby so he could sit in her lap and see the ocean. Maybe the darting sea gulls would hold his attention for five minutes or so.

Five minutes was about the extent of his enjoyment, and he began to fuss and wiggle in her arms just as Neil came out of the cottage and joined her on the step. Still wearing only his swimming trunks and a towel, he made mincemeat of her irritation with him just by virtue of how very good he looked wearing nearly nothing.

"Madigan is incommunicado," he said sourly. "Either that or she's left instructions at the desk not to put through any calls from me."

"She wouldn't do that. She's probably already left the hotel."

"She has avoided my calls before." He ran one end of the towel over his hair, disheveling it into appealing disarray. "You shouldn't have talked me out of hiring Sam Spade."

Krista spared a glance for him as she turned a fidgety Robby and let him stand in her lap. "Okay, I'll take the blame for not insisting you hire a *male* detective, but frankly I don't think Madigan has done so badly."

"She hasn't done badly at all," Neil agreed. "She's just so mouthy." He draped the towel across his knees. "Her name is Prudence, by the way. I believe we had a bet on what her initials stood for, so now I owe you five dollars."

"I thought the bet had something to do with her trench coat."

"Then you owe me five dollars."

Krista gave him a frown. "Deduct it from my baby-sitting fee."

Neil leaned back, his arms bent and resting on the stair behind him, revealing a smooth, tanned expanse of muscled chest. Krista looked away, wondering how she could be so irritated with him and yet want so much to make love to him again.

"The bill for all this is probably going to amount to more than it would have taken to send the Kid to Harvard."

"You can afford it," Krista said, bracing her elbows against her sides to support Robby's energetic bouncing. "In fact, this is probably the best investment you'll ever make."

She felt his gaze slide skeptically to her. "Which one? You? Or the Kid?"

"Don't play games with me, Neil. You've been in a foul mood all day. It isn't my fault and it isn't Robby's fault that you're having second thoughts. Here." She plopped the baby into Neil's lap, stood and walked up the stairs. "The two of you can fuss at each other for a while. I'm going for a swim."

"Wait. We'll come with you."

Krista didn't even pause. "Please...don't do me any favors." She let the screen door slam behind her, but when she came out again, ready to buck the waves—

whether familial or ocean—she found Neil and Robby waiting with a smile. At least, Neil was smiling. Robby was still bouncing like a short-leashed yo-yo.

"Think of us as your lifeguards," Neil said. "We'll keep a lookout for sharks, jellyfish and bodybuilders."

Relief trickled through her. She didn't think his mood had actually improved, but he was at least making an effort to be more pleasant. "How thoughtful," she said with a slow smile. "I suppose you two men think you can handle any danger I might face on the beach."

"Allow us to demonstrate our right hook." Neil grabbed Robby's hand, and they jabbed the air together. "If any ninety-pound weakling bothers you, he'll have to answer to us."

Krista laughed and loved them both so much it hurt.

THE PHONE WAS RINGING when they came back from the beach. Neil was carrying Robby, so Krista entered the cottage first and picked up the receiver. "Hello?"

"Hello?" The voice on the other end of the line was feminine and foreign, flat and mechanical. "This is the operator. Will you accept a collect call from Stephanie?"

"Stephanie?" Krista repeated the name as her heart started to beat a little faster and a little harder. "Yes, operator. Yes, I'll accept the call."

"Hello?" The voice changed to an American accent and a soft, girlish sound. "Is this—?" She reeled off the phone number just as Madigan had done earlier and then giggled nervously. "Uh, I guess it is or you wouldn't have agreed to pay for the call, huh? I'm really sorry to call collect, but I couldn't put this on our hotel bill. If Jason saw it, he'd ask all sorts of questions and I wouldn't know how to begin explaining, and since we're going home tomorrow morning, he'd be bound to see it on the bill. So I'm really glad you didn't just hang up the phone as soon as you heard my name.... Oh, by the way, I'm not really Stephanie. But I guess you figured that out, huh? I thought you might not know me if I used my real name and—'' The flow of words stopped abruptly. ''Who are you, anyway? I was supposed to call Dr. Blanchard. Neil Blanchard.''

Krista swallowed and motioned for Neil to come into the house from outside. ''He's here.''

''Oh. Well, good, because this is the only number I have written down. Someone, a private investigator actually, gave me this number—well, to be honest, she gave me *another* number first, but then this afternoon she gave me this number instead and told me if I wanted to get in touch with him, I should call. But I don't really know why I'm calling. There just isn't a lot to say, and Miss Madigan told me he wanted to wring my neck, so it's a good thing I'm calling long-distance, isn't it? But really, none of this is my fault. I didn't know anything else to do, and it's just unfortunate that he got mad about it because I didn't mean for him to get upset. What time is it there?''

''A little after 4:00 p.m. You can speak to Neil now.'' Krista started to hand the phone to Neil, but stopped when a loud ''No! Wait!'' shrieked across the wire.

''You said you wanted to talk to him,'' Krista said, pulling the receiver a short distance from her ear.

''*I* never said that. Madigan said I *should* talk to him, but that's not the same thing as *wanting* to. I only called because I was afraid he'd call here and Jason would answer, and then, there I'd be in the very middle of the *worst* disaster of my *entire* life. But Jason went down to the sauna and so I thought this would be the best time to talk to the man, but really, I'd much rather talk to you."

"But Dr. Blanchard is right here."

"No! Don't put him on the phone or I'll hang up! I will. I'll hang up as quick as anything. If he's mad—and Madigan said he was—then I don't want him to yell at me. I hate that. Jason sometimes does it and I just get cold chills all over my body. So whatever you do, don't put him on the phone."

Krista rolled her eyes and held the phone so that if Neil, leaning close, could also hear. "If you don't want to talk to him, why did you call?" she asked as gently as her own inner conflict would allow. This was Carrie. The long-lost Carrie. The woman who had more of a claim on Robby and Neil than Krista would ever have. Her hand shook slightly and she forced herself to steady it. "The two of you need to talk."

"I know," Carrie whined all the way from Jamaica. "At least, I guess I know. This is the most awful mess, and I thought everything was going to be fine once I married Jason. But I really don't want to talk to Dr. Blanchard. I mean, what am I going to say to him?"

"How about starting off with what you intend to do next?" Neil grabbed the phone and shifted the baby into Krista's arms in one smooth move. "Then maybe we can progress to why you didn't contact me when you first found out you were pregnant? Then maybe we ought to go over—"

Robby didn't like being passed around and he didn't like the tension around him either. He let out a whopper of a cry. And above the crying, Carrie's voice echoed into the room. "Oh, my God. It's a baby."

"*Our* baby," Neil corrected. "Yours and mine, Carrie. Now let's talk about the best thing to do for *our* baby, shall we?"

There was a moment of complete and unexpected silence. Then a click and the empty buzzing of the phone.

Chapter Twelve

"Before Robby came along, women never hung up on me." Neil bent to pick up a seashell and toss it back into the tide. "Telephone conversations ended with 'good-bye' or 'I'll see you later,' not a rude click and a buzzing noise."

"You've said that at least a dozen times since this afternoon," Krista said as she walked along the beach beside him. "You said it when it happened. You said it while you fixed Robby's bottle. You said it before you changed clothes. You said it on the way to the lodge. You said it before the waiter took our order, twice during dinner and again before we got up from the table."

"That's only eight times, nine including just now."

"Well, frankly, Robby and I are getting tired of hearing it." Robby agreed with a bubbly gurgle as he turned his head to nuzzle Krista's neck beneath the cotton baby blanket Neil had insisted on draping over him and her shoulder.

"Well, excuse me. If we were on the phone, I'd hang up."

"But we're not on the phone. The three of us are on our honeymoon."

"Does that mean I can't hang up on you?"

"Not if you want this trip to look authentic."

"Why didn't I know before now how ruthless you are, Hartley?"

"You weren't paying attention."

"Hmm." He liberated another shell from the sand and skipped it out to sea. "What do you think of the honeymoon so far?" he asked.

"I'll turn in my comment sheet on the last day." She offered him a frown. "But really, Neil, you should have warned me I'd have to give you a grade."

"Not me," he said with a snap. "Timmerlea. What do you think of the resort?"

She sighed and, as suddenly and as quickly as it had left, the strain of the last few days returned. Neil wished he knew how to make everything all right between them again, really all right, the way it had been before. Ever since the wedding . . . no, ever since he'd told her they were going to be married . . . she had worn this air of reserve, a certain cool detachment. For a while this evening, it had vanished, but now he couldn't seem to make a move out of its suffocating presence. He didn't like it, but so far, nothing he'd done had been able to get past it. Was it possible he was just doing all the wrong things?

"The resort is lovely," she said after a moment. "Quiet and quaint. I can hardly believe we're only a three-hour drive from home."

"I don't think they get too many children here. Did you notice the way everyone looked at Robby tonight? As if they were surprised to see a baby in the lodge dining room."

"He did attract a lot of attention. Of course, he is too cute for words."

"I wonder if any of those people who smiled at him would like to give him some attention around midnight. You have to admit he isn't at his peak of 'cute' then."

"He'll develop a better schedule as things settle down. His life hasn't been exactly smooth and uneventful during the last month or so."

"His mother is crazy." Neil shoved his hands into the pockets of his jeans. "She hung up on me."

"So you've said."

"Well, I can't understand why she did it. And that bothers me."

"Maybe it upset her to hear Robby crying."

"Oh, sure. That probably upset her as much as abandoning him did." His strides lengthened unconsciously as the tension and resentment built in him again. He had to stop and wait for Krista's more even pace to catch up. "I suppose I'll call my attorney tomorrow morning as soon as I've talked to Madigan. I probably ought to tell her to keep digging around and find out all she can about Carrie and her new husband. There might be something that would help—"

"Give it a rest, Neil." Krista climbed the bottom step of their cottage and turned to him. "Robby is not a problem you can keep attacking from forty different angles. Stop trying to figure out how you can *win* custody of him and start trying to figure out whether you really *want* custody of him. There is a difference, and you owe it to him to know, going in, which it is."

Neil paused, eye to eye with her, the sweet, seductive scent of her surrounding him with a whole set of sensations that had no relevance to the conversation. None at all. "What is that supposed to mean?"

She cupped her hand at the baby's shoulders and held him steady as a brisk ocean breeze lifted the corner of the blanket. "It means that you love a challenge, Neil. You love the solving of a problem more than you love having the answer. You should give at least as much thought to what you want as to how to go about solving the next step in this equation, because the solution may be more than you bargained for."

"You don't think I should keep Robby, is that it?"

Krista closed her eyes for a moment and he almost lifted his hand to touch her cheek, to brush the wayward tendrils of hair away from her face but, of course, he didn't. "I didn't say that, Neil. Forget it. Just forget I said anything at all."

She turned and walked up the remaining step to the porch and into the cottage. He started to follow, to argue his position and get her to say that he was right. He was doing the right thing. For Robby. For himself. For her. But he didn't think she would say that, so he didn't follow her. He stopped when he reached the porch and walked to the end of the structure. He chose a perch on the railing, in the shadows, where he could watch the nighttime ocean and the panoply of moonlight and white-fringed surf.

It looked different here than from his deck at home. Funny that a few miles along the coast could make a change in one's view of a vast and changeless sea. Not so funny actually, he thought. Look how a few days had changed his view of himself and his life.

The screen door opened and Krista came out onto the porch. He knew she didn't see him at first and he seized the opportunity to study her in private. Look how these few days had changed her, he thought. Or perhaps only his perspective had changed. Before he had coerced her into sharing the responsibilities of caring for Robby, she had carried herself with an almost haughty determination. The scent of business had clung to her, her mode of dress had broadcast her ambition, even the very feminine sway of her hair and her hips had been practical and productive. As an assistant, he couldn't have asked for more. But since the moment Robby had arrived, he'd asked for more and more and more and wondered when she was going to cry "enough."

She turned and he knew she saw him simply because of the instant stillness that framed her. "I put him to bed," she said softly. "He's fussing a little, but I think he'll go on to sleep."

"He ought to be tired out." Neil turned his head toward the view, if only because watching her made his throat ache. He had promised himself that he would keep the honeymoon platonic. Last night he had all but forced her into his bed. He'd been angry with her, although now he couldn't recall why. But he would not lose control like that again. As she'd reminded him, sex was not a part of their deal. From now on, he was through pushing her for more than she wanted to give.

She let the screen door close quietly as she took a couple of steps toward him. "You're probably a little tired, too. What with the drive and all the frustrations you've had today."

He tapped his knee with the flat of his hand, feeling a sudden, taut energy burgeon inside him. "No, the truth is, I'm keyed up. I was just thinking about going for another swim."

"Oh."

There was a world of meaning in that one word, but Neil didn't know if it held disappointment or disapproval. "I guess I shouldn't leave Robby, though."

"I'll stay with him. I don't care to swim anymore to-day, anyway."

Neil's lips curved in a humorless smile. "That's not the point, is it, Krista? It's my responsibility to stay with him, not yours. I'm not going to ask you to make any more sacrifices for me."

"That has a noble sound to it."

"Not really. If I wanted to go for a swim, I probably would, whether you had volunteered to stay with Robby or not. I'm a selfish man, used to doing what I want, when I want."

"Do you expect me to argue?"

"I expect honesty from you, Hartley. Nothing more." He glanced at her and offered a rueful smile. "That's obviously not true, isn't it?" He paused, drinking in the sight of her standing in the pool of light from the doorway and looking so incredibly desirable that his mouth went dry just at the thought of holding her close against him. "Believe or not, I was only thinking of a swim to give you a little time to your-self."

She smiled and took a step forward, bracing her arms against the porch railing for support. "And here I thought a honeymoon meant spending time together."

He didn't answer that. After all, how many times had she pointed out that this was not a *real* honeymoon. "The couch makes into a bed. I'll sleep there."

The silence that followed his announcement was louder than a foghorn on an early morning in San Francisco.

"Is that my cue to invite you to join me in the bed?"

"I said I wasn't asking you to make any more sacri-fices for me."

"Hmm." She bent forward slightly, angling her body in a smooth and unconsciously seductive curve. "And here I thought I was making all these 'sacrifices' for Robby's sake."

"Well, sleeping with me is no longer on the list of selfless offerings."

"My mother would be disappointed to hear that."

He thought for a moment he'd misunderstood. "Your mother? Is *she* planning to show up and take my place on the couch?"

Krista turned, reversing the drape of her body against the railing, bracing her arms behind her and smiling more seductively than Neil had thought possible. "She wouldn't dream of spoiling our honeymoon. I just meant that she sent this really trashy little bit of lingerie with me, and she's bound to ask if I wore it to bed. My mother isn't shy about asking things like that."

"Lie to her. I won't contradict you."

"I meant that she'll most likely ask *you* what you thought about it. She really is not shy."

"So? Show it to me. Then I'll be able to give her my honest opinion."

Krista seemed to consider that, and Neil grew slightly uncomfortable beneath her regard. Didn't she know how difficult this was for him? He was trying his damnedest to keep a friendly distance when all he could think about was how much he wanted to kiss her, stroke her, make love to her. Hell, he thought he was making quite a sacrifice, and she didn't even seem to notice how much it was costing him.

She had unfastened the belt and undone three buttons down the front of the dress she had worn all evening before he realized what she was doing. His heart did a dropkick and ended up in his throat. "Hartley," he said in the best warning tone he could muster. "Don't play games with me. Not tonight."

Her expression was a long way from innocent and he knew in his gut that this was some kind of harebrained test, devised to probe his willpower and consequently drive him insane. She unbuttoned two more buttons. "You said I should show you the lingerie my mother sent along as a wedding gift . . . so you could form an honest opinion."

"You're wearing it?" His voice was fast deteriorating into a raspy croak. "Under your dress?"

Her smile had to have originated in the Garden of Eden and Eve could not have done it better. "Where else? Do you want to see it or not?"

He could feel the flat of a nail pinching into his shoulder and knew he was no longer simply leaning against the wood, but using it as a brace to support himself. An ambience of danger pervaded the ocean-scented air and told him he was in trouble. With any more assistance from her, he was going to flunk this test in a big way. "That could be a particularly dangerous question to answer, Hartley."

"I think this place needs a little danger," she said softly. "Don't you?" The dress, unbuttoned almost to the hem, dropped from her shoulders like so many inhibitions sliding away and left her standing before him in a lacy net of sultry black seduction.

He sincerely hoped his jaw wasn't hanging slack and loose, but he didn't seem to have much control over it . . . or any other part of his anatomy. "Hartley . . ." he said, although it came out sounding like a groan.

She raised her arms and did a slow spin for his inspection. "Like it?"

"Your *mother* bought that for you?"

"Mmm-hmm. Pretty imaginative, isn't she?"

He wasn't about to comment on that. Not when his imagination was short-circuiting in all directions. "You wore that all during dinner?"

She nodded, and, for the first time, a hint of a blush stole across her cheeks. "I intended to throw it away, but... I didn't."

"You certainly made mincemeat of my little speech about sacrifices and sleeping on the couch."

Her gaze met his across a too-wide expanse of weathered porch. "I know the realities of our situation, Neil. I know there will be an end to this marriage, but is that a good reason not to enjoy at least some of the benefits while it lasts?"

Sex was not a benefit, he thought. It was a responsibility and one that they had no business playing around with. There was too much emotion already at risk between them. But hell if he knew how he was supposed to resist her. With or without that skimpy bit of willbreaker, she was... irresistible. "Are you doing this for Robby's sake?" he asked, although he knew she wasn't.

"No." She advanced on him with a hesitance he found endearing and tantalizing. This was not the first time a woman had made an effort to seduce him, but he certainly had never been so intrigued by an attempt. This wasn't like the Hartley he knew. She had married him for Robby's sake, and yet, for the first time, he had to wonder if perhaps she cared for him a little. Obviously, she shared the attraction he felt. Obviously, too, she intended to make this honeymoon as authentic as possible. Did she think the marriage might become a real one, once the questions about Robby were resolved?

The thought scared him, just as Robby's crying spell that morning had scared him, made him feel helpless in the face of the responsibilities he'd blindly assumed. What was he doing here on a honeymoon with a woman who, until a couple of weeks ago, he had thought of simply as a close personal friend? How had he become a husband and a daddy without ever consciously stating that he wanted to become either one? The questions whirled through his mind as Krista stopped beside him and laid her hand possessively on his thigh. The questions and the doubts stopped, though, the moment she leaned in to press her lips to his.

A groan of pure longing broke free of his throat, and he brought his hands to cup her face so he could kiss her long and slowly. In the space of a frantic heartbeat, he took over the seduction. She had excited him, tempted him past the point of reason, and he could wait no longer. He lifted her into his arms and carried her inside the cottage, pausing only to open the screen door and ease it slowly shut behind them. This was one time he definitely wanted Robby to sleep for hours.

In the tiny bedroom, he lowered her to the bed and followed her down, wanting her more than he could ever remember wanting a woman. Was it the steamy scrap of lingerie she had worn specifically for this purpose? His heartbeat quickened at the thought of practical, down-to-earth Hartley putting on such a feminine tool and wearing it all through dinner. She had been planning this moment for hours, and that thought filled him with a sweet and heady desire.

His mother-in-law's gift was appreciated and discarded with abandon. Neil kissed it off...not that there was much fabric involved. Krista arched her back, bringing the slender curve of her throat to his mouth, requesting the pleasure of his lips against her skin. He allowed his hand to skim the surface of her stomach and follow the curve of her waist upward to the ripe fullness of her breast. She inhaled, as if drawing sustenance from his touch, and beneath his hand, she trembled.

A strange and powerful emotion knotted inside him with her response. He wanted to possess her and he wanted to protect her—a paradox, and yet, not a contradiction at all. As he lowered his head and nuzzled the soft swell of her breast, drawing the nipple between his teeth with exquisite gentleness, he knew he could be both master and slave. He could lead her beyond sensual promise and follow her into fulfillment. He was no more in control of her than she was of him, and yet the rapid-fire beating of his heart was entirely at her command. And if he moved his hand here... and here, touched her there... and there, her pulse raced as if she hadn't the power or the will to suppress its reply.

He tasted her, taunted her with flyaway kisses and tried to pretend that he had set the pace. But as her seduction took hold, as she began to work her magic on him, every movement drew him farther from shore, cast him into a rip current of passion that both startled and surprised him. He couldn't fight it, so he joined the force of the tide, followed the directions of her urgent hands, the insistence of her lips, and made imperative demands of his own. He didn't know who was swept away first, whether he rode the current or whether she drew him into a drowning pool of white-hot energy and fierce intensity. He knew the experience was new and somehow fragile and, as the world exploded into searing release, as she cried out with him, he surrendered to the emotions that rocked him with awesome force.

It was over too soon. And, too soon, the afterglow of contentment and release was spent as well. She murmured to him, nonsensical phrases, whispered words that were more a soothing noise than a source of meaning. He whispered back, answering her in kind, holding her close and conveying his admiration and respect for her in a language that was silent but sincere. He had a silly impulse to talk about the future. Their future. And Robby's. Not next week or next month, but a year from now. Two years from now. Ten. But then she was asleep in his arms, and the impulse faded into a wiser procrastination. There would be time for talk tomorrow, he thought. Or the day after.

After all, the honeymoon had only just begun.

KRISTA OPENED HER EYES to a dismal dawn. Something was different this morning. She felt it, sensed it, before her mind was clear enough to fathom what it was. Next to her, Neil sighed in his sleep, and she smiled a little at the thought that waking up in bed with him was certainly a departure from her normal routine.

Across the room, she could see the black net lingerie she had worn the night before, draped carelessly on the small wooden dresser. It looked innocent enough in the wan light, hardly the instrument of seduction it had been last night. Krista blushed a little at her boldness, but couldn't feel a shred of regret.

Sometime yesterday afternoon, somewhere between frolicking on the beach and Neil's suggestion that they have dinner in the resort's main lodge, she had realized that she was actually, legally, and completely married. True, Neil had presented his proposal as a temporary measure, a means of securing Robby's future and not as a lifetime commitment. She had agreed to those

terms. But that didn't mean she couldn't try to change
his mind. She had a few weeks to convince Neil that he
was cut out to be a husband, as well as a father. He
might have shuffled the deck, but in the process he had
handed her a couple of aces. Last night she had played
one of them, with better than pleasing results.

She stretched a little beneath the covers and the warm
circle of his arm. The bed was small, much smaller than
the one they had shared at his house. But cozy. Decidedly cozy. If she tried, she could curve her body into his
without even rumpling the sheets. The bedroom, too,
was small, one square in a larger square that was the
whole cottage. And, against the background rumble of
the ocean, the place was as quiet as a church at midnight.

Quiet.

The nagging sense of something missing changed to
a jab of awareness. It was morning, and Robby had
slept through the night. The idea was wonderfully
troubling. Were babies supposed to sleep *all* night?
When did they stop waking up for a two o'clock feeding? Had Neil gotten up with him at some time during
the night and she slept right through it?

Not likely.

What if something was wrong? What if he had
stopped breathing . . . for real?

She was out of bed instantly and padding across the
bare wood floor into the room where they had placed
his crib. "Robby?" she said softly as she entered.
"Wake up, Robby. You slept all night."

The baby didn't stir. He was crumpled beneath the
baby blanket, a mound of padded diaper and a wrinkled nightshirt, tummy down, his face turned toward
the opposite wall. Krista's hand shook as she reached

out to touch him. "Robby?" Her voice rose with a moment's panic, but as she saw his sudden jerk, the telltale movement of his legs under the cover, she sagged with relief. He was okay. It was only her imagination that wasn't breathing. And now, of all things, she had awakened him from a sound sleep. He'd probably cry for hours . . . and she couldn't blame him.

Did all new mothers act so silly?

Robby rocked, his feet tucked up underneath him, like a turtle all drawn inside its shell. When he didn't make a sound, didn't offer to give even a token cry, Krista frowned. She leaned over the crib again and brushed her fingertips across his smooth little cheek. Smooth, *hot* cheek. She laid her hand flat against his skin and felt the instant, dry heat of fever. A high fever.

"Neil." She turned abruptly, not knowing if she should pick up the baby or leave him, sick and stirring, in his crib. Hesitating in the doorway, her eyes on the crib, she released a slow, quivering breath. "Neil," she called. "Neil, come in here."

He was beside her a moment later, wearing nothing but an expression of sleepy concern. "What is it?" he asked with a barely suppressed yawn. "Is the Kid still asleep?"

"He's sick." She grabbed Neil's arm and pulled him closer to the crib. "Feel him, Neil. He's burning up."

Neil bent over the portable crib, touching Robby's head and then slipping his hand under the blanket in an attempt to gauge body temperature. "He is hot. Did you just find him like this?"

"Yes. I woke up and realized he hadn't cried once during the night. I was afraid he wasn't breathing or something, but he moved around when I touched him.

Then I felt how hot he was. Do you think it's serious? What could be wrong? I don't know the first thing about sick kids."

Neil frowned and continued rubbing his hand over the baby's back. Robby began to cry in a pitifully weak imitation of his usual lusty wails, and Neil rolled him over onto his back. He didn't know the first thing about healthy kids, much less sick ones. He had no idea if Robby was deathly ill or only experiencing one of the myriad ailments that accompanied childhood. But the kid had a fever. That much was easily apparent. Something ought to be done... and clearly, Krista expected him to decide what.

She hovered at his elbow, alarmed and trying not to be. Neil felt the sickening rise of his own helplessness. What the hell was he doing with a baby, he thought. "I guess we'd better get him to a doctor," he said.

"EAR INFECTION," the doctor at a nearby clinic pronounced gruffly. "Both ears involved. I'll give you a prescription for drops and an antibiotic. He'll be cranky for a day or two, might not sleep much, but by Wednesday, he ought to be back to normal. You from out of town?"

Neil blinked at the switch from diagnosis to chitchat. "San Diego," he answered. "Is an ear infection serious, Doctor? Will it affect his hearing?"

The older man squinted as he looked up from scribbling on a prescription pad. "Could," he said after a moment. "But it isn't likely. I see twenty or more cases of this a week. Most kids get over it, no problem. That's not to say he might not have a lot of trouble with this kind of thing and end up with scar tissue and some loss of hearing. But at his age, I wouldn't worry too much about that. Just be sure he takes all of the medicine and take him on in to your regular pediatrician in a couple of days for a checkup. Just for your own peace of mind."

"What about the fever?" Neil wanted to know. "Doesn't he need a prescription for that?"

The doctor frowned and tore off the top page of the prescription pad. "Once you get a dose of this anti-biotic down him, the fever should begin to taper off. If it hasn't gone down some by evening, you might call your own doctor and see what he recommends. A tepid bath is good for fever, but his isn't all that high at the moment. If it does go up, try a bath. Sponging him off will make him feel better. And that'll make you feel like you're doing something to help." The doctor stood, handed the prescription to Neil and patted him on the shoulder. "Take my advice, son, and calm down. The more you fret, the more he's going to fret. This baby is going to be all right. You can stop worrying. Trust me, I've been a doctor for a lot of years. I know these things."

Neil was reassured to some degree, but his feeling of helplessness had not gone away. "So, what do we do with him? Should we keep him in bed? Or feed him a special kind of formula? Should we keep him bundled up or make sure he's not too hot?"

The old doctor chuckled as he headed for the door-way of the examining room. "Do whatever you nor-mally do with him. I doubt he'll want to eat much and I don't recommend giving him any chicken soup, but other than that, just use your own good sense." He cast a wise eye on Krista. "Young lady, you may need a lit-tle extra rest, seeing as how you're going to have to deal with father *and* son." He left the room, chuckling.

"I think we should see another doctor," Neil said as the door closed. "I don't think he knows what he's doing."

Krista began folding the baby blanket around Robby, who did, miraculously, seem better. "I think we ought to go home. He'd probably be more comfortable there, and I know *we* would."

"You're right." Neil immediately saw the logic in that. A honeymoon cottage was no place for a sick baby. "We'll go back to Timmerlea, pack and be home this afternoon. Then we can take Robby to another doctor. Do you know a good pediatrician?"

She lifted a patient gaze. "I have a friend who's a dermatologist and I can give you the name of my gynecologist. But, up until today, I haven't had much need for a pediatrician. Can we please worry about that once we get home?"

"Of course." He placed the carrier seat on the examining table so she could put Robby in it. "Mary Nell will know. She has grandchildren. She's bound to know which pediatrician is best."

"Her grandchildren live in New Mexico, Neil."

He frowned at that unexpected complication. "It can't hurt to ask her. Don't worry, Krista. We'll find one."

"We need to find out if and when Robby had all his immunizations. Do you think Carrie kept up with that? Surely she did. No one would be that irresponsible. This could have been a lot more serious than an ear infection."

Neil didn't like to think about that. Carrie had already demonstrated her lack of concern for her son, but it seemed ridiculous to think she wouldn't have taken care of something as basic as checkups and immunizations. Krista was right. It was something he had to know.

And just as soon as he found out how to contact Carrie, he'd ask her.

The helpless feeling sank its roots a little deeper into his heart and he couldn't help wondering if every man was caught unprepared for the amount of responsibility that was delivered along with a baby.

"THIS IS MADIGAN. I'm back in town. You can call me at the office."

The message spun into the bedroom at home, along with a half-dozen other magnetic messages, half of them from Krista's mother, who was offering to babysit on various and variable occasions in the future.

"Your mother is taking this grandparent bit pretty seriously, isn't she?" Neil asked as he reset the answering machine. "She seems to have formed a strong attachment to Robby already."

"Yes," Krista agreed with a pensive nod. "You realize, don't you, that she will want to remain his grandmother even after you and I—" She hadn't meant to mention that, to remind him that their marriage wasn't a permanent arrangement. "I mean, it would be cruel to..."

Neil was looking at her in a strange and oddly tender way, and Krista couldn't seem to finish a sentence. "I understand, Hartley," he said. "Something can be arranged. Something that will, I hope, please even you."

There was a note in his voice she didn't recognize, a tone of reassurance that she didn't dare hope meant what she wanted it to mean. "Good," she said as she laid Robby on the bed and laid her hand against his cheek. "My mother will be happy about that." She glanced up at Neil. "He doesn't feel as warm now. The medicine must be helping."

They'd purchased the antibiotic and eardrops at the clinic because it was handy, and Robby had been given a teaspoonful of the orange stuff and four drops in each ear of the white stuff. And he was, already, improving. Krista could tell by the increasing activity of his feet. He had been fussy on the ride home, but at least he wasn't lethargic.

"I'm going to call Mary Nell about the pediatrician." Neil picked up the phone, then set it down again. "I think I'll go in to the office instead. I've got to see Madigan, anyway, and find out what she has for us."

"I thought she told you that on the phone." Krista didn't like the thought of being left alone with the baby. What if the fever returned, got higher, sent him into convulsions? What if he got worse all of a sudden? What if—

"She was supposed to get some pictures of Carrie, as well as information about where Carrie is going to live, where her husband works, an address or two for future reference, anything of interest." He made a face. "And probably a lot of useless information that isn't of any interest at all. But any of it might prove useful in a custody hearing. I may drop in and talk to our attorney, too. Then, I'll go on to the office. Don't bother with dinner. I'll bring something home."

"But, Neil—"

He came around the bed, interrupting her protest with a swift kiss on her cheek. "Don't worry about the doctor. I'll take care of finding someone, and we'll take Robby in to see him first thing tomorrow."

"But what if he gets worse while you're gone?"

Neil bent over the baby. "He looks a lot better, Krista. And if his fever comes back up, give him a bath, like the doctor suggested." He straightened and turned toward the door.

"But, Neil..."

He barely paused. "If anything happens, call me. You have my number."

As he walked out, leaving her alone with the baby, alone with the responsibility, she thought about throwing in the towel. Or possibly throwing the *How to Raise a Healthy Baby* book at his head. Or maybe she should dial his number and hang up on him. Robby cooed softly, gurgling as he did when he wanted to be picked up.

With a sigh, Krista turned and lifted him into her arms, loving the sweet, warm feel and the soft, powdery scent of him. Who was kidding whom here? she wondered. The Blanchard men had her number, all right.

Chapter Thirteen

"I'm going to be a little late," Neil said. "Don't worry about dinner. I'll get something downtown. Do you want me to bring anything home?"

Krista was beginning to know this speech by heart. She'd first heard it on the afternoon they returned from Timmerlea. So far, in the four days they'd been back, she'd heard it three times. On the one day she hadn't heard it, he'd simply forgotten to call. It had just slipped his mind...or so he'd said. Then he'd smiled and said something about how he wasn't accustomed to having to "report in" or having anyone to "report to."

"No," she answered now. "I don't want you to bring anything home. Magdalena prepared a meal, and I've already eaten. I knew there was no point in waiting for you."

His voice picked up a note of self-defense. "Krista, this business does not run itself, and you know I can't be away from the office for days on end...as I have been lately."

As if it were *her* fault. "You were scheduled to take this whole week off, Neil. It's certainly a good thing we came back early, so you could be there to *run* the business."

"What is wrong with you?" he asked, none too nicely. "You know as well as I do this job is not a nine-to-five affair. You've worked your share of overtime."

"And just look at me now. I've gone from overtime employee to full-time mother substitute. I'm working twenty-four hours a day, Neil, and without the extra benefits, too!"

"That isn't fair, Hartley."

It wasn't. She knew it, but damned if she was in any mood to be fair. "Look, Neil, you said we should get married in order to convince the courts that you could and would provide a stable home for Robby. At the time you proposed the plan, I thought it made sense. Now I think I was crazy to agree. Maybe I just wanted to be a part of any plan that would help him. I don't know. But now I'm stuck. You're out doing what you've always done, and I'm here making it easy for you to do just that. I'm not really your wife and I'm not really Robby's mother. I've gone from having a career to being a slave."

"Krista, that isn't true. I want—"

"You want to live as you've always lived, Neil. With no one having any claim on you or your time. You want someone else to handle all the little complications, so you don't have to."

"Hey, you're the one who resigned, Hartley. You're the one who said it was time for a change. I gave you a change of career. You wanted to be a mother. I gave you the job. It isn't my fault that you don't like it."

"That is not what I said."

"That is exactly what you said."

"I don't think so. As usual, you're just not listening."

"How can I *not* be listening when you're not—" He caught himself, and his subsequent pause writhed with frustration. "Do you want me to come home?" he asked tersely. "Is that what this is about?"

He didn't understand, damn it. She wanted him to *want* to come home. She wanted him to *want* to leave the office behind. She wanted him to *want* the family he had. But what if he did understand and simply did not want what she wanted? "No," she said softly in defeat. "No, don't come home. Go to your meeting. I'll fulfill my end of our bargain. But, Neil, I think we need to talk."

"Nothing good ever begins with the words 'we need to talk.'"

She ignored that. "It's time to find a nanny for Robby."

There was a pause, as if he were searching for a hidden meaning. "We've discussed that already, Krista. He does not need another stranger in his life right now. Maybe in a few months, when the custody issue is settled. But not now. Look, if you're getting cabin fever, go somewhere. Take him with you. It will be good for both of you to get out of the house for a while."

Her irritation returned like the perennial dandelion and she fought the impulse to hang up on him. She'd done *that* twice already this week. The atmosphere around the Blanchard household was becoming thicker than the odor of an aging cheese. "As a matter of fact, we have been out. Robby had an appointment with his new pediatrician this morning. Dr. Adson said the infection is gone, his ears look fine, and he weighed fifteen pounds and three ounces."

"I missed the damn appointment." Neil's chagrin carried clearly across the phone wire and did nothing to soothe her. "You should have called and had Mary Nell remind me. I got involved in a lengthy discussion with Dalton and forgot all about meeting you there. No wonder you're so angry."

No wonder, she thought. As Mary Nell had predicted, Neil had gotten someone else to handle the responsibility of taking care of Robby. And she had no one to blame but herself. "You should have been there, Neil. You could have shared my frustration in filling out the New Patient Information Form. I don't even know Robby's birth date, much less any of the other information asked for."

"I'm sorry." He sounded sorry, but that wasn't much comfort. "It will all be over soon, Hartley. Carrie will have to answer our petition for custody. She can't avoid us forever."

"No." Krista rubbed the furrows frowning had made in her forehead. "No, I suppose not."

"I'll be home as soon as I can. I'll cut the meeting short and . . . well, I'll be there."

"I'll see you then," she said and replaced the phone in its cradle. *It will all be over soon*. Words of comfort. Words of reassurance. Distressing words. Because, as frustrated as she was with Neil's abandonment of responsibility, she really did not want this to end. She did not want it to be over.

The ringing of the doorbell jarred her. It would most likely be her mother. Phyllis dropped by every day for one reason or another. Usually her reason involved a present for Robby. She had bought some outfit that would look precious on him. Or she'd seen some adorable stuffed teddy bear that she thought he just had to have. Krista rubbed away the last traces of irritation on her face and went to meet her visitor with a smile and the pretense that this was one, big, happy household.

Magdalena stalked past the front door as Krista approached. She did a good job of keeping the house clean, but the influx of visitors did not set well with her. She had made it clear to Krista—in a very few words—that she didn't answer the telephone or the door and she would not, under any circumstances, watch the baby. Still, Krista smiled politely as the plump woman ambled down the hallway to the back of the house and whatever she found to do in the laundry room.

As soon as Magdalena was out of sight, Krista opened the door and stood there in some surprise. It wasn't Phyllis. It was a young woman, a blonde with wide blue eyes and a tentative expression. "Hi," the woman said. "I'm Carrie. Is Dr. Blanchard home?"

A tremor shook Krista from knee to heart, but she held fast to the door and tried to conceal her panic. "Carrie?" she repeated. "You're . . . Carrie?"

The woman nodded and glanced over her shoulder, presumably at the midsize car she had left parked in the middle of the drive. "Is my car okay there?" she asked. "It's a rental, but I'll move it if you think it will be in your way. I did sort of park right in the middle of your driveway, didn't I? Oh, well, I won't stay long. I have to get back. My . . . my husband is waiting."

"Oh." For the life of her, Krista couldn't think of another thing to say.

"Is Dr. Blanchard here?" Carrie asked again, smoothing her flyaway hair away from her eyes. "Neil Blanchard?"

"He lives here," Krista acknowledged. "But, uh, he isn't here now."

"Oh, good." The blonde seemed to sag with relief. "I was hoping maybe he'd be at his office. I don't really want to see him, you know. My sister started this, and I really wish she hadn't. Things have been such a disaster, and I don't know what to do about it. When Jason finds out, there's no telling what will happen." She rammed her hands in the pockets of her denim shorts and looked expectantly at Krista. "May I come in? You must be the housekeeper."

"No, I'm—"

"It's all right," Carrie interrupted with an assurance that seemed shaky at best. "I'm a harmless person, really. And I just got back from my honeymoon, but I expect you know that. Dr. Blanchard would have told you. Are you the housekeeper or just a friend of the family?"

Krista blinked, unable to think past the realization that Robby's flesh-and-blood mother was standing in front of her. "I'm not the housekeeper," she said. "And I'm not a friend. I'm Dr. Blanchard's . . . wife."

"Ooooh." Carrie looked at Krista a little closer. "You don't seem his type, but I only met him once and I wasn't quite myself at the time."

"You were Stephanie."

Carrie's lips curved with amusement. "Wild stories travel almost as fast as news, don't they? Actually, I was never Stephanie. I only pretended to be her because . . . well, it was more fun and I didn't think she'd find out and I certainly never thought things would turn out the way they have."

In quick decision, Krista stepped back and motioned for Carrie to enter the house. "I think we should talk, Carrie. If you don't want to deal with Neil, maybe you should give me some answers."

"Answers?" Carrie stammered a little on the word. "I can't give you any answers. I don't understand why these things happen to me. One minute I'm having a good time and the next minute my entire life is one giant disaster."

"Robby is not a disaster." Krista thought she sounded very much like a protective mother, while Carrie sounded like a windup doll.

"Robby? Who's Robby?"

"The baby. We named the baby Robert Neil and call him Robby for short."

Carrie smiled. "That's a cute name. I like it much better than the one I picked. I mean, they come in the hospital after you've just had this baby and want to know what his name is and well, frankly, I can't think that fast. So I told them to give me the forms and I'd send in a name later." She looked around the room with interest. "I like your house," she said as if the subject was a natural progression of the conversation. "Did you do it yourself? Decorate it, I mean. Jason and I are buying a house, but we don't have the same tastes at all, so who knows what it will look like. He likes simple things, you know, but I'm partial to frilly curtains. But this is nice." She gestured and then stopped in mid-movement. "Wait a minute. Neil wasn't married. I distinctly remember that he was not married and didn't even have a girlfriend."

"It's been a year since you met him, Carrie." Krista didn't know whether to sit down or remain standing. "A lot of things can happen in a year."

Carrie giggled nervously. "Ain't that the truth? I'm a perfect example of that. Jason tells me I should keep a journal, but honestly, I can't see the value in keeping track of things I'd just as soon forget."

"Is Robby one of the things you're trying to forget?" Krista asked, growing anxious and impatient with the chatter. "It certainly looks that way."

For the first time, some of the animation in Carrie's expression dulled and her lips tightened in a near frown. "I haven't done a very good job as a mother, have I? If I'd had time to plan, maybe I'd have done better, but there wasn't time, and these people kept asking me and asking me if I was positive I wanted to give him up for adoption and I didn't know if that was the right thing and then this other woman in the hospital told me I would regret it and so I changed my mind at the last minute. But I had to keep working and I didn't have any baby things for him and then Jason called and I couldn't just blurt it out over the phone that I had this baby and . . ." Her voice trailed off in miserable indecision. "I guess that sounds like a pretty weak excuse, doesn't it?"

Krista answered with silence, and Carrie wandered over to the sofa where she picked up one of Robby's toys that had been left there. "This is his," she said. "I guess he has a lot of toys and things here. I should never have done it, you know, but Neil was so nice to me that night. And I didn't mean any harm by it. How was I to know Stephanie would give the baby to him? I wasn't going to ask for money or anything like that. I just wanted the baby to have a father he could be proud of and so, when that woman in the hospital asked for the father's name I just—told her."

Krista absorbed that slowly, swallowing hard as the implications sunk in. "You mean . . . Neil isn't his father? You didn't sleep with him that night at Melinda's house?"

Carrie blinked as if she had to think about it. "Well, I slept with him, but I didn't *sleep* with him. And I really wasn't thinking about making him 'Father of the Year' then. It just . . . well, when the man who got me pregnant turned out to be very married *and* the father of four children besides, I just couldn't see ruining his marriage. He was going through a bad time and he really loved his wife and kids and I liked him a lot, so it seemed kind of unnecessary to stir up a hornet's nest in his life. Especially when I planned to put the baby up for adoption. But then, like I said, I changed my mind and the woman came in and wanted the father's name for the birth records and—" she shrugged "—I guess I made a slight error in judgment."

Slight, in this instance, was such a gross understatement that Krista didn't know where to begin attacking it. She rubbed her temples instead and grimaced when she heard the unmistakable sounds of Robby waking up from a nap. "What do you intend to do, Carrie?" she asked. "You must know Neil wants custody of the baby."

"He does?" Carrie seemed surprised at that. "But it isn't his baby."

"He doesn't know that. And it wouldn't make any difference, anyway. He wants to keep the baby."

"Oh." Carrie frowned. "Are you sure? I mean, men are funny about that kind of thing. You know how protective they are when it comes to their sperm. I know I've heard Jason say any number of times that he would rather have his frozen than to use another man's—" She stopped talking as Robby's cry for attention got louder. "Is that the baby? Could I see him?"

Krista did not want Carrie anywhere near him. "I don't think that's a—"

"Where's his room?" Carrie was already on her way down the hallway toward the bedroom, and just as she reached the doorway, the phone began to ring. Krista hesitated, but maternal instinct won out and she followed Carrie. The phone trilled a second summons as she stopped to watch the blonde bend over the crib and say, tentatively, "Hi, there. Bet you never expected to see me again, did ya?"

"Here—" Krista moved into the room "—I'll get him up."

But Carrie wouldn't move out of the way. "You don't have to. I'll just stand here and talk to him. I think I may have forgotten how to hold him, anyway. It's been so long, and I was never very good at it. Boy, he's really grown, hasn't he? And he's gotten a lot cuter, too. Your phone is ringing. Aren't you going to answer it?"

Krista was torn, but she didn't want Carrie to get the idea that she was afraid of her. "I'll get the phone," she said. "It'll just take a minute."

Reluctantly, looking over her shoulder all the way down the hallway and into the master bedroom, Krista went to quell the intrusive ringing of the phone. "Hello?" she said.

"I cancelled the meeting." Neil's voice came through the line with a tone of conciliation. "Get your party dress on, because you and I are going out for the evening. I've made reservations for dinner and the theater. Your mother is going to baby-sit. So, no excuses."

"Oh, Neil," she said. It was a sweet gesture, an unlooked-for peace offering, but she had too many other things on her mind to appreciate it. "Carrie is here."

"What? What did you say?"

"Carrie is here." She thought she heard footsteps in the hall, and cupped her hand over the receiver. "Look,

I can't talk now. Maybe you ought to come..." Was
that the front door? "Wait," Krista said as she cocked
her head to listen. The house was too quiet all of a sudden, with only the faint noise of Magdalena's favorite
game show coming from the television in the back.

And then Krista heard the faint but unmistakable
sound of a car engine. She dropped the receiver and ran
for the door...just in time to see Carrie's rented car
back out from the driveway. With her heart in her
throat, she ran for Robby's room, knowing, even before she saw the empty crib, that he was gone.

PRUDENCE MADIGAN WAS ONLY half listening to the
prospective client seated across the desk from her. His
wife was having an affair. He wanted evidence. He also
wanted a sympathetic ear, which she was providing because she felt too lazy to end his recital of marital ills.
His wife thought he was bland and unexciting, he was
saying. Pru tried to look shocked as she fought a yawn
and wished she could get more assignments like the
Blanchard case. A few more days in the Caribbean
would suit her fine. The tan she'd barely managed to get
was already beginning to fade.

When the phone rang at her elbow, she answered with
gratitude. "P. G. Madigan," she said.

"Madigan!" It was Neil Blanchard, and he sounded
upset. "Carrie has taken the baby. Give me every address you were able to find on her, A.S.A.P."

Prudence was already reaching for her bottom drawer
and the file. "What do you mean, she took the baby?
Took him from where?"

"She went to my house, talked to Krista and left with
the Kid. Now tell me your best guess as to where I'll find
her."

"I'd say Stephanie's apartment. I don't know if she's back from making a movie in Texas, but I'll bet Carrie is staying there one way or the other."

"I hope you're right. What's the address?"

Prudence read it off to him. "Listen, I'll meet you there. You might need the other addresses and phone numbers in the file. How soon are you leaving?"

"I'm in the car now. I should be there in ten minutes, maybe less."

"I'm on my way." Madigan hung up, grabbed the file, slung her purse over her shoulder and headed for the door, realizing only as she reached it that she had forgotten the client. "Emergency," she said over her shoulder. "I'll have to get in touch with you later, Mr. Bland."

"Brown," he called after her. "The name is Brown."

WITH A SHAKING HAND, Krista scribbled down the address Neil gave her. "I'm leaving right now," she told him.

She was in her car and on the road in less time than it took to repeat the address in her head. Alternating between reassuring herself that Carrie wouldn't hurt Robby and telling herself that Carrie didn't possess a single ounce of common sense, Krista drove as fast as she dared. She hoped Madigan was right about the address, hoped that the apartment was indeed Carrie's destination. But less than ten minutes had elapsed between the time Robby was taken and the time Neil had called back with the address. She couldn't have taken him very far.

Krista grimaced and pushed the gas pedal a little closer to the floor. She could have taken him anywhere. What if they never found him? What if Madigan had gotten the wrong address? The worried thoughts pounded her heart relentlessly until she was a mass of conflicting emotion. If anything happened to Robby, she thought, she would pull every blond hair from Carrie's head . . . one handful at a time.

THE ARGUMENT WAS ALREADY in progress when Krista entered the apartment. Her first sweeping glance was to locate Robby, and when she saw him, she relaxed. His expression indicated that he was a little wary of the new surroundings and of the woman who held him on her lap. Krista couldn't decide who looked more uncomfortable sitting there, Robby or Madigan, but at least he was all right. Her heart finally loosened its hold on her throat.

"Krista." Neil acknowledged her presence and moved to her side. "I'm glad you're here. Let me introduce you. Carrie you've met. Her husband, Jason James. Her sister, Stephanie Starr, who is sometimes called Sally. And, of course, you know Madigan."

Krista nodded at each person in turn and wondered why Neil was being polite. These people had stolen Robby. They didn't deserve a proper introduction. "Why did you take the baby?" she asked bluntly. "You had no right to do that. You scared me."

"I'm sorry," Carrie said as if that absolved her. "I didn't mean to scare you, but I had to tell Jason about the baby and since there never seemed to be an opportunity, I thought if I just showed him the baby, then he'd ask me how I happened to have a baby and then I could tell him. Really, I only meant to borrow him for a while . . . the baby, I mean. But Jason has only been yelling at me ever since I got here and then—" she nodded toward Neil "—he shows up and he starts yelling, and honestly, I'm just trying to do what I can to change the mess I made."

"You're a disaster, Carrie." Stephanie tossed the verdict from her position on the couch. "An utter disaster."

"*Why* didn't you tell me *before* we got married?" Jason tapped his foot on the linoleum floor and his hand against his knee. "I cannot believe you kept this from me for weeks. Honestly, Carrie, this is the stupidest thing you've ever done."

"Well, excuse me, Mr. Wonderful. I guess you've never made a mistake, huh?"

"I can think of one *big* mistake I made, and it has your name written all over it." Jason stood and stalked into the kitchen, which was only an alcove in the small apartment.

Carrie pushed out her lower lip in a demanding pout, crossed her arms at her chest and turned her back on everyone.

"I need something to drink." Jason opened and closed a couple of cabinet doors with unnecessary force. "Stephanie, do you have *anything* in this refrigerator?"

Stephanie rose and followed her brother-in-law into the kitchen, ignoring her sister's chilly glance. "There's frozen orange juice in the freezer. Anyone else want something? Water or juice. That's the extent of my hospitality. I've been out of town, you know."

Krista looked up at Neil with a question. "Can't we just get Robby and get out of here?" she whispered. "Why are we standing around, listening to them yell at each other?"

"Carrie has as much right to that baby as I do, Krista. Let's see how far we can get with diplomacy before we start pulling Robby in all directions." He nodded toward Carrie's rigid back. "When Madigan and I got here, she was stammering out that same idiotic story, trying to explain why she hadn't told her husband about the baby."

"Do you think she wants to keep the baby?"

"Hard to tell. So far there's been a lot of nothing said, but very little of any substance. There have been so many interruptions, it's hard to know exactly what has been said and what hasn't. I'm just waiting my turn, and Madigan, I think, is waiting to either protect me or to hear the punch line. I'm not sure which."

Krista glanced at the private detective who was looking on with interest. "No one's talking now," she said. "Tell Carrie you intend to ask the court for legal custody, and let's get out of here."

He frowned, but he did approach Carrie and, in a voice that brooked no argument, he spoke to her. "It will be easier on all of us, Carrie, if you'll agree that I should have custody of the baby. I don't want to fight you in court, but I will if you make it necessary."

She turned to look up at him, and Krista could see the huge tears forming in her eyes. "You can't have custody," she said. "He's not your baby. I just put your name on the birth certificate because you were nice to me and because I couldn't give the real father's name because he's married and has other kids and—"

"Carrie!" Jason took two steps to reach his wife and grab her by the upper arm. "Do you mean you slept with someone else? Someone other than...*him*?" He jerked his head toward Neil. "This is unbelievable. *Un-be-liev-a-ble!* How many men were there altogether? Two? Ten? A hundred and forty?"

"*Two* hundred and *fifty*!" she snapped. "And what difference does it make to you, anyway? At the time, I wasn't married to you. I had every right to sleep with any man I chose. And I did. So there!"

Jason released her arm angrily and stalked back to the kitchen. "She's right, Jason," Stephanie said. "You couldn't expect her to be faithful to you when you'd jilted her and left her standing at the altar."

"Oh, thanks a lot for bringing that up," Carrie said, following the words into the kitchen. "As if I don't have to remember that humiliating experience every single day of my life, you have to bring it up at every opportunity."

Jason raised his voice. "We're married now, you know. And I don't think it was such a humiliating thing for me to do. I told you the night before that I was having second thoughts, and you just didn't listen to—"

As the disagreement continued, Neil stood, silent and somber and very still. Krista moved to his side and touched his arm. "Let's go," she said. "You can't talk to these people. They're still so immature, they can't think of anything except their own problems. They certainly aren't thinking about what's best for Robby."

Neil lifted his head, and she saw the storm gathered in his blue eyes. "I'm not his father," he said. "He isn't mine."

Krista sighed her impatience with the argument which was still going on in the alcove and tried to draw Neil aside. "That doesn't matter, Neil. You love him. You've taken care of him. Let's just get him and get out of here."

Neil's jaw clenched and he shook free of her touch. "We can't do that, Krista. I'm *not* his father. Can't you understand what a difference that makes?"

"Don't be ridiculous," she said. "The fact that you're not his biological father doesn't change anything."

His lips tightened and the expression in his eyes grew colder. "It changes everything, Krista. Everything."

She stared at him, not believing, not wanting to believe he meant it. Did it mean so much to have fathered a child? Was contributing to the gene pool more important than an emotional bond? "You don't mean that, Neil. You can't mean that."

"I didn't even *sleep* with him!" Carrie shouted from the kitchen, her finger pointing straight at Neil. "Well, I *did* sleep with him, but I didn't have sex with him. And there is a difference, Mr. Know-It-All Jason. Ask him. Go on. Ask him if we had sex. He'll tell you I didn't sleep around...even though I had every right to because of what *you* did. But I didn't. Not even when I was pretending to be Stephanie so people wouldn't really know who I was."

"If you didn't sleep around," Jason shouted back, "how did you end up with a baby?"

"By accident, you idiot!"

Robby started to cry at that point, and Krista looked at him with the horrible knowledge that she was helpless to stop the flow of events that would determine his future. If Neil didn't love him enough to fight for him, how could she do it on her own? She couldn't. There was nothing she could do for Robby. Or for herself.

"Uh, he's crying." Madigan rose awkwardly, with Robby held ineptly between her hands. "Someone needs to take him."

Neil strode across the room and lifted Robby into his arms. As Carrie and Jason walked into the room, still fighting with one another, Neil motioned for Krista to take the baby. She almost obeyed the silent command, almost stepped in to let Neil walk on her doormat heart one more time. "No," she said. "No, Neil. If he isn't your responsibility, he certainly isn't mine." She spun on her heel, taking care to tune out Robby's cries, carefully avoiding looking at anyone. The door seemed a thousand yards away, but finally, somehow, she reached it, opened it and walked outside, away from the raucous scene inside the apartment, away from Neil's betrayal, away from the two people she loved most in the world.

Chapter Fourteen

As a place to hide from the world, Timmerlea Resort was perfect. As a place to think long and hard on the whims of fate, it was suitably quiet and peaceful. As a place to escape from Neil, it left a lot to be desired. His memory was in the cottage, on the shore, in the main lodge—wherever she was, he was there as well. She tried to occupy her thoughts with the future, what career path she wanted to pursue, where to send a résumé, places she might like to live. And then she would remember her wedding day or the day they'd discovered Robby on the desk or a million other sweet moments, and her heart would break all over again.

She had handled it poorly. She recognized that. Somehow, she should have been able to persuade Neil that being a married man with a child was a wondrous thing. She should have been able to convince him that fatherhood was the ultimate challenge, that responsibility was a prize in itself. He'd *married* her and she hadn't known how to make that an advantage. In that one moment, in that tiny little apartment, with Carrie spouting nonsense, she had looked at him and known it was all over. He no longer had any need for her.

It will all be over soon, he'd assured her. And it was. Robby would stay with his mother. The marriage would end as he'd planned for it to end from the beginning. Her abrupt journey through a fairy tale was finished and, unlike Cinderella, there wasn't going to be a happily ever after.

Tired of the melancholy, Krista stopped her walk along the beach and stooped to pick up a broken shell. For some reason, it reminded her of Robby, and instead of tossing it out to sea, she stuffed it into her pocket and looked for another shell to throw. She found a conch shell, but it was too large to throw and too large to fit in her pocket, so she left it where it was and began the search for another. Digging in the sand, at least, gave her something constructive to do.

"You didn't say goodbye."

Startled, she glanced up and tipped back her head so she could see out from under the wide brim of her hat. Neil stood there, feet slightly apart, arms crossed at chest level, dark hair mussed by the sea breeze, his eyes hidden behind a pair of sepia-toned sunglasses. Her heart scampered to her throat and she couldn't think of a thing to say. He was here. And even if he'd come to put a legal end to their marriage, she didn't care. Somehow, this time, she'd do it right. She'd seduce him, beg him, kidnap him...whatever she had to do to make him stay.

"What is it about me, Hartley? Why are women so eager to hang up on me and walk out on me without so much as a goodbye? Do I need a crash course at Miss Manner's School of Charm? Have I lost all of my suave playboy style since you came along?"

She squinted up at him and hoped, absolutely, that she didn't lose her balance. It was a cinch she couldn't stand up... not steadily, anyway. "I came along nearly two years ago, Dr. Blanchard." She managed a whispery, but good imitation of her old business voice. "How long ago did you get your first hang-up?"

He smiled, a slow, delicious curving of his lips, and her stomach tied itself in a love knot. "About the time I started to fall in love with you, I think. I can't believe it took nearly two years for you to get my attention."

Fall in love with you. Fall in love with you. The words cavorted through her, and she laid a hand on the warm sand to steady herself and to keep from toppling over in joyous delight. "Maybe my heart wasn't really in it."

He took a couple of steps and stooped down beside her, putting them on more equal terms. "You didn't half try," he said. "Why, I had to drag you to the altar, kicking and screaming, and even then you'd only agree to it under false premises."

"Now, wait a minute. If you expect me to believe that you actually, *truly,* wanted to get married, you have some tall explaining to do."

His lips curved again just before he leaned in and kissed her full and freely. Whatever was holding her upright caved in at that point, and if he hadn't grasped her arm, she knew she would have crumpled like a puff pastry after the first bite is taken. "Hartley," he said slowly and very, very close to her lips. "In the nearly two years since you came along, have you ever known me to do anything I didn't actually, *truly* want to do?"

True statement. Completely true. She couldn't dispute it, but she couldn't quite believe it yet, either. "Not without an ulterior motive."

"I guess you won't believe me if I tell you I fell in love with you so fast, I didn't have time to invent a good ulterior motive."

She shook her head and the hat slipped. Holding the hat in place with one hand, she used the other as a brace so she could get to her feet. Her knees tingled, but whether it was from the length of time she'd had them bent or because Neil was so close, she didn't know. "That would be a little out of character for you, Neil. We both know that."

He rose, dwarfing her in height and casting a shadow she knew she could never escape. "Why did you run away, Krista?"

She pulled off the hat and shook her hair free. Then, trailing the hat, she started walking, knowing he would fall into step beside her. "I realized it was over," she said. "Everything between us had happened because of Robby, and when you denounced him, I knew there was no reason for me to hang around. If you couldn't be his father, then I couldn't be your wife."

"I don't think we're talking about the same thing here."

With a sigh, she glanced in his direction. "Neil, the moment you found out you weren't Robby's biological father, you relinquished your claim on him. You said...and I quote...*'It changes everything.'* What was I supposed to do? Stand there and hear you tell Carrie that it had been a pleasure to baby-sit her son, but you had other places to go, other people to see? I wanted to take Robby with me so much I ached with it, but I had less right than anyone. Except that I might have been the only one who really loved him."

Neil's strides lengthened, then settled back to an even pace with her own. He started to say something a couple of times, but stopped, and Krista wondered if things could possibly work out for them if they didn't have Robby as a bond.

"How I got this shady reputation for being a love 'em and leave 'em kind of man, I don't know, but I know for a fact I have never given you any reason to think so poorly of me. Finding out I wasn't Robby's biological father did change everything. I thought I wanted custody because it was my responsibility, my duty. When that reason was gone, I had to make certain I *wanted* Robby."

She turned to him in surprise. "Neil, I—"

"Why would you think I didn't love Robby? I got up with him as many nights as you did. More, even. I changed diapers, fixed bottles, sang lullabies. I walked the floor, hired a detective, consulted an attorney, did every single thing I could think of to win custody of that baby. I will confess that I used my best persuasive powers to get you to help me, but I did not shove my responsibility off onto you. Regardless of what you think."

"What was I supposed to think when you *told* me you were going to marry me?"

"That I was unsure of your feelings for me, but I knew I could play on your feelings for Robby. And once we were married, I was confident I could make you fall in love with me. When I found Robby in my office, I didn't know how to do anything but work hard and play hard. In the space of a few weeks, I learned whole new concepts. I learned that I wasn't as disastrous at being a parent as I'd thought I was. I learned that coming home at night to a beautiful, desirable woman is a very nice feeling."

She was melting again, hearing things she never thought she'd hear, feeling emotions she'd thought belonged only to a princess in a fairy tale. "Oh, Neil," she said. "Why is everything so difficult?"

"This isn't difficult." He reached for her and pulled her into his arms for a blistering kiss. "We have it easy, sweetheart," he said after he'd caught his breath again. "One—we're already married. We don't have to be engaged, plan a wedding, get a license, invite our relatives to the ceremony or do anything we don't want to do. We're already on our honeymoon. What could be better?" He took her chin in his hand and tipped up her head as he pulled off his own concealing sunglasses. "And two—the second not-difficult thing about us is that we already have a son. No trying to get pregnant. No nine-month waiting period. No labor and delivery. We have a baby. Now, what was so difficult about that?"

"Robby?" she whispered, blinking back a mist of emotion. "We have Robby?"

His smile held a precious promise. "We have Robby. It took a lot of maneuvering, some quick thinking on Madigan's part—she wondered aloud at a very appropriate moment what the consequences would be to Carrie if I wanted to challenge her naming me as the father. With hardly any help at all, Jason translated that into a civil suit where he might be liable for some punitive damages, and the next thing I knew, he was all for us adopting the baby."

"They're rather shallow people, aren't they?"

"Shallow or immature or both. Whatever, it worked to our advantage. Carrie agreed to let us adopt him. Actually, you will be the one who adopts him. My name is already on the birth certificate, which also keeps this from being difficult. Our attorney assured me it can all be handled quickly and with relative ease. A new birth certificate will be issued and, voilà, he's ours."

"Where is he now? You didn't leave him alone in the cottage, did you?"

"Give me a break, lady. Do I look like Disaster Dad to you? Our son is with his grandparents, safe, sound and spoiled rotten." Neil pulled her close again, tightening the embrace with a gathering emotion. "And he's going to stay with his grandparents until you and I have had our honeymoon. Any questions?"

Krista looked up at him and smiled. "Do I tell you now or later that I love you?"

His hands slid down to capture hers in the same tender way he captured her lips. "Now *and* later. You know how demanding I can be."

"I'm looking forward to making a few demands of my own."

"Your mother sent you a present."

Krista frowned. "Is it black and so sheer no respectable woman would ever put it on?"

"It's red and I'm really hoping you will shed respectability for at least an hour or two. I've been looking for a disrespectable woman all my life."

"Lucky you found me, isn't it?"

He squeezed her hand and drew her into a slow walk toward their honeymoon cottage. "I'm lucky Robby found you for me. What a kid. Do you think he's a child prodigy?"

"I think he's an only child who would really like to have some brothers and sisters."

Neil smiled at that. "I believe that's why your mother sent the little red nightie."

"She's a very smart woman."

"Is she going to ask for my opinion of her present this time, too?"

Krista walked up the steps and pulled him after her. "You can count sheep on it."

"I have a better idea," he said as he lifted her into his arms and carried her across the threshold.

HAPPY VALENTINE'S DAY

James Rafferty had only forty-eight hours, and he wanted to make the most of them.... Helen Emerson had never had a Valentine's Day like this before!

Celebrate this special day for lovers, with a very special book from American Romance!

#473   ONE MORE VALENTINE
by Anne Stuart

Next month, Anne Stuart and American Romance have a delightful Valentine's Day surprise in store just for you. All the passion, drama—even a touch of mystery—you expect from this award-winning author.

Don't miss American Romance
#473   ONE MORE VALENTINE!

Also look for Anne Stuart's short story, "Saints Alive," in Harlequin's MY VALENTINE 1993 collection.

HARVAL

Harlequin is proud to present our best authors, their best books and the best for your reading pleasure!

Throughout 1993, Harlequin will bring you exciting books by some of the top names in contemporary romance!

In February, look for *Twist of Fate* by

Hannah Jessett had been content with her quiet life. Suddenly she was the center of a corporate battle with wealthy entrepreneur Gideon Cage. Now Hannah must choose between the fame and money an inheritance has brought or a love that may not be as it appears.

Don't miss TWIST OF FATE...
wherever Harlequin books are sold.

BOB1

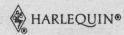

The most romantic day of the year is here! Escape into the exquisite world of love with MY VALENTINE 1993. What better way to celebrate Valentine's Day than with this very romantic, sensuous collection of four original short stories, written by some of Harlequin's most popular authors.

**ANNE STUART
JUDITH ARNOLD
ANNE McALLISTER
LINDA RANDALL WISDOM**

**THIS VALENTINE'S DAY, DISCOVER ROMANCE
WITH MY VALENTINE 1993**

Available in February wherever Harlequin Books are sold.   VAL93